I0633052

# *Praise for Pegasus Flying*

"Author Denise McAllister's stories of Katy McKim gift the reader with a heroine to root for. She's always ready to right a wrong, bring justice, and help her friends according to the tenets of her faith. Which she does in Pegasus Flying, in spades. And to keep the party going, there's Detective Matt Hartman who has romance on his mind."

— **C.K. CRIGGER, SPUR AWARD-WINNING AUTHOR OF *THE SPEAKER OF CLOVIS CREEK***

"A strong-minded young woman follows her own path leading into mayhem and mystery within the world of show horses in this intriguing romance."

— **VICKY J. ROSE, AUTHOR OF *TREASURE HUNT IN TIE TOWN***

# Pegasus Flying

# Also by Denise F. McAllister

## Wild Cow Ranch Series

*Maverick Heart*

*A Wild Cow Winter*

*Follow a Wild Heart*

*Cowgirls and Rustlers*

*A Wild Cow Wedding*

*Wild Cow Christmas*

## Rafter O Ranch Series

*Home is Where You Are*

*A Fiery Match*

*Finding My Destynee*

## Katy McKim Mysteries

*Stalker or Saint*

# Pegasus Flying

## KATY MCKIM MYSTERY
### BOOK TWO

## DENISE F. MCALLISTER

**Pegasus Flying**
Paperback Edition
Copyright © 2024 Denise F. McAllister

CKN Christian Publishing
An Imprint of Wolfpack Publishing
701 S. Howard Ave. 106-324 Tampa, FL 33609

cknchristianpublishing.com

All rights reserved. No part of this book may be reproduced by any means without the prior written consent of the publisher, other than brief quotes for reviews.

This book is a work of fiction. Any references to historical events, real people or real places are used fictitiously. Other names, characters, places and events are products of the author's imagination, and any resemblance to actual events, places or persons, living or dead, is entirely coincidental.

Paperback ISBN 978-1-63977-483-8
eBook ISBN 978-1-63977-482-1
LCCN 2024933748

*To God, family, friends, readers, writing organizations, and all others who support my work and dreams—thank you very much.*

*To all those who have lost loved ones from this earthly life, my prayer is that you cherish their memory, feel peace, and will be blessed to be reunited with them in a heavenly place one day.*

*Pegasus Flying*

# CHAPTER 1
## Getting to Know You...

KATY MCKIM HAD BEEN DATING MATT HARTMAN FOR A while now, through lots of challenges—stalking, loss of family, as well as restoration. She sensed him now scanning her face and auburn-colored hair and was grateful for his presence in her life...although they were still learning about one another. It was tough at times getting to know each other.

"I need money, Matt. Everyone needs money. Plus, I enjoy writing and staying busy. Having a purpose. Like you do with your job."

She was referring to his profession as a private investigator. That's how they had met. He had helped her with a lot of different obstacles in her life in the short time they had been together. Hoping that all the weird, crazy stuff, as she called it, was behind her and that her life would now settle down and become somewhat normal like other people's, Katy tried to explain to him about her passion for her new work venture.

"But Katy, you received the insurance payment to rebuild your barn. And you won the jackpot at the

Golden horse show. You could use some of it to fix up your parents' house...excuse me, *your* house...and make it your own like you wanted to do. Why don't you take a break before going back to work?"

He just didn't understand. Although they had started a relationship, and she really did care for him, she always reminded herself that she was a woman alone and had to support herself. What if they broke up someday? Then she certainly would be on her own again.

Sure, things might progress between them, even making their way to the altar one day. And yes, some women might strive for that and be satisfied in a role where the man took care of everything, financially and otherwise...although the world had been changing for a long time. Now young women were keen on having their own careers, business, and direction. Sometimes even without a man.

Katy respected their decisions, but she wanted to be a partner with the man in her life and pull her own weight. Her parents had taught her to be self-sufficient, to work hard, not to rest on her laurels, but to keep at it till the day was done. Then get up in the morning and do it all over again.

But her parents weren't here to root for her, to be in her corner, to talk out any problems she might encounter along her life's journey. They died a couple of years before surrounded by mysterious circumstances. Turns out their murder, by carbon monoxide poisoning while they slept, was arranged by someone she had known and who had turned out to be a psycho stalker. She told herself, you can't make this stuff up. Truth is stranger than fiction.

Detective Matthew Hartman was the private investi-gator who had worked that case—not the murder of her parents, but the Golden State National horse show where Katy was showing her horse. Both stories seemed to be tied together. A dangerous stalker was at large, drugging horses and people. It had been a scary time and Katy wanted to put it all behind her and move on with her life.

Their discussion continued as they navigated around the kitchen like a dance and prepared breakfast together in Katy's ranch house.

"Matt, I want to get back to work. I enjoy writing articles for the magazine. It's been a dream job for me. Work from home or wherever I take my computer, reporting on horse shows, equestrian fashions, and equipment. I'm excited that I'll get to pitch story ideas this time. There's a new publisher and I already sent him word that I'd like to do a spread on top-level owners, their ranches, trainers, everything. My old boss at the magazine said it sounded great."

Stopping their kitchen maneuvering and standing face to face, Matt put a hand around her waist and stroked her hair and cheek.

"Katy, I'm just trying to watch over you. I want the best for you, especially after all you've been through. But I won't stand in the way of your dreams. If this is what you want, I'll support you however I can."

She accepted his kiss as he leaned closer.

"Thanks. That means a lot. And besides, if you and the boys are not going to let me in on your detective work, then I'll have to find my own." She grinned.

"What does that mean?"

"You know exactly what I mean. You, Andre, and Shawn all working together at Kleos and not letting me in on the action."

She was half teasing, but half serious too.

He set out a couple of mugs and plates. Oftentimes they ate breakfast at the kitchen island rather than in the dining room.

"We're all trained detectives, Katy. Or, in Shawn and Andre's case, ex-military guys experienced in special ops. We've talked about this. I'm still working my own cases with the police department and helping Andre and your brother on some of their cases. They get into some dangerous situations that I don't think you should be involved with."

Her life had been somewhat complicated. After her parents had died, Andre Patron, her brother's military buddy, was there to console her. Her brother, Shawn, had gone missing during that time. To Katy, it was a dreadful season of her life, one she never wanted to relive. Now "the guys" were back together working private military, or civilian cases with Andre's company, Kleos.

"I'm not saying I want to get into combat with a killer, but I could lend my brains to the operation. Didn't I help solve the Golden horse show case? You've got to give me some credit for that."

He smiled and nodded. "Yes, you did give me some insight on the Golden show. But as far as working with us now in detective work, your brother and Andre voted it down."

"What about you? What's your vote?"

He tilted his head, and she knew he was watching his words. "Let's just say, maybe you should go ahead and write articles for the magazine."

"Oh, I see, you think that'll be tamer, safer. Right?"

"Katy, let's not fight. Let's enjoy our time together today."

"Who said we were fighting?"

She smiled and gave him a peck on the lips, then turned back to the frying pan where she was scrambling eggs.

Matt poured two coffees. "So, what's on the agenda today? Something fun, I hope, especially if you're going to be busy Monday."

"Maybe we could go downtown and walk around, have lunch. You said you've never been on the Sundial Bridge before, which I find hard to believe. It opened in the early 2000s. How long have you lived in California?"

"Uh, pretty much my whole life. But I'm always working, Katy."

She touched his shoulder. "It's really cool, kind of a must-see, at least once in your life. I know you'll like it."

"Okay. Sounds good. Do we need to do anything around here before we go?"

"Just eat breakfast. Afterward, we can give Cash and the other horses some hay. I might turn them out and call my neighbors to check on them while we're gone. I think Stan and Lily are home today."

Cash was her show horse, but she didn't pamper him like some people did. Her father had always taught her that horses needed to be horses and were the happiest when they had pasture time. Cash spent a lot of time outside with her neighbors' two horses and they all were best buds. Occasionally, when the weather was bad, like lightning, she'd bring the horses into the barn.

Matt set the full mugs of coffee at their places and pulled out a barstool in front of a plate of eggs.

"This looks great." Matt grabbed the little bottle of Tabasco sauce.

"You're kind of addicted to that stuff, aren't you?" She grinned.

"Don't leave home without it, I always say."

"Maybe it's from your Hispanic roots. You grew up in Chula Vista, right?"

"Yeah, pretty close to Tijuana. But I've always been a little mixed up on my roots. My mom claims Hispanic. My dad says the Hartman name is German, but someone else in the family said English. One grandmother was Irish...or maybe she was a great-grand, and there's even some French mixed in there, believe it or not."

"Well, I like Heinz 57. Maybe even more so than Tabasco sauce."

She gave him a wink and passed the bacon as well as avocado toast, a favorite for both.

"I'm glad you're not one of those girls who doesn't eat, Katy. They skip meals and only eat lettuce or a spoon of yogurt."

"I've had my moments of not eating, like at horse shows. You're not saying anything about my figure, are you?"

"No, Katy. Gosh, you're perfect."

She thought it cute how he squirmed a little at her teasing.

"I don't know about that, but I work it off. Ride my horse. Muck stalls when Cash and the neighbor horses stay in. I've been working in the garden, too, trying to revive it. So, I need to eat. Fuel my body."

"Well, keep up the good work, sweetie. You're healthy and fit...and, I reap the benefits of your cooking. The garden's looking good, by the way. I'm sure your parents would be very proud."

She used to tear up whenever they were mentioned, but a couple of years had passed since their death. And she knew Matt was a compassionate man who only spoke reverently and sincerely about them. She often heard him say he wished he had known them.

"I hope so," was all she said as she finished her breakfast.

He touched her hand when she rested it on the counter.

"So, we hike a little, walk across the bridge, have lunch. Anything else you want to do or see downtown?"

"Yeah. The magazine office. I think it's in the same old building as before. I just want to make sure. Even though my work is mostly remote, I'll go in once in a while for meetings."

He stuffed his mouth but talked around the food. "Sure. Let's find it while we're there. And hey, you still up for visiting my sister tomorrow?" He waited but she seemed to be off somewhere in her mind. "I mentioned it before, not sure you heard me."

She took a sip of her coffee. "Sorry. Yes, visit your sister and squeeze the new baby. Sounds good."

"And church," he added.

She wasn't sure about that. "Do we have time? She lives about an hour from here, right?"

"Yes, not too far from my apartment in Willows. The church is close to their house. She asked if we'd meet there, then have lunch at her place. I don't get to see her that often because of work."

She couldn't resist his eyes. He was so kind and never asked for anything selfishly. Why not do this one thing to make him happy?

"Sure, Matt. If you want to."

"I think you'll like the church."

They had talked a little about how she was easing back into her faith. When her parents died, she blamed God for not protecting her sweet, good mom and dad from evil. And when her brother, Shawn, went missing and was presumed dead, that just sealed the deal. How could she believe that God loved her family if He couldn't keep them safe?

Little by little, though, with Matt's help, she realized that evil wasn't God's fault and that it saddened Him when his children were hurting. She was willing to give Him another chance.

After finishing breakfast and quickly cleaning the kitchen, Katy got her neighbor on the phone and hit speaker. Matt sipped the end of his coffee and watched her.

"Morning, Lily. Matt and I are headed downtown. If I put Cash and your boys out in the big pasture, will you and Stan be able to check on them and bring them in later if need be?"

"Sure, Katy. We'll be glad to. We're home all day. Doing chores and cooking. My daughter might come by later."

"Thanks, Lily. We appreciate it."

"Have fun, you two."

They were such good neighbors. About the age of Katy's deceased parents, Stan and Lily Beck had been there when the psycho from the Golden horse show had set fire to the barn, or paid someone to do it. That was still being decided by the authorities and Katy did not look forward to seeing the criminal again in a court case, but it was inevitable since Katy had been the targeted victim.

There were a lot of charges against the perpetrator who was being held in jail, no bond. Accused of being the mastermind behind the drugging of horses and people at the Golden horse show, she had also been instrumental in Katy's brother, Shawn's, mysterious disappearance for nearly a year, which led to the belief he was dead. The biggest charge in Katy's mind was the killing of her parents in their own bed of carbon monoxide poisoning, to which the criminal pretty much confessed.

It was all so unbelievable. Overwhelming at times for Katy. But she had been trying to put it all behind her now. And with Matt's caring devotion, she was finally getting some peace.

## CHAPTER 2
# *Sundial Bridge*

AFTER TURNING HER HORSE AND THE NEIGHBORS' TWO horses out in the big pasture, Katy went back in the barn and saw that Matt had placed a flake of hay in each of their feeders for when they came back in later in the day.

"Thanks for the help."

"I topped off their water."

"Good. They should enjoy themselves out there. It's a nice day. And I'm sure Stan and Lily will check on them in a while."

"All right. Let's get going on our adventure. To the bridge we go."

Matt froze in place with a faraway stare, thrust his arms out straight with pointed fingers, one forward and one back, and balanced on one leg. At first, she wasn't sure what his intended pose represented, but he kind of resembled a hunting dog.

"You are too funny."

"Gotta make you smile so you'll keep me around, ma'am." He touched the brim of his ball cap and nodded to her.

"My truck or yours?"

"I've got your chariot awaiting, m'lady." He did a little bow.

He was right. Kept her smiling.

They got on the road and Katy enjoyed the beautiful scenery along the way. The sun flickered through the trees like an old-timey projector and she had to look away before it made her dizzy. She gazed at Matt's strong arm on the wheel, then his profile. He was a handsome man.

DOWNTOWN REDDING WAS ABOUT thirty or more minutes from her parents' farm, *her* farm now. It had been in her dad's family before that. He and his father had built the barn which survived many storms, mostly rain since snowfall was less than five inches every year in their protected valley. The barn was even still standing after the fire that the crazy stalker had intended for total destruction of property and livestock.

Katy always caught herself after she called someone "crazy" in her mind. She did have sympathy when it was obvious someone had mental health issues and she sincerely hoped they would get the care they needed so they wouldn't harm others or themselves. It's just that her stalker had exhibited such wacko behavior when they were hell-bent on wreaking havoc in Katy's life that she had a hard time thinking of them as anything normal.

*Oops, guess I shouldn't call anyone "wacko" either.*

She was daydreaming as all kinds of topics ping-ponged around in her brain. Matt occasionally glanced at her, but she liked how they didn't have to talk all the time. They were comfortable in the silences. She leaned her head back and watched the trees blur past.

As they entered downtown, she sat up straight.

"Before we go to the bridge, let me look for the magazine's building. Go slow. It's next to a good coffee shop."

"Is that it over there? Pegasus?"

Matt slowed in front of an old red brick building, and Katy viewed a striking new logo sign over the door depicting a flying white horse against a blue-sky background.

"Yes, that's it. *Pegasus Publications*. Used to be called *Cali Horse Shows*."

"Do you want to stop? There are a couple of people going in."

They saw a tall man in a cowboy hat hold the door for a young woman in tight jeans and a fringed top. Katy felt a tingle crawl up her arm when it seemed the man was looking directly at her and Matt, which was strange as he didn't look familiar to her at all.

"No. Keep going. Straight through town. There's parking near the bridge, at the bistro or turtle museum. And lots of hiking not too far."

Matt turned his head toward her. "Are you okay?"

"Sure. Why wouldn't I be?"

"I don't know. You said that really fast. I thought you wanted to stop at the magazine office."

"I'll be there this week. I just wanted to make sure it was still in the same building."

He grabbed her hand. "Remember, Katy, I have a 'Spidey-sense' and know when you're fibbing."

She frowned. "I don't know what you're talking about. Now, let's go have some fun, Spider-Man. You're not afraid of heights or bridges, are you?"

"I ain't afraid of nuthin', ma'am. Except maybe you."

He squinted his eyes and showed all his teeth as though he were a snarling animal.

There were other instances in their time together when he had put on that funny accent. She wanted to swat his arm, but instead just giggled and shook her head.

He drove on to find a parking space.

"Do you know about Pegasus in mythology?"

"I remember a little from school," she said. "He was a white stallion with wings."

"Did you know his mother was Medusa, the one with the snakes coming out of her head?"

"Eww. I don't remember that."

"His father was Poseidon, god of the sea and horses. Maybe earthquakes too."

"You're kidding. I must've totally missed that in class."

"Yep. And it gets creepier. Pegasus came out of his pregnant mother's neck after Perseus beheaded her. Talk about a dysfunctional family."

"I think you're making some of that up."

"I'm not. It's true, Katy." He made a cross on his heart. "For real. I wouldn't lie to you."

"Sure, you wouldn't, Spider-Man. Oh, there's a space." She pointed to a vehicle backing out.

"Okay, Miss Navigator. More about Pegasus later."

"No, thank you. I don't want to have nightmares about his mother's snaky hairdo."

She smiled at him and gathered her tote and hat as she got out of the truck. "Why didn't you call me your copilot instead of navigator?"

"Because God's my copilot." He grinned.

She didn't have any comeback for that and thought it sweet that he was religious. Her parents had raised her and her brother to attend church, but when they died, she held it against God as though he had orchestrated the whole thing. However, Matt told her God never meant anything for her harm, that He loved her unconditionally, that the Enemy was the one who rained down death and destruction upon the people of Earth. She was trying to understand this better and patch up her relationship with God. She wanted to feel the same kind of joy as Matt seemed to embrace in his life.

## CHAPTER 3
# Matt to the Rescue

It was a beautiful clear day with an ocean-blue sky, a little crisp, just the way Katy liked it. They parked at the Turtle Bay Exploration Park and first went to the museum where Matt paid for two tickets.

He held her hand and she enjoyed walking together like tourists. It was such a change from ranch work and horse showing and gave her mind a break from all the drama that had taken place in her life in recent months. She watched other people, some with kids to corral, and she wondered if that scenario would ever be in her future.

"Kinda crowded, isn't it?" Matt squeezed her hand, and she liked how the warmth enveloped hers.

"It's the weekend. But it's not too bad really. It's still early."

They followed the flow of people through the aquarium and were fascinated by schools of colorful fish darting around frenetically, and slow-moseying turtles on man-made banks above the water as they hunted bugs. A reptile habitat showcased a plethora of snakes and Gila monsters, which she hurried by.

Outside was an exhibit of birds including the yellow-billed magpie that was Katy's favorite. "So pretty, isn't it?"

The list on the wall of other animals to observe included fox, badger, raccoon, bobcat, porcupine, beaver, and skunks. "When I was a kid my dog got into a skunk," Matt said. "It was the worst smell I've ever been around."

Matt read almost every word in the exhibit that detailed the construction of the bridge as well as the Shasta Dam. "Amazing how it was built," he commented.

Katy mostly wanted to hurry on to the next display. "So many things to see." She read aloud from the colorful pamphlet designating herself as their tour guide.

She told him about the underground caverns, a room with artifacts from early settlers, samples of different animal furs since the fur trade had been big in the area, as well as an art gallery and botanical gardens.

"The bridge is free. It takes about fifteen minutes to walk across which includes time to look around. It's two hundred seventeen feet high and spans seven hundred ten feet across the Sacramento River. It's the world's largest working sundial. Incredible, huh?"

Matt nodded. "Yeah. Amazing."

Katy continued highlighting facts from the pamphlet.

"There's a glass-like surface so we'll be able to see through to the river below. It took eleven years to complete, and cost $23.5 million. In July, thousands of swallows swoop out from under the glass walkway where they build their nests. After we get across the bridge, we can come back for the car. Then drive a short way and park near the river. There are some nice hiking trails, only a couple of miles each way."

Matt wore a light backpack containing water and snacks as well as bug spray and sunscreen.

"Were you a Boy Scout?"

"What?"

"Well, you're always prepared." She chuckled.

"Prepared is my middle name."

"Matthew Prepared Hartman?"

"You got it."

There were quite a lot of people on the bridge, but they flowed among them easily. Katy was excited to share this experience with Matt and remembered coming to the bridge when it had first opened. She was a child then and life was good. Her parents were alive and her brother was both a pal and a nuisance, but that was normal for a boy, she thought. Back then, Shawn had threatened to pick her up and toss her over the railing into the river below. All Katy had to do was make a scared face and her father pinched the top of her brother's shoulder. Just a little threatening reminder for him to go easy with his sister.

"Look, Matt!" She pointed over the side to the river below. "Isn't it beautiful?" Then she stood on the clear part of the bridge where she looked through to the water below.

He came alongside and wrapped his arm around her waist. "Yeah, it's amazing."

They walked once across the bridge, then back again to their vehicle so they could park closer to the trails. When they got on the trail there was a bit of an incline, but it was an easy and pleasant hike.

Katy's gaze followed the bridge towering into the sky. "Pretty incredible. Are you glad we came?"

"Yeah, for sure. Thanks for suggesting it. After living

in the state all these years, I can finally say I walked on the Sundial Bridge."

She smiled, but the moment was interrupted by high-pitched yelling and crying.

"What in the world is that?" Katy asked.

"I think it's up ahead. C'mon." And Matt was off at a fast jog in the direction of the wail.

They came across a small group gathered around a young girl who had tripped on the trail. Blood covered her face, elbows, and knees and tears flowed down her face.

"How can I help?" Matt kneeled and asked the adults around her.

A woman, presumably the girl's mother, said, "She fell over a root or something."

"It'll be okay," the mother's friend said comforting the girl.

It didn't appear there was a father with the women. A young boy a few years older than the injured girl stood on the outskirts of the group with what Katy thought to be a guilty expression. Or at least a sorry look of compassion. She wasn't sure which.

The mother spied the boy and yelled at him. "I told you to stop running. Now look what you've done to your sister. She's only six. You're supposed to watch out for her."

It reminded Katy of her and her brother at that age. They were always horsing around and ended up in some misadventure. Shawn reminded her not to "cry like a girl." So, she did everything in her power to appear as tough as him. There were times, though, when she couldn't keep the tears at bay.

Matt dropped his backpack and asked Katy to open it and retrieve some water and a cloth. She handed it to him, and he asked the mother's permission to assist after saying he had some first aid training as a former police officer. The mother nodded her okay.

He carefully got closer to the little girl's level on the ground. "I'm sorry this happened to you, but don't worry. We're all going to help get you cleaned up. Can you tell me where it hurts?"

She blubbered and pointed to her puffy lip and chin, both dripping blood. Then showed him her elbows and knees. Her shaky voice squeaked out with, "My shirt..." as she pulled at the shoulder of a white, bloodstained T-shirt emblazoned with hearts and a cute Disney animal of some kind, maybe a gray mouse with big ears. Or a bear?

Her mother said, "It's her favorite. Lilo and Stitch who, I think, is a dog, or a sci-fi robot, or something. I'm not really sure what it is." The woman's hands shook, and her eyes were moist.

The girl whispered, a little defiantly. "He's Lilo's friend."

Matt knelt down. "I'm sure your shirt will be fine. Just needs washing. Now let's take a look at your scrapes. I'll be gentle and, if it's okay with you, I'll put a little water on those spots so we can wash away the blood. Okay?"

She nodded at him through pools of water flooding her eyes.

He gingerly dabbed and wiped the areas on her elbows and knees. After somewhat cleaning her up, he demonstrated with his own arm and asked, "Can you move yours back and forth? Like this. Now your leg. Do you think you can stand? I'll help you."

Katy watched him work and felt her heart expand. She hadn't known about his gift for communicating with children and thought she'd file that knowledge away on her internal list of positive attributes when it came to Matthew Hartman.

When the little girl attempted a standing position, she faltered and he caught her. She winced and teared up again.

"Hey, no worries. Do you like horses?" He was right beside her and gave a big smile.

She nodded a little, but asked, "What? Why?"

"Horses. We don't have any here, but you could think of me as your rescue pony. I will carry you back to the start of the trail and we'll call for some real first aid people to take a look at you. They'll fix you up as good as new. I promise."

The mother interjected. "She likes ballet dancing more than horses. She has a recital next week."

"Oh, okay." Matt kept his smile bright for the little girl. "We'll get you all mended so you can *hopefully* dance at your recital. How does that sound?"

In his training as a police officer, he was always told to add "weasel words" such as "hopefully" when dealing with the public. Never guarantee or promise, at least as far as health issues or recuperation time, since no one knows the future.

Her tiny voice said, "Okay."

"I'm not a doctor," he said, "so he or she will make the final decision. But I can tell you're a very strong little girl, and probably a good ballerina too. I feel pretty confident that you'll be good as new very soon."

The girl gave him a big smile. "I can do twirls."

"Wow. I bet you can."

To the mother Matt said in a low tone, "I don't think anything's broken but a doctor should make that determination." Then he noticed the boy hanging back from the circle around his sister, so he put in a good word for him. "Don't be too hard on your son. I recall my boyhood and stuff just happens with kids. They usually bounce right back."

Now the mother teared up. She pulled her son close for a hug and thanked Matt.

With the little girl clinging to his back, hands around his neck, legs around his waist, Matt and his patient were in the lead, with Katy close behind carrying the backpack. The group hadn't gone very far on the trail, so it wasn't long before they reached the parking lot at the beginning point. There they were met by an ambulance and EMTs.

The mother explained. "My friend called ahead and told them about the accident."

"Great," Matt said. "Your daughter will be in good hands."

"I can't thank you enough." She hugged Matt tightly.

"Glad to be of help. Take care now."

The EMTs told him "good job" and talked to the mother about the merits of further treatment at the hospital including X-rays to rule out any possible injuries not visible in their exam.

Soon Matt and Katy were back on their own.

"Well, aren't you the big hero, mister?"

"Just there at the right time."

"Humble too." She kissed his cheek.

They had had a wonderful day together, in spite of the little girl's accident. Although Katy hated that the girl got hurt, she was grateful to have witnessed Matt's handling of the situation. He was polite and caring with the mother and daughter, and even put in a good word for the brother. He showed calm leadership under pressure and humility at receiving any praise for his heroics. Yep, she'd keep him in the plus column.

Instead of having lunch at one of the restaurants in the park, they decided to head home to Katy's ranch. Besides checking on the horses, she wanted to do a little computer work. And he mentioned he might put some hamburger patties together for their trip to his sister Angel's the following day. He knew her husband Luis would like having ready-made burgers to drop on the grill. Matt said he'd send a text to confirm.

"Let's go this way to the truck, through the botanical gardens." Katy grabbed his arm, and he moved closer to her.

As they came around a bend in the richly landscaped walkway, a man wearing a suit and holding a professional-looking camera held up one finger to his mouth and let out a "shhh." A wedding ceremony was in progress.

"Oh." Katy stopped short. "Look," she whispered. "How pretty."

They couldn't hear every word, but Katy surmised that the event was nearing the end.

The bride wore a beautiful white, halter-style dress, with rows of cascading satin and tulle reaching the floor. The groom was handsome in a trim black tuxedo and shiny patent leather shoes. Both were beaming with smiles and seemed locked on each other's eyes as if the crowd of family and friends was not even present.

Katy listened as they vowed to stay true for the rest of their lives and to love and support each other. She felt a twinge of envy that the couple seemed dedicated to each other and no doubt felt very sure about their decision. At least she hoped they did.

Would that ever happen for her? She always had so

many doubts and what-ifs floating around in her brain. What if the groom left her or cheated or fell out of love with her? What if he died? She was acutely familiar with the devastating heartache of losing her parents and then almost losing her brother. She'd rather be alone than go through all that again. Or would she? Would that really be living at all? She made a mental note to look up the quote about "...better to have loved and lost than never to have loved at all." It made a lot of sense. Humans weren't meant to go it alone through life.

After they got home from their day of playing tourists, they tended to the horses and spent a quiet evening together enjoying a simple dinner. Later, they turned in...to separate bedrooms—she in hers and Matt in the barn loft. There would be church in the morning and Katy's mind filled with thoughts of that and a million other things as she placed her head on the pillow.

# CHAPTER 4
## *Church and Babies*

FOR MOST OF KATY'S CHILDHOOD AND TEEN YEARS, SHE attended a nondenominational church in their small ranching community along with her parents and brother. She recalled having a lot of fun at the various youth activities—car washes, 4-H-type shows with farm animals, and, as she got older, dances like the fall festival.

Because the elder McKims held leadership positions in the church, albeit volunteer, she couldn't help but feel spied upon since church members who only had the best of intentions sometimes scolded her and her brother for various wrongdoings. Eventually the report got back to her parents. It was almost like being a "PK"—preacher's kid—without being on the payroll. Seemed to her there were a lot of rules to abide by. Although, all in all, she hardly ever took a misstep away from being a good girl. Her brother...that was a whole different matter. He could be a downright hellion at times.

Now Matt had invited her to his "traditional" church where his sister and her husband attended. She wasn't sure what to expect, but she had heard the stories of a lot of up-and-down movements—kneeling and standing. She told herself to try and maintain an open mind.

He helped her out of his truck and held her hand as they walked to the entrance. Katy hoped her attire of white cotton peasant blouse, blue jean skirt, and blue-and-tan cowgirl boots was appropriate.

When they left her house, Matt had said, "Of course, you look great. Nowadays people dress casually. It's not like my mother's church, which is a lot more old-school."

She had scowled a bit. "I'm not sure if that makes me feel better or worse."

"What'd I say?"

She wasn't upset. She knew men didn't really have a clue when it came to women's clothing, at least most men.

Inside the doorway, she watched as Matt dipped a finger in a holy water bowl mounted on the wall and made the sign of the cross on himself—finger to forehead, heart, then each shoulder. She touched the water but just cupped her hands together politely and scanned around to see if anyone was watching. Otherwise, she was determined to follow his lead.

As they made their way down the center aisle, Katy recognized Matt's sister who turned around in her seat and gave them an excited wave.

When they reached the row, Angel, with a full smile, whispered and patted the velvety seat of the pew, "Here, I saved you seats."

Matt let Katy go in first so she could sit next to Angel. The two women clasped hands and gave each other a cheeky hug.

"I'm so glad you came, Katy." The big smile on Angel's face did not look like it was leaving any time soon.

"Thanks for inviting us."

Katy leaned forward so she could see around Angel to Luis, the husband, who was cradling a sleeping baby in his arms.

Katy gently touched the baby's arm. "So sweet. How old is he now?"

"Six months already." Angel beamed.

The baby was dressed like a little man. White shirt, blue bow tie, blue striped pants covering his diaper, bare feet with the sweetest toes that would probably be wiggling if he were awake. His headful of dark curls drew Katy in like a magnet. She had to stroke his hair. His bluish eyes, now shut, would most likely change to brown within the next few months.

Luis smiled and whispered, "Let's see if he'll stay this way all through the service. If he wails, I'll have to take him out."

People settled into their seats and quieted down after visiting with fellow members. A priest walked across the altar to the podium.

Into the tiny flesh-colored microphone taped to his cheek he said, "Welcome to all. Let us sing and praise our Heavenly Father. May the joy of the Lord be upon your faces and in your hearts." He held his arms out wide.

Katy liked his jovial appearance—gray, spiky hair, gray trimmed beard, and round midsection. His green brocade robe was not too glitzy, but rather understated. She watched him carry out the steps of the Mass assisted by two altar boys. The statues around the church were intriguing to her. She and Matt's family sat on the Joseph side or the right facing the altar. A beautiful image of Mary, the Blessed Mother, was on the left, at her Son's right hand. And, of course, Jesus was on the crucifix in the center.

Katy thought about that. Some churches chose not to

place Him there since Easter signifies that He rose from the dead and was no longer on the cross. But she meant no disrespect in her thoughts. Perhaps this church was just showing remembrance of the cruel act that had occurred during His ministry.

Matt squeezed her hand and smiled. Then they all stood. Then kneeled for a time. Up again to recite the Lord's Prayer. Then everyone sat for the priest's message...sermon, or as this church called it, the homily.

He spoke about forgiveness and how it really frees the person who makes the decision to forgive. The offender oftentimes has no idea how their deed has hurt another, or maybe doesn't even care and has already moved on. Katy thought of the person responsible for the death of her parents. It was unthinkable for her to forgive that horrible deed. How could she? Her mother and father had been ripped from her life and now she would spend the rest of her years without them. Robbed of so many days, of wonderful memories they could have made together.

The priest continued but Katy's mind wandered to the stained-glass windows and other decor. For the small community of Willows, it was apparent that some individual, group, or religious body had contributed to the adornment and upkeep of this facility. It wasn't a rural pop-up like a cowboy church at horse shows, nor a supersized megachurch like Katy had seen on TV. And she was sure it was unlike the modest church Matt had described as the one his parents attended close to Chula Vista, where they had been members all their lives, where Matt and his sister had been christened as infants.

When the time in the service came for communion Katy wasn't exactly sure what to do. Drawing on her experience with the nondenominational churches, she remembered they sometimes observed communion once a month or as the "Spirit led" them. Sometimes those congregations came forward, or other times they stay seated and passed the trays of small white wafers and plastic sealed cups of grape juice.

Here, the priest explained that those not of the faith could join the procession forward and instead of partaking of the "elements," as he referred to the wine and wafer, they could cross their arms across their chest and receive a blessing. Katy followed Matt and did that, but felt kind of odd when she noticed she was the only one folding her arms.

She understood Matt's church observed Holy Communion every Sunday and the members formed a line to head to the altar where the priest offered a sip from the chalice of wine and a round white wafer representing Jesus's body. She wondered if the wine presented a problem for recovering alcoholics. Maybe they abstained. And what about the spread of germs in today's paranoid culture? She tried to quiet her brain from meandering questions.

When the service ended, and even before, she heard some of the kneelers being kicked up to clear the way for people to exit their rows. Katy couldn't help but stare and thought the noise was rather rude to others, and to the priest, who stayed till the very end. Why were they in such an all-fire hurry to get out?

After chitchat with a few people Matt and his sister knew, and a thank-you to the priest who had come around to the front door for goodbyes, Matt and Katy followed in his truck to Angel and Luis's house. It took a few minutes to get going as they waited for Luis to securely hook the baby into his car seat.

"Jon-Luis is a nice name. It was sweet of them to use Matthew for a middle name," she said.

"I want to call him J.L."

She frowned. "Is your sister okay with that?"

"Not exactly. But I'm gonna be the funcle."

"The what?"

"The fun uncle."

She shook her head. He was a nut. But kept her smiling.

The house was located down a country road on the outskirts of town, about twenty minutes from Matt's apartment. There were trees around and even some green grass surrounding the building.

Matt had told her that Luis Martinez taught wood-working at the local high school and coached football and other sports. He and Angel loved kids and the loss of their first baby had been devastating but they struggled through it with the help of their family, friends, and faith. Having Jon-Luis gave them another chance to be parents. No wonder Angel's smile was so big and ever-present.

They put on a big spread for lunch. Everyone gathered around the kitchen as Luis brought in a tray of pulled pork from the grill and set it on the stovetop.

"I started it early this morning and let it warm slowly while we were in church," he said. "I've also got those burgers you brought, Matt. If we don't eat everything, you can take some plates home."

Angel came near to Katy. "We're having tacos with flank steak. There are lots of different toppings. I hope you like everything."

"Smells great. I'm sure I'll love it. What can I do to help?"

Matt squeezed her shoulder.

"You want to hold the baby? Looks like he's starting to stir." Angel leaned down to the infant carrier and unhooked the straps between his legs.

Katy hadn't had a lot of experience with children during her lifetime. But they sure were sweet. She reminded herself, maybe she thought they were sweet because she hadn't been in the thick of things—dirty diapers, red-faced screaming.

"Sure. And if I get into any trouble, Matt will bail me out."

Angel placed the baby in Katy's arms and directed her toward the couch to sit.

Immediately Katy started to baby talk with him.

"Oh…hello, little man…don't you have beautiful eyes and long lashes?" She nodded her head at him. "Yes, you do…very beautiful. All the little girls are going to be after you someday." She kept nodding and he watched her intently. Then his mouth opened widely, and she got very excited. "Look! Look! He's smiling at me."

Luis chuckled. "It might be gas."

"My little buddy, J.L., would never give any trouble. And he does *not* have gas." Matt smiled but then his sister batted his arm.

"I told you not to call him that. It's Jon-Luis."

Katy knew they were just teasing. The family warmth wrapped her in a cocoon, and she loved it even if it was a little bittersweet for her. She didn't mean to be greedy, but she couldn't help wishing her parents could still be here, wishing her brother didn't have a dangerous job that took him all over the world, and wishing she knew where her life was headed.

She tried to be grateful for what she did have, not for what she didn't. Every day. Count your blessings one by one. Just like her mom and dad had taught her.

## CHAPTER 5

### *Drugstore Cowboy*

A FEW DAYS LATER KATY WAS STILL BASKING IN THE memories of a great weekend. Matt had gone back to his apartment in Willows but called every morning and every night. They reminisced and commented on the fun time they had spent together.

First, on Saturday, she and Matt had taken in all they could at the Sundial Bridge, the turtle museum, and did a bit of hiking until they came across the little girl who had fallen on the trail. Matt had really proven he had hero attributes. It was so nice to get away and play tourist in her own city. For a few hours she had turned off her pestering thoughts and didn't dwell on the past, about losing her parents and brother, and dealing with a mentally unbalanced stalker. She had a lot of fun with Matt and knew she was lowering her guard and getting closer to him.

On Sunday, she had an interesting time at his church and enjoyed the visit to his sister and her husband's home. The baby, Jon-Luis, was simply a doll.

Now it was time to get back to work and prepare for the horse show she'd be attending in a couple of days.

She had written articles the last few years for *Cali Horse Shows* and even though it was a small company, her colleagues there had become dear friends. They were understanding when her parents died and she took a leave of absence. Now she was coming back, but the magazine had undergone a restructuring and her friend had sold his interest to a new owner from Portland.

Rebranding was taking place and Pegasus Publications would change the name of the magazine to *Pegasus*. Being that it was a horse publication, it kind of made sense. Although, after the mythological story Matt had shared with her as they drove through town on the weekend, the name kind of gave her the willies. Images of Medusa's snake hair danced in her mind.

The previous owner and her dear friend, Wes Stevens, had asked her to come in for a meeting so he could introduce her to the new owner before her first assignment at the horse show this weekend. It was really one of her suggested ideas rather than an assignment, included on her list which he had approved months ago. Wes was one of her biggest supporters and one of the kindest men she'd ever known. That is, after her father, and now, Matt. They were like a different breed compared to some males nowadays. But she didn't want to be gender biased since it was the same for females too. Seemed like the whole world had gone nuts lately.

Not too far from Redding, the small town of Libertyville was a little sleepy this Thursday morning. Katy carried a coffee and laptop into the restored historic house-turned-office of Pegasus Publications after parking her truck.

A pretty girl at the counter smiled. "Good morning. How may I help you?"

"Hi, I'm Katy McKim, here to see Wes Stevens and Brett Barker."

"Oh, hi, nice to meet you. I'm new but am a big fan of yours. You write the best articles. Have a seat and I'll tell him you're here."

"That's very sweet of you to say. Thanks very much."

Behind the counter were a few desks and a couple employees in the open, big room. At the end of the room was the owner's office. The door was uncharacteristically closed, obviously the new owner's practice.

The receptionist picked up her phone and announced Katy's arrival.

After fifteen minutes, she said to Katy who had taken a seat, "I'm so sorry. He must've gotten tied up. It shouldn't be too much longer."

Katy sipped her lukewarm coffee. Late people bothered her, but she tried to maintain patience. "Thank you." She smiled at the girl. Wasn't her fault. And why did she keep saying "he" instead of "they?"

Finally, the back-office door opened and out flew a slim blonde woman, speed walking and obviously exasperated. Her eyes met Katy's and the receptionist's, but she quickly jammed black sunglasses on her face as she yanked open the front door to exit. Katy and the receptionist shrugged to each other.

The receptionist's phone beeped and she picked up. To Katy she said, "You can go on back now," and pointed toward the new owner's office.

*Well, I guess no escort or greeting.* Usually, her old boss Wes would come out of his open-doored office, happily call for Katy to join him, and never would have kept her waiting. Or he'd come to the front and walk her back with him.

She didn't let it bother her too much. It wasn't like this was a big city with formal offices, but she still got a rudeness vibe. And who was that skinny blonde that ran out in such a huff?

The office door was shut so she slightly knocked and opened it. As she entered, she saw the man behind the desk, booted legs propped up, a phone to his ear. He held up one finger for her to wait. She felt her insides start to seethe, but she determined to push the feeling away. However, she wasn't going to stand as though she were in the principal's office, so she slid into a chair in front of his desk and set her laptop bag on the floor.

After a minute the man pressed the end button on his phone and set it on the desk. Boots swung around to the floor and he got to his feet. She noticed how tall and fit he was, as though he lifted weights and watched what he ate. For some reason she remembered an oversized T-shirt her mother used to wear for bed sometimes: "Real Men *Do* Eat Quiche." She had been on a kick of making different flavored quiches, some with ham, some with all veggies, which her husband loved. But when she got the T-shirt for him at a cutesy gift shop, he emphatically told her there was no way he would wear that. It was a play on words from the 1980s when a book had claimed men do not eat the foo-foo egg dish because it wasn't masculine.

The new owner wore dark blue pressed jeans, Western shirt and jacket, and bolo tie with a silver longhorn medallion. The longhorn conjured an image in Katy's mind of a devil with horns. She'd seen others where the horns were wider set and they didn't look scary at all. Maybe it was the flaming red jewels inset for eyes on the one he wore. She turned away from their threatening glare only to notice his huge silver belt buckle that sported an unfriendly skull. She wasn't sure what to make of this guy.

He just needed a cowboy hat to complete his image, but she doubted he ever got dirty or worked with livestock. Glancing around the office she saw what she thought might be a brand-new silverbelly hat on a rack attached to the wall, exactly where Wes Stevens used to hang his hat. But Wes's was well worn, well used, and well earned. Everyone in their small town knew how proud he was of the multigenerational lineage of his ranching family.

With an outstretched hand, the man behind the desk said deeply, "Brett Barker."

"Nice to meet you." She stood and shook his hand for a nanosecond. And because she was genuinely perplexed, she added, "Where's Wes?"

The man ignored her for a few seconds as he tapped his phone and smiled to himself. She had no clue what he was doing but found it as another rude point against him.

"I told him it was counterintuitive. I knew he had already discussed the business transaction with you, told you I was the new owner, so I thought it best to just cut to the chase."

He smiled a society smile, all teeth, no sincerity. She kind of hated when people said "counterintuitive" as though they were flaunting a college education.

"I see." She gave one nod. No light in her eyes.

Still flashing a wide smile, he extended his palm toward her chair. "Well, you sure are a pretty little lady. Have a seat. Let's talk about your future. Shall we?"

She stretched her closed lips into a minuscule smile

and before she could say a word, he started what Katy considered a rehearsed speech. Maybe one to show he had the upper hand.

"So, Katy." He settled into his high back red leather chair, different from the wooden one Wes used to have like the old newspaper guy that he was, and again Barker propped his booted feet atop the desk. Rude again, Katy thought. "I have a whole new vision for this magazine." He gestured in a flamboyant manner as though he were addressing a boardroom of executives. "We're not going to remain just a little agro pub. I want to build something more upscale. Grander. We should attend prestigious horse shows. Cover high-society events. Polo and even high-dollar horse sales. Maybe Keeneland."

Her brow furrowed and her mouth hung open a little. "Keeneland? That's racehorses. In Kentucky. Kind of far for us, wouldn't you say?"

His straight nose lifted as though he smelled something unpleasant. "I suppose so. But the world is smaller now what with the Internet. Do you have a problem with that?" His persona took on a change, heading toward the unfriendly zone.

She had to speak her mind. "But that's not our target market. People have been reading our magazine in this area and a few surrounding states for years—California, some Oregon, Nevada. Western horse showing mostly, some English. Definitely not polo." She shook her head, then added, "Does Wes know about any of this?"

Her latest remark seemed to irk him. When he spoke, he seemed to enunciate each word carefully.

"Wes Stevens is retired. I told you I have a brand-new vision. I want to take this magazine places. Nationally. Do you still want to write for us, Ms. McKim?"

Was he threatening her job? She determined to hold her own and remain professional.

"May I ask about your experience, Mr. Barker? Wes told me you managed a magazine before. Where was that?"

"I *owned* the publication. It was in Austin. Texas, that is." His words came out in a staccato cadence.

She obviously had ticked him off and probably should have held her tongue but couldn't resist her next zinger.

"Some people say Austin isn't really a part of Texas. It's more...shall I say, like Portland. Oregon, that is."

She noticed his ears got red first, then his neck before the color crept into his jawline.

"We also had an office in Portland," he deadpanned. "Are you expressing a political opinion about those cities, Ms. McKim?"

Okay. So, no more first-name basis, or "pretty lady" labels. *I guess I got his goat as my dad used to say.* She'd have to look up the derivation of that idiom.

"I'm sure the people that live there enjoy their lifestyle. It's just different from the horse scene where we are located. That's all I'm saying."

He gave a menacing stare. "I believe I've said...a couple of times now...that I have a *new vision* for this publication. Now why don't you tell me about the current story you're planning to work on."

She took in a breath and straightened in her seat. "This weekend I'll be covering the Rolling Hills horse show in Corning. I'll turn in the story and photos within the next week or so."

Again, he picked up his phone instead of interacting with her.

"Okay. Not a big show. But I'll be there too. I want to

meet a few people, shake some hands. I've got to be visible and let the people know about our rebranding and new ownership. If you know of anyone there of any importance, be sure to introduce me to them."

It was a surprise to her that Barker would be at the show, and she wasn't happy about the idea. But she gave a smidgen of a smile and said, "Sure thing." Then she pretended to pay attention to the time on her phone and said, "I have some errands in town if that'll be all."

"Yes, we're done. I'm very busy myself. I'll make a list of assignments and email them to you."

He turned his chair back to her.

She had to stand her ground.

"Uh…I don't really work on assignment. Wes agreed I can choose my own stories…"

Barker abruptly turned back to her, his phone to his ear. Instead of holding up a finger this time, he showed his palm, pretty much dismissing her. His eyes almost appeared like the longhorn's glaring red jeweled eyes in the bolo tie.

She grabbed her bag and walked out of his office trying her best to not let the bad words in her head spill out of her mouth. *What a jerk.*

# CHAPTER 6
## Sad Memories

LATER THAT NIGHT AFTER ALL THE CHORES WERE DONE around the barn and house, Katy was tired and just wanted to relax in bed with her e-reader. Although, as much as she loved reading, it always put her to sleep after a short while.

Matt called as she was pulling on her stretchy pajama leggings. She was still wound up from her meeting with Brett Barker and started sharing the details with him.

"Whoa, Katy, I've never heard you talk like that."

She hit the speaker button on her phone. "Well, he was. A real jackass. I could've said a lot worse. I don't know how I'm going to work with someone like him. He was arrogant, misogynistic, patronizing...didn't even let Wes come to the meeting. Said he'd email me assignments. The nerve. And you should have seen how he was dressed. Like *GQ* meets rodeo. My dad would have called him a drugstore cowboy. His boots were adorned with bison although I doubt he's ever seen one in person."

"So, you really didn't like him?" He tried holding his snickers in but wasn't very successful.

"Matt, this is not funny."

"Babe, it's just that you're on a tirade. You know I support you one hundred percent and I'm sorry you have to work with him. But I'm sure you'll figure out something. Maybe this is just your first impression, and he's trying to show that he's the boss. Later you both might even develop a friendship."

She was glad they weren't on video chat or else he'd see her rolling her eyes and shaking her head at his remarks.

"Now you're stretching it. I'm sure that'll never happen in a million years. Friends? Humph."

"There is another option, you know."

"What's that?"

"You could quit. You don't have to work with him. This is freelance, right? Write for another magazine."

"But I've gotten to know all the people on the show circuit—the exhibitors, vendors, show personnel—they know me and this magazine. Wes built a good reputation over the years. I'm not even sure there's another glossy publication like this one in our area. There's a little *PennySaver* kind of four-page newsprint thing that accepts advertising if you want to sell your chickens or pigs. I don't think I could write for them."

"Now, Katy, that's a little silly, don't you think? I'm sure there are tons of good publications. And with everything being remote nowadays, it doesn't have to be in your own backyard. You could write for an online magazine."

She let out a big sigh. He just didn't understand. And she was too exhausted to explain any further.

"Matt, I've got to get some sleep. I have an early start tomorrow."

"Sweetie, you know I care about you. I was trying to encourage you, but I guess I flubbed it. I'm just saying you can do anything you set your mind to."

She was quiet so he filled in the gap. "Did you reserve a motel?"

"Yes."

"Will you call me tomorrow night?"

"Yes."

"I'll miss you, Katy. Maybe I could drive to the show."

"No. I'll be working anyway. I'm only going to stay a couple of nights. I'll be back Sunday afternoon."

"Do you need me to do anything for you around the barn?"

"No. Thanks, though. The neighbors said they'd look after everything while I'm gone."

"Okay. Sounds like you've got things covered. Call me anytime, if you need anything. You're not upset with me, are you, Katy?"

"No. We're good. Good night, Matt."

"Good night, sweetie."

In their relationship they hadn't said, "I love you" to each other yet, but Katy felt that would happen pretty soon. She did care about him. A lot. It's just that she was used to doing things on her own, and as lonely as that got sometimes, she didn't want anyone to dictate how she should feel or act. Even though she knew Matt wasn't controlling like that, she still had some trust issues to work out.

～

SINCE THE NEIGHBORS would be doing chores for her this weekend, she only had to get herself up and out the door in the morning. It was about an hour ride to the show, and she wanted to get there early enough to cover as many classes as possible.

The drive was nice through trees on both sides of the road, some kind of oaks, and the air was cool this time of morning. It gave her time to think—about Matt. Was he "the one," the true love of her life? What would it be like if they got married? Would they have children? Live at her ranch?

She tried to contain her imagination. They were still in the dating phase, she thought. Sure, he often stayed at her place, but it was platonic. He usually stayed in the barn loft bedroom or sometimes in the guest room in the main house. She wondered how long it really took to know all about another person. To her, marriage was a lifelong commitment. And she knew Matt felt the same.

Then her mind darted to her brother and Andre and their line of work. She didn't really want to be a professional detective like Matt, but she seemed to have a genuine knack for fitting puzzle pieces together, human pieces. And although he may not have totally admitted it, she believed she had been a real help to Matt at the Golden horse show. He had been an investigator on the case involving horses that were drugged at the show where she was an exhibitor. That's when they had first met.

And then there was the memory of her parents. The thought of them always brought a tear to her eye and she was grateful for this time alone on the drive. Even though it had been more than two years, the loss was still as fresh as the day it had happened.

She was the one who had found them in their bed.

After college she had lived on her own with a girlfriend, but more recently had returned to her childhood home and lived with her parents. Her brother Shawn was away on one of his secret paramilitary missions. She wasn't really sure what he was doing or what city or even country he was in.

Some young people might be strongly opposed to living with their parents, but Katy actually liked hers. They were kind, funny, hardworking people. The three of them enjoyed similar things—nature, animals, growing vegetables, riding and caring for horses, going to church. And her parents—Howard and Dorothy McKim—didn't intrude on her life. They encouraged her dreams and accepted her as an adult. If she went out with her friends, she respected her parents and came home at a decent hour or called if she was planning to spend the night elsewhere.

Her dad was usually the first one up in the morning with her mother following closely after him. He put the first pot of coffee on, then got to the barn and pasture to feed the animals, collect eggs, and do whatever needed to be done. Mrs. McKim started biscuits, bacon, and eggs or pancakes or both and chopped melon, strawberries, and other fruit. She was a big proponent of her family eating healthy food to keep them going all day long. Some days she continued her preparation to include fixings for lunch and dinner.

The night before, Katy told her parents she'd be visiting a girlfriend. They went to see a chick flick, although Katy would rather have seen an action movie, then she spent the night at the friend's. When she got home the next morning around nine, she fully expected her father to be at work around the ranch, and that breakfast would be long over but the aroma of bacon lingering. To her, that was the smell of family and security, of fond, childhood memories.

But that day when she walked in the back door to the kitchen there was no bacon aroma, no laughter or banter between her parents, no sounds whatsoever. Except for maybe the sounds carrying from the barn of a mooing cow that hadn't been milked yet.

A weird kind of chill vibrated up Katy's back and neck. Something was wrong.

She had planned on heading to the barn, but for some unknown reason she felt compelled to check upstairs first. So, she went to her parents' room. The door was slightly open as usual. She tapped on it politely. No answer so she slowly pushed it the rest of the way open.

Her parents were still in bed, which was so odd. Were they sick? A quilt covered their bodies to their waists, like two mounds in the pasture. It was nearly three hours past their regular waking time. As she came closer, she saw they were curled facing each other, on their sides, heads on their pillows.

There was no snoring—her dad was famous for that —nearly bringing the roof down around them. She didn't know how her mother ever got any sleep.

"Mom? Dad? You okay?"

She tiptoed closer and felt like an intruder. Maybe they *were* sick.

That tingling returned like electricity zapping through her body. She was really worried now. It was too quiet.

She went to her mother's side of the bed and leaned closer. Her mouth was open slightly and her skin appeared reddish. She normally was paler since she stayed indoors more than her husband and Katy, although she did get out when her help was needed or if

44

it was time to work in the garden. Katy didn't recall her mother having a rash or sunburn the day before.

"Mom?"

Katy touched her shoulder, but there was no response.

"Oh, God, please no." She whispered to herself.

This couldn't be happening. They couldn't be dead. How is that possible? Both of them? Together?

She was making her way around the bed to her father's side when she realized the room smelled, not exactly of death, but something rancid, like a rotten egg. It wasn't overpowering, but she was wary and went to open the window.

By then tears were streaming down her face although she hadn't noticed when they started and could hardly feel them.

"Daddy?"

He also had a red skin tone and when she touched his arm it felt cold and stiff.

Katy stumbled to the floor beside the bed and covered her face with her hands.

"Oh my God, please don't take them. Please. Please."

She wanted to shake her parents awake but knew she shouldn't. She had to call someone. She needed help. Where was Shawn? How could she reach him and what would she tell him?

She went into their bathroom, threw up in the toilet, then splashed cold water on her face, and called 9-1-1.

It was the worst day of her life.

## CHAPTER 7
# Horse Show Intrigue

As PLEASANT AS THE DRIVE COULD HAVE BEEN WITH THE
winding road and pretty morning, she wished her mind
hadn't taken her down the tragic memory lane. But she
often thought of her parents, especially first thing when
still in that half-sleep, half-dream state at home.

She couldn't bring herself to sleep in their master
bedroom where it had happened. Instead, she had
remodeled her childhood room. In the future, she might
consider remodeling theirs, maybe turn it into her office
instead of sitting at the kitchen island with her laptop.

Thank goodness she finally arrived at the Rolling
Hills show. Hopefully, it would take her mind off the
past.

People were already getting an early start—lunging
and riding, brushing and bathing horses. She waved at
some familiar faces.

Many arenas did not have a designated room or
office for show personnel. Volunteers and paid staff set
up their laptops on a table inside the arena. The secretary kept track of placings and matched those to

exhibitors' numbers and names. This arena was fortunate to have a separate small building, similar to an extra-large storage shed or mini cottage, to house a few people.

Katy parked near the show office and started to gather her notebook, camera, and small bag when she noticed a stocky man next to the building speaking animatedly to a young woman. He was pointing and gesturing almost in her face, and he touched her elbows as though he might shake her. Both wore the dark blue jackets, khaki pants, and cowboy hats of the judging team.

Katy decided to wait in her car with the window down another minute to watch the confrontation through her dark sunglasses. The man's voice rose and Katy heard him say, "Listen, just do as I say or you'll regret it."

The woman pulled back and tried to free her elbows from his grasp, but he held her tight.

Katy hated bullies. She gathered her belongings, exited the truck, and walked quickly near them as she headed for the office door.

"Everything all right here?"

The man glared at her. "Just a private conversation."

Katy connected with the woman's eyes. "You okay?"

The woman nodded and moved away from the man, then hurried out of sight. The man stared at Katy and put dark glasses on as he also left the scene quickly.

*That was weird.*

In the office she greeted an old friend who acted as show secretary at many horse shows in the area.

"Hey, Sally, how are you doin'?"

The plump woman peered over the top of her readers and gave Katy a big smile along with a lazy shrug.

47

"Oh, same old, same old. You know how it is. Lots of stressed people at a horse show. Everyone wants something."

Katy nodded.

"You doin' okay, Katy? It's been a while. You're lookin' good, as usual."

"Aww, thanks, Sally. Trying to hang in there. You too. I like the blonde." She gestured to the woman's hair.

"Gotta keep my hubby on his toes." When she laughed, her belly kind of jiggled. "You here for the magazine? I always liked Wes."

"Well, we've got a new owner now. Brett Barker."

"Oh, that's right. I heard about him. Barker was schmoozing around last night at the motel bar. Tall guy, right?"

"Yes. Tall. Sharp dresser."

"I don't know about that. He didn't look like a real horseman to me. Too clean."

The two of them grinned and laughed as only old friends do. Katy had to agree with Sally's assessment of her new boss.

"So how long until they start horsemanship?"

Sally glanced at her phone. "Maybe forty-five minutes. You have plenty of time. If you get there before I do, say 'hey' to my Jimmy. I know he'd like to see you. He's helping set up. Part of his honey-do list."

"You guys make such a good team. What would we all do without you?"

As Katy turned to walk out, Sally called after her.

"Oh, Katy. I wanted to say we were sorry to hear about what happened at the Golden show. But so glad you and those horses turned out safe. And that stalker or whatever she was…Glad she got put in jail."

Katy didn't like talking about that dark time in her life.

"It's still being hashed out. There will be a court case…not only about the Golden horse show…but also her involvement in my parents' death."

Katy stared out the window.

"Oh my gosh. I'm sorry to bring up a sad subject, Katy. I'm just glad you're all right."

"Thanks. I appreciate it. Well, I'd better get to work, or I might be out of a job." She smiled.

"Never. You're too good," the other woman said.

Katy smiled and put her hand on the doorknob, but then stopped in place and turned back.

"Sally, one more thing. And forgive me if this is totally none of my business."

"What is it?"

She hesitated. "It's just that…before I came into the office, I saw a man and woman…I think they were judges. The man was talking to her pretty harshly. I couldn't hear everything they said. But the young woman seemed upset."

Sally spoke in lowered tones although no one else was in the office.

"Yeah. They were in here before you, checking on the schedule. That guy can be kind of brusque. And she's still pretty young to be a judge, but I hear she worked real hard to get her card. I'll keep an eye on them."

Katy smiled. "Maybe this should stay between you and me. I could be mistaken. I don't even know either of them."

"It's okay. You can always ask me anything."

"Thanks, Sally. Appreciate that."

The woman's eyes went over the top of her readers again and she smiled.

"Besides, we're old friends. Gotta have each other's back. A lot of weird things go on behind the scenes at a horse show."

"Don't I know it."

Katy thought about all that Sally's statement held. And all that had transpired at one of her last big shows.

*I could write a book.*

# CHAPTER 8

## *Blind Judge?*

WHEREVER KATY WENT AT THIS SHOW IT SEEMED MANY people knew her. It wasn't like she was outgoing and made friends easily. But she'd been around for years and genuinely liked and cared about other people. She took the time to listen to them and ask about their family and animals. People appreciated her kindness in a sport that was sometimes cutthroat.

As much as she wanted to linger and chat with folks however, she disciplined herself to politely move on and find a spot in a low bleacher row, close to the rail where she could have an unencumbered view of the action in the ring.

The first class getting ready to show was halter. She wasn't an expert but she was familiar with the class. It wasn't one where she would enter her horse, though. Cash wasn't what you'd call a halter horse. He was tall and lean. She always thought some of the halter horses were like body builders, Arnold Schwarzeneggers of their sport. Many exhibitors spent big bucks on the right feed, extra supplements, body spray shines, and everything under the sun. Some of those horses were not turned out in their pastures like "regular" horses in case they played too rough and nicked their bodies. They had to almost be a perfect specimen in the show-ring so their off hours were restricted. Katy felt sorry for them. Sure, they were well taken care of, but did they get to act and play like others? She had an open mind and knew their owners would have a different viewpoint and argue their halter horses had a wonderful life and were happy.

She had done her research to learn what it meant to have a top-notch halter horse, plus she had watched many classes over the years. They were divided by age and sex. About fifteen horses entered the three-year-old mares' class. Katy watched each one parade into the arena to form a long, straight line, their handlers to one side holding a leather lead. The horses did not wear saddles as this class's purpose was to show off their physical beauty and correctness.

Exhibitors had just a minute to get their horse "squared up." They were allowed to carefully maneuver their horse in to the right position to form an evenly balanced picture. Sometimes it only took a nudge from the toe of their boot. Other times they had to bend down, grab a hoof with their hand, and place it in the soft sand where it best represented how a halter horse should look.

There were two judges for this class. One was the big man she had seen outside the show office earlier, and the second was the young woman he had been harassing. At least that's how the interchange appeared to Katy. Often-times, when there were two judges, points earned were doubled for the entrants.

Wearing the customary dark jacket and khaki pants, he reviewed the line. The exhibitor, not the horse, wore the entry number on their back. So, in the beginning, the person turned their back to the judge so that he could write their number on his form. Then, it was the exhibitor's job to do everything to show the horse in the best light. Sometimes it meant a little tug on the lead, but not too much to upset the horse or make it move the wrong way. Everything was extremely subtle.

Katy knew all these nuances and remembered the number one faux pas to avoid at all costs was for the exhibitor to walk in front of the judge, blocking his or her view of the horse. The person showing the horse had to continually move away from the judge's line of vision when he or she walked around the horse. It was a little comical to Katy and she thought of the exhibitors as toy soldiers standing at attention in their show attire, booted feet planted solidly together, and waiting for the judge's nod or movement around their horse.

Most of the horses stood like beautiful statues, a testament to their training. However, these were three-year-olds, still young, and occasionally one got impatient and moved around or even acted skittish. The judge would have to count off on the score. It was heart-breaking for the exhibitor who had put a lot of work and training effort into getting their horse ready for today's event.

Katy had her eye on number 247, a striking chestnut-colored, or some called it sorrel, horse from Parkhill Stables that checked all the boxes to be a perfect halter winner. She knew the owners who were meticulous with the care of their horses, including supervised pasture time which contributed to the animal's mental health as well as physical making it a well-rounded individual.

She recalled this particular horse had proven itself by winning other competitions. Success would increase its value for the owners and when it was time to sell, they would, hopefully, recoup some of their investment.

There was maybe only one other horse in this class that came close to 247, but Katy thought it didn't measure up to be awarded first place. The rest of the horses were so-so, in her opinion, some better than others, some antsy or had poor conformation. None of them deserved to be in the top three.

The whole crowd seemed to be of the same mind and rooted loudly for 247. And that's why it was especially stunning when the announcer called out that first place went to a horse that Katy deemed as being number five or six down the line.

"What?"

She turned her shocked face to a woman seated next to her whom she didn't know, to which the lady just shrugged her shoulders and shook her head back and forth.

Everyone was confused.

Katy made a note on her pad. This wasn't right. Was the judge blind?

She turned around to view the crowd and noticed that many people were visibly upset and grumbled among themselves. Their faces displayed unbelief, confusion, even outrage.

The next class got ready to start and Katy left her seat in the bleachers to walk among the people, maybe hear their comments and opinions along the way. She also saw Brett Barker and figured she should at least say hello to him since technically he was her boss. He was talking and laughing with some girl but then got a call on his cell phone so stepped away a few feet to answer.

As Katy approached, his vision took her in but he held up that one finger again to signal her to wait. He'd already used that gesture with her before in his office and it was really starting to annoy her.

Into the phone he said, "Sure thing. Let's have lunch sometime to discuss. Take care."

He punched a button and returned the phone to his pocket.

"Hello, Ms. McKim. Seems like the phone never lets me alone."

"You're a busy man."

"Always."

"What did you think of that last class?" she asked. "Kind of out of left field, wasn't it?"

He held his nose in the air and his eyes took in the people around them, not her, which she thought was rude. In fact, she was starting to associate that word with a lot of his behavior.

"You mean the winner? Well, they always say judging is subjective. It's one person's opinion."

She sighed. "It was so obvious to the audience who should have been first place. The one they placed was more like sixth or lower."

He moved his head a little closer to hers, invading her personal space, which she did not like at all.

"Ms. McKim, you need to learn the politics. Watch what you say. And don't get at odds with the ones pulling the strings."

She frowned at him. "I always believe in honesty, not politics. And rewarding people for their hard work. I've been around horse shows my whole life."

"In a fairy-tale world, that's how it works," he said with a laugh that was way too loud. He obviously wanted people to notice him, she thought, a classic lover of the limelight.

"I'm going to make the rounds," she said.

"Take a lot of photos, Katy. That's what people like. Oh…and of course your article too. Send it to me as soon as it's done."

She awkwardly forced a half smile, didn't say a word, and turned on her heel to get away from him. *What a jerk.* Try as she might, she really didn't care for his personality.

Coffee—that's what she needed right now. As she made her way to the concession food truck, she came across Sally from the office, her arms full of notebooks and paperwork.

"Need any help?"

The older woman was breathing heavily. "Oh, thanks, Katy. I'm okay. Just dropping a few things off, then gotta get back to the show. I'm on a quick break right now. You doing okay?"

Katy first confirmed that no one was around to hear her. "I'm good, except that was a really weird halter class. Everyone thought Parkhill Stables should have placed first."

Sally whispered. "So did I. In fact, an appeal has been filed by the Parkhills. Something just smelled fishy about that outcome. Hey, don't mention the appeal to anyone. Nothing's official yet."

"I won't, Sally. You know I keep confidences."

"Of course I do, Katy. Hey, listen, I've got to run. See you later?"

The woman's new hairdo was sticking up in all the wrong places. Probably a homemade job, Katy thought, which endeared the woman to her even more.

"Sure thing, Sally. Take it easy."

A few people stood in front of her in line at the food truck and when it was her turn, she placed her order.

"Coffee, and one of those blueberry muffins, please. Thanks."

When she stepped to the table for napkins, and stirred cream and sugar into her coffee, she noticed the same young woman who had run out of Brett Barker's office the first day she met him. A few tables and chairs had been set up on a section of asphalt near the food truck and the blonde girl sipped on a diet soda and dabbed her eyes with a tissue. Had she been crying?

Katy slipped her sunglasses on, sipped her coffee, and watched her. Shapely figure but super thin, trendy tight jeans torn to shreds, tall boots—not exactly a horse-woman, more like a wannabe runway model. Katy stood next to a concrete column of the arena building and sometimes slipped behind it so she wouldn't be spotted. Brett Barker suddenly appeared and sat close to the blonde. He made a bit of a ruckus when he forcefully yanked his chair across the rough surface. She was like a startled deer and barely looked at him, instead tore little pieces from the paper napkin on her lap.

As luck would have it, Katy could hear a little bit of their conversation, mostly because of Barker's deep voice.

"I thought I told you to stay back at the motel. I'm busy here."

"I was bored, so I took a taxi. I can't stay in that motel all day and all night." She pleaded with him, but he only appeared more annoyed.

"If you stay here, then go sit in the bleachers and watch the horse show. I have meetings so I can't enter-tain you."

With that, he got up from the table and left her sitting alone.

Her mousy voice was nearly inaudible. "Please...I just wanted to talk with you."

Katy's mind reeled. *Unbelievable. Huge jerk. And too old for her.*

She ducked behind the column so he wouldn't see her as he stormed off. Should she go talk to the girl? Sit with her? Console her? Katy wanted to, but maybe she should just stay out of it. It was none of her business.

# CHAPTER 9
## Something's Fishy

IT WAS A NICE VENUE WITH A LARGE, AIR-CONDITIONED arena for the show classes, and another covered arena outside for warm-ups and practice.

Katy needed to get a lot more material for her article so she watched a few more halter classes and after that a horsemanship class was in the ring. She liked this one. It reminded her of the kind of riding she did in trail classes and around her ranch on a daily basis.

Her phone buzzed in her pocket, and she was happy to see by the screenshot of his handsome face that it was Matt.

"Hey, how ya doing, sweetie? Having fun?" He always sounded upbeat to her, and she liked his cute terms of endearment.

"Hmmm...yes and no."

"What does that mean?"

She got up from her seat and headed outside away from people. Speaking in a low voice, she said, "Well, I saw one class where the judge obviously made the wrong call for first place. I asked Barker about it, and he essentially said you have to play the political game and not say anything. Then I saw him with a young woman, girl-friend or whatever. He was rude and initially wanted her to stay back at the motel all day, but if she was going to be at the horse show then to leave him alone. Can you believe that? What a jerk."

Matt paused, then spoke evenly. "Katy, please tell me you're not sneaking around playing lady detective, listening to other people's conversations."

"You know that's a sexist thing to say, don't you? 'Lady detective.' I can't help it if I hear stuff. And that thing with the judge who made the wrong call, everyone in the arena was shocked. They would all agree with me."

"Ka—ty."

She could almost see his head tilting down and his eyes watching at her from under furrowed brows. He sounded like a parent to her, the same way her father spoke when she was up to no good.

"Promise me you'll just do your job and not get into any trouble. You know that judging is a subjective thing. It's one person's opinion. The audience doesn't always agree with the calls the judges make. Katy? Are you listening to me?"

"I hear ya. Hey, I've got to get back to the arena and watch the next class."

"All right. Be careful. I can't wait to see you again."

"Me too, you." And she ended the call.

SHE WATCHED MORE classes as the day progressed, made her notes, and took a lot of candid photos around the showgrounds as well as a few winners in the designated space in front of the Rolling Hills horse show background. Some of them were joined by their entire families including trainer and other supporters. Katy always thought horse shows were a great environment for young people instead of them hanging out at some mall or staying holed up in their bedroom with a video game never seeing the light of day or another human being. Taking care of a horse taught them responsibility and participating in a show encouraged teamwork and good sportsmanship. Or at least that's the way it was supposed to work. There were always jealousies and bad behavior too. That was human nature.

In the ring now was a procession of eighteen horses gliding on the rail in unison. It was a big class and each entry listened for the announcer's instructions. "Walk your horses, please." "Go at a jog, please." "Lope your horses." And then the riders hoped, or prayed, that the cues they gave their horses were imperceptible to onlookers, especially the judge, and that the horse would perform perfectly and not freak out at some spider or whisper from the crowd, imagined or otherwise.

Katy remembered hearing one old joke that equated a Western pleasure class with watching paint dry. Be that as it may, slow and relaxed was the criteria. The idea was for the rider to train the horse to go in a nice, smooth, slow gait as though they were on a pleasure ride in the countryside. This certainly wasn't as dramatic or exciting the way jumping or running barrels was.

If watching the horses go round and round as though on a live merry-go-round was a bit boring, something about this class that piqued Katy's interest was the judge. She recognized the same large man who earlier, in her humble opinion, had made the wrong decision, a very suspicious decision, in the halter class. He was also the same man who had been engaged in a heated exchange with the young woman outside the show office who also wore judge's attire. Katy determined to keep an eye on him. She pulled out the show sheet program and noted his name was G. Granger. Lots of red flags were waving in her mind about him. Was he crooked? Or just ill-equipped mentally to award the best entry with the highest placing.

The group of eighteen horses seemed to float around the ring, nose to tail, not too close but there wasn't much room to spread great distances between them either. Most kept a slow, almost mechanical, or sleepy pace, their heads low toward the ground and barely bobbing. Katy wondered if the horses were happy in their job. They didn't choose it, but they dutifully followed orders. Occasionally, a horse's speed was too fast to stay in the neat line and the rider was forced to bring it to an imaginary lane on the inside, thus passing the others. This action was sometimes counted off an exhibitor's score since the goal was for all horses to move in the predetermined manner.

Again, Katy had her favorite and it just so happened to be another Parkhill Stables entry—a beautiful palomino-colored horse with a luxurious, flowing tail. It looked like the horse's real tail, but then again, the rules allowed the wearing of fake ones so Katy wasn't positive. It wasn't only the tail that caught her eye. The horse was cooperative with the rider and appeared to truly enjoy this activity. It also fit the criteria the judges were looking for—quiet, soft, and smooth, on a loose rein with light contact. Katy imagined this horse would go around without a bridle if asked.

And that's why she felt sick to her stomach when the judge—Granger—placed the horse fourth. Katy had seen the first-place rider jerk back on the bridle in an almost cruel way to get the horse's attention, when the judge's back was turned of course. Some people did things like that, small corrections, but if caught for excessive use there could be consequences.

Katy couldn't believe it. This judge was a piece of work. Did he have something against Parkhill? Or, was he favoring specific others, perhaps in exchange for payment? She felt she had to say something. But whom could she trust?

It was almost lunchtime, and the show was on break. Katy contemplated speaking confidentially with Sally, the show secretary.

She headed to the office but stopped in her tracks when she saw Granger standing outside a side door of the arena. Actually, she heard him first, a loud belly laugh. She sharply turned her head to follow the sound.

*Oh, my gosh.*

Granger was chatting with Brett Barker. And they appeared to be enjoying themselves, in a "good ol' boy" kind of way. Katy thought about that phrase and even though Northern California was different from the southeastern states where some folks, mostly men, who lived in the country were characterized as belonging to an unofficial club with an unspoken set of rules where if you belonged you could reap special benefits...California had their version too. You pat my back, I'll pat yours. Or scratch. Or do special favors. Even Hollywood and other places like that had the Old Boy Network for people of money.

She didn't want them to see her, but needed to get closer, so she ducked behind a horse trailer that was parked next to the building. Creeping around, Matt suddenly was in her head. She didn't think he'd approve.

*I'm not doing anything wrong.*

She carefully peeked around the edge of the trailer. Luckily the two men were busy laughing, and one patted the other on the back. There you go, she thought, just like that colloquial expression.

Then...and she could hardly believe what she was witnessing...Barker passed a thick white envelope to Granger who quickly pocketed it in the navy jacket he wore, a judge's jacket, one which, in her opinion, he didn't deserve to wear.

Katy assumed the envelope contained money, but of course, she couldn't be sure.

Still, she thought, *what slimeballs*.

Before she could stop and think about what she was doing, she held her cell phone up and snapped a few photos. She could always enlarge them later to get a better look.

But then she nearly dropped the phone when a voice behind her asked, "What are you doing, Katy?"

## CHAPTER 10

# *Daughter*

"OH, MY GOSH, SALLY. YOU NEARLY GAVE ME A HEART attack. Don't sneak up on me like that."

She planted her palm to her chest as she exhaled, put her phone away, and tried to compose herself.

"Looks like you're the one sneaking around, Katy. What exactly are you doing anyway?"

"Shhh, not so loud. I don't want them to hear us."

"Who? Gordon and your boss?"

"Is that Granger's name? Gordon?"

"Yes. He's a judge."

"I know he is. I wanted to talk to you about him. But not here. Can we talk in your office?"

Sally's arms were full, like before, with a big notebook and folders. She huffed at her heavy load.

"I'm just coming from my office after a quick sandwich. I need to get to the arena. It's probably kind of empty since we're still on lunch break. Let's go in there."

Katy nodded and started slowly walking with Sally, but turned one last time to peek toward the men and was startled when she thought Barker was staring right at her.

"C'mon, hurry up," she said to Sally who gave her a confused look.

"What is going on with you, girl?"

Inside the big arena only two riders were in the ring practicing. Actually, they were mostly chatting as they walked their horses side by side.

Sally dropped her belongings on the table where she sat during the show.

"Now tell me what's on your mind, Katy. We have maybe forty minutes. I need to get organized but I'm listening."

"So, you agree that Granger's choice of first place was pretty quirky, right? And you said the Parkhills are filing an appeal for that halter class?"

Sally nodded. "Yes, a lot of people have expressed the same thing. But most times, once a judgment is made, it's final whether it's the correct one or not."

"Did you know the same thing happened in Western pleasure? Also, with a Parkhill horse."

"I heard about it. I was away for a few minutes. Someone else was filling in for me."

"How much do you know about Granger? How long has he been a judge?"

Sally moved her notebook and stacked papers. "He doesn't live around here. I don't know much about his background. His judge's card checked out, though."

Katy kept an eye on the door.

"I saw Granger and Barker talking when you found me near that horse trailer."

"Talking is not a crime, Katy."

"Barker passed him an envelope."

"So? It could've been some kind of paperwork. You don't know what was in it."

"It just seems strange, Sally. Suspicious."

"Why don't you ask your boss?"

Katy rolled her eyes.

"Sally, you and I have been friends for a long time. We trust each another. Please don't share this conversation with anyone else. And about my new boss? Let's just say, I haven't figured him out yet. For some reason, my Spidey-sense is tingling."

"Spidey-sense?" The older woman laughed. "You want me to take you seriously? And then you say something like that?"

"You know what I mean. Red flags. Suspicions."

"Okay. I won't say anything if you promise me one thing. Just be careful with your lady detective work."

"I cannot believe you just said 'lady detective.'"

"What? What's the matter with that?"

"Never mind." Katy shook her head. "Hey, I think I'll grab a snack before the show starts. Do you need anything?"

"No, thanks. I'm good. Just remember what I said, Katy. Be careful and make sure you have evidence before you pass judgment."

"All right. I'll see you later." Katy started to walk away, then turned back. "You know, you sound just like someone else I know."

Sally winked. "That handsome, young detective you're dating? Maybe you should listen to him."

~

THERE WAS a small diner on the grounds, but Katy liked the food truck for quick things. She went up to the window and ordered a taco and water.

When she turned toward a picnic table to sit for a few minutes someone bumped her and knocked the water bottle out of her hand.

It was the blonde woman she had seen with Barker earlier.

"Oh, my gosh, I'm so sorry. What an idiot I am. Here, let me get that for you."

The girl was all discombobulated and rattling her words out like confetti shot from a gun.

Katy touched her shoulder to try to calm her and accepted the water bottle.

"It's no problem really. Don't worry about it. Here, let's sit. My name is Katy. What's yours?"

The girl's eyes darted left and right as though unsure she should speak to a stranger.

"I'm...uh...uh...Melanie."

"Nice to meet you, Melanie. Did you get any food?"

The girl held up a small cookie. "Just this."

"Mmm, looks good." Katy picked up her taco. "This little thing is mostly just a small wrap, one skimpy chicken strip, and a smidgen of cheese. But it's okay. I don't need a lot right now."

Melanie slowly bit into her cookie, about the size of a mouse morsel, all the time watching Katy. She quickly dabbed the corners of her mouth with a paper napkin although there were no visible crumbs, then put the cookie down and wrapped it up in the napkin. Her skinny physique was evidence that she didn't eat many cookies in her daily life, and probably not much of any other food groups either. The thought of anorexia passed through Katy's mind, but she was no expert on the subject.

Perhaps, though, she could befriend the girl and learn more about her relationship with Barker. But she'd have to tread lightly, she told herself.

She nonchalantly eyed the girl's skintight jeans and high-heeled boots.

"Those are pretty. Are they comfortable?"

Melanie grimaced a little and shook her head. "Not exactly. But they were a gift."

"Oh. From your boyfriend?"

"I don't have a boyfriend." The girl nibbled just a few grains of her cookie.

"Oh...uh...sorry to presume. I thought I had seen you before at Brett Barker's office. I write articles for his magazine."

"Thought you were a little familiar." The girl politely smiled.

"So, he's not your boyfriend?"

"What? Eww, no. He's my...uh...uh...father."

Katy nearly choked on her miniature taco. "Father? Oh, my gosh."

"Do you realize you just said 'oh' about three times?"

Katy chuckled. "Yeah, I guess I do that when I'm nervous. Repeat myself."

They both laughed.

"What do *you* have to be nervous about?"

"Well, technically, I suppose he is my boss. Although I'm really freelance."

"Don't worry. I understand. He can be intimidating. I'm just getting to know him, and he scares me."

Katy was perplexed. "What do you mean, 'just getting to know him'? Your father?"

"He hasn't been around for years. I didn't know he

was my dad. He didn't know I was his kid. And I've been…uh…uh…away."

Katy felt she was intruding on personal territory. "You don't have to tell me anything. But you also can tell me whatever you'd like and I promise to keep it confidential."

"Thanks. I appreciate that. I don't have a lot of people I can talk to."

Katy finished her mini-sized taco in two swallows and crumpled the paper in her fist.

"If you don't mind my asking, where is your mother?"

The girl's eyes clouded, and she stared off into the distance.

"She died almost a year ago. That's how he found me. A lawyer contacted him because my mother left a letter with instructions for him to take care of me. I was in a rehab…"

"I'm sorry."

"Not for drugs. Eating disorder. I have issues with food and body image."

"I hope he's treating you well."

"He deserves some credit, I guess. He didn't walk away from me completely. They were only married about a year and that was nearly twenty years ago. She never told him she was pregnant so he didn't know I even existed. I think he's still trying to figure out the father thing."

They both sat for a minute, silent. Then the girl said, "Gosh, sorry to unload my personal business on you. I'm not sure why I told you all that."

"It's a lot to process. You need someone to talk to. I hope it works out for both you and your dad."

"Thanks."

"So do you like horses?"

The girl let out a small laugh.

"Honestly, I'm afraid of them. Had some bad childhood experiences. But I was hoping to spend some time with…uh…him…sorry, sometimes I don't know what to call him. Seems weird to call him 'Dad' or 'my father.' Turns out, he's pretty busy with the show and all. So, I'm just gonna hang out. Maybe he'll have time for me later."

Katy felt more than sorry for the girl. She had lost her own parents but that was due to a tragic incident beyond anyone's control. Well, except for the criminal. Here, Melanie had a flesh-and-blood father right in front of her but he didn't have any time for her. Must be heartbreaking, Katy thought. And it just solidified her opinion of Barker. A jerk of the highest degree.

She couldn't help but want to protect and befriend Melanie.

"I move around the show a lot and take photos for my article. But whenever I camp out to watch classes, you're welcome to sit with me."

"Thanks. I'd like that. You're really nice."

The two smiled at each other and Katy felt good about showing the girl some kindness. She seemed so fragile and said she didn't have many people she could talk with.

Suddenly a stern voice invaded their bubble of newfound friendship.

It was Barker. His eyes were slanted, and his teeth clenched. "What are you doing, Melanie? Go inside and wait for me." He pointed toward the indoor arena.

"I…uh…was just talking to…"

"Go!" He pointed again.

Melanie's eyes widened and pooled with liquid as she peeked at Katy.

When the girl moved away, Barker came uncomfortably close to Katy's ear and pointed his index finger.

"You stay out of my personal business. Stick to your article." He almost growled.

"We were just talking. Maybe you need to chill."

The red in his face told her he was close to exploding. She smelled his minty breath as he came close again. She had noticed him chomping on those things on several occasions. Was he trying to quit smoking? Alcohol? Or, just a nervous habit? His sparkling white teeth almost turned into fangs in her imagination.

"Do *not* tell me what to do. That article of yours had better be good. I can always find someone else. Writers are a dime a dozen."

He glared, then turned on his pointy, drugstore cowboy boots, and marched off.

*Yep, still a jerk.* She knew there were a lot worse words she could call him, but "jerk" would have to do. Katy shook her head.

## CHAPTER 11
## *Granger*

KATY'S PHONE VIBRATED IN HER POCKET AS SHE WALKED toward the indoor arena so she stopped and lingered outside. She never liked talking on a cell phone in a grocery store or in a group of people and thought it rude when others did although many had no qualms about it.

She often heard strangers, family members, or roomies describing items in a store to confirm they were picking up the correct size or brand.

"Do you want the one with the orange packaging? Large size? It's buy one, get one free. We should stock up. What do you want for dinner?"

While Katy agreed it was a convenient way to communicate and effective in avoiding mistakes, it just seemed weird to hear everyone's business. She figured she must have inherited some of her dad's old-school genes. Her brother, who was knee-deep in technology what with his military training, had no problem talking on a cell phone out in public, that is, if he was in his "regular guy" persona. He was also able to turn on his stealth-mode personality if necessary and talk in code to certain parties.

Her brother aside, it bugged Katy to be forced to listen to people's conversations.

In a restaurant, she once heard a diner recount every detail of how frustrated they were with a coworker.

"I don't trust her one bit," the diner said in a loud voice. "Tells everyone my business. And doesn't finish her work assignments. Always on personal calls. Drags me down. I've had about all I can take. I'm for sure gonna need a glass of wine after the day I've had."

Who needs to hear details of some stranger's life? Don't we each have enough of our own stuff to contend with, without being subjected, against our will, to listening to a blow-by-blow account of other people's lives? Katy wondered, what did we all do before cell phones came along? She didn't always hop on her soapbox, but sometimes the world was just too much.

So, she tried her best not to be an annoyance to others, stayed away from the crowd, and didn't hit the speaker button.

"Matt. Hi. What's going on?"

"Hey, sweetie. Things okay at the show?"

"Very surprising. I'll tell you more about it later. What are you up to?"

"I got together with Shawn and Andre to help with one of their cases. We have a question for you."

"Okay."

"Are you familiar with Fowler Feed?"

"Yeah, I've heard of it. New to the area. I don't use them at my ranch. Why do you ask?"

He was quiet for a moment. "Do you think it's possible to hide drugs in feed bags?"

"I guess anything's possible nowadays. How do they do it? Did you find drugs?"

"Not yet. We're following up on tips from an informant. They carefully open the bags, hide drugs in plastic, and reseal the feed bags. Or, they tamper with those tubs of feed or supplements, and hide drugs. It's a way of transporting interstate and avoiding inspection."

"Wow, you're kidding."

"Remember, this is all confidential. We thought you could keep your ears open since you're the most connected among us to the horse industry."

"Will do, sir. Does that mean you're going to deputize me?" She chuckled.

"I don't think we're quite at that stage yet, Katy."

"Let me know when you think we are. I'm going to need a gun, my own vehicle, a badge, an expense account..."

She liked having a boyfriend to tease and joke with although she was realizing with each passing day the most important aspect of their relationship was that he sincerely cared for her well-being and future. It was nice to have someone in her corner, especially after so many years of being on her own.

He cut her short. "Yeah, yeah, Miss Smarty-Pants. How's your drugstore cowboy?"

"Humph. Let's just say, 'the plot thickens.'"

"Sounds ominous. I can't wait to hear all about it. When are you coming home?"

"I want to catch a few more classes tomorrow. I'm deciding whether to head back in the afternoon or stay tomorrow night. I had planned to be here till Sunday, but now I'm not so sure it's necessary."

"Is everything okay, Katy?"

"Yeah, sure. I'm just thinking maybe I've seen enough. I'll let you know tomorrow."

"All right. Just be careful. I want you back in one piece. So does Cash."

"Is he okay?"

"Yeah, I checked with your neighbors. They said everyone is happy."

"You didn't have to do that, Matt. I was going to give them a call."

"I told you I'd help, and I knew you might get busy at the show."

"Thanks. I appreciate it. Hey, I've got to go. Talk to you later, okay?"

"Sure, sweetie. Later."

Katy clicked the call off and blended in with a group of people and horses entering the indoor arena. Technically, the building was called the "coliseum" and for a split second she thought of what it must've been like in ancient Rome in the historic Coliseum, gladiators fighting one another to the death, and Christians facing the jaws and teeth of hungry lions determined to tear their bodies apart. Banding together, unified in faith, the believers clung to each other and the hope of eternal life free from earthly pain.

She was grateful to be living in modern times when this building was used for family entertainment—one day, car show or craft show; today, horse show. But even this benign endeavor had its carnivores lurking around each corner, or so it seemed.

Katy took a seat in the first row of bleachers, which gave easy access to the rail if she wanted to get a close-up photo of certain horses in the ring. And she could also keep an eye on Barker and his daughter who were situated across from her near the end-gate. Barker was all smiles when people passed them and sometimes shook hands like a politician. But Katy's internal radar picked up on the secret moments when Barker's face was deadpan, and his daughter's expression showed uncomfortable pain and longing.

Next up was a Western riding class where horses were challenged to change leads throughout a designated course—from a walk to a jog and lope, over logs and rails, also called pylons. Katy enjoyed this class and thought it was somewhat similar to the horsemanship class. Even though each rider had the same routine to accomplish individually, watching them succeed or fail was interesting, at least for people in tune with horse showing and all its nuances, until it became boring.

Katy was almost reaching that point. She had been around horse shows most of her life and was knowledgeable about the intricacies, but yes, sometimes she got a little bored. So now, even though she was still taking notes and snapping pics for her article, she also decided to pay close attention to what was happening behind the scenes and would keep a close eye on Barker and his daughter...and that questionable judge, Gordon Granger, who, she just realized, was sitting in a folding chair on the side of the arena judging this class. Next to him was the young woman judge. Katy really wanted to talk to her. She read the program and saw her name was T. Stone.

There were twelve horses and riders in this class and six of them had already taken their turn. Some gave a flawless performance, a few had minor bobbles, and others had major errors. The next one up was a Parkhill Stables entry, so Katy paid special attention and sat tall on the edge of her bleacher seat.

Parkhill was known for its award-winning horses

due to years of experience in exemplary care and nutrition and well-researched training. The entry in the ring now was yet another superb example of that legacy, performing to the epitome of perfection. Surely horse and rider would be rewarded for their hard work.

But no, it wasn't to be for Granger was in charge of this class. And, try as she might, Katy could not figure out what he deemed as a fault, if he were being honest, that she and the whole crowd did not see. There had to be some other explanation at play here, and Katy was determined to find the truth. Wasn't that her primary goal as a journalist and horse-loving advocate?

She watched the interchange between the judges, Granger and Stone, through the lens of her prized digital camera and wished she could read lips. The young woman held her clipboard at an angle and appeared to be showing it to Granger, presumably her marks for the entries. At one point, Granger shrugged and held out his hands, palms up as if to say, "Who cares?" or maybe "Just do as I say." When Judge Stone detached her scoring sheet from the clipboard, Granger snatched the paper from her. Katy could not be sure what their conversation included, but she had a sick feeling. Something was not right. And she wondered if anyone else in the audience noticed the scene.

If he was fudging the results and had any sort of bias against Parkhill Stables, or if he was possibly receiving payment to recognize other horses with the top awards, how was Katy going to prove it? Even Matt had reminded her that judging was a subjective practice. Although Katy agreed with that, to a certain extent, she also knew it was based on a point system—manners and disposition of the horse, response to the rider, quality of the gaits and lead changes, and light contact from the rider's hands via the reins to the bit. There were also various errors that counted as negative points and were deducted from the overall score.

She wondered if she could get a hold of the judges' paperwork and verify how many points were given to each horse, originally. Maybe Sally, the secretary, could help her. She had to try.

Just then she realized the class was over. The judges stood and Granger walked over toward the lineup of horses, but first handed a small sheet of paper to the ring steward who carried it to the announcer's table. Over the PA system, Katy heard first place awarded to a horse she had witnessed make at least a couple of mistakes. In her opinion, and probably the rest of the crowd, she believed the horse deserved fourth or fifth place.

She noticed Granger wrinkle up other sheets of paper and toss them in a trash can by the announcer's table, then he pasted on a toothy smile and sauntered over to the mostly young women in the lineup. It made Katy's skin crawl. If he patted any of their boots, as he grinned up at them on their horses, she promised herself she would file an objection against him.

The woman judge, Stone, walked out of the arena without a word to anyone. Katy wanted to follow but first, she had to figure out how to retrieve Granger's notes, and presumably Stone's, from the trash without arousing suspicions.

## CHAPTER 12
### *Sleuthing*

PEOPLE AT A HORSE SHOW WERE ALWAYS MOVING ABOUT. IF a friend or family member rode in a certain class, their entourage sat in the bleachers and rooted for them. When done, the group dispersed in various directions—either headed back to their stalls to get ready for the next one or to eat, rest, take care of the horse, or any number of reasons.

Katy noticed bunches of people on the move, and she contemplated her dip into the trash can. First, she searched her tote bag for paper, tissues, anything to mask her true goal. She ripped pages from her notebook and crumpled them. She planned on tossing them in, then leaning over to retrieve Granger's papers. Could she do it without looking like a fool?

She slowly made her way down the bleachers and watched for a group of people to converge around the fifty-gallon trash can to give her cover. Next to it she held her bag at her chest, flap open, and grabbed a few pieces of her own would-be trash and tossed them in.

Then, like an actress, said to herself, "Oh darn, not that one," as though she had made a mistake. Leaning over the bin, and thank goodness it didn't have a covering lid, she quickly grabbed nearly all the papers in there and hoped they would include Granger's and Stone's original scoring sheets.

A deep voice next to her said, "What in the world are you doing? Dumpster diving?"

Barker.

*Sheesh. Him again.*

She looked up. "I dropped something by mistake."

"Really? Maybe your whole article?"

He chuckled loudly and beamed at other people as though he were on stage delivering a comedy routine and expected applause.

Face flushed, she struggled to contain the anger bubbling up from her chest and threatening to exit her mouth in words she might find impossible to retrieve.

"Excuse me." She pushed past him, then had another thought that might shut him up. "Say hello to Melanie for me."

She was right. He glared at her and turned on his heels in the other direction.

*Good.*

Now where should she go to examine the papers? To the show office and talk to Sally? There might be people coming in and out. To her motel room where she could spread the papers out on her bed? Hopefully none would be too germy…or drippy, ugh, gross…from the trash.

That's it. To the motel.

But first, she'd find the woman judge and have a chat with her.

Entering the show office, she found Sally busy at

work, her concentration going from a stack of papers on the desk to staring at a computer screen and keying in some information. She glanced over her reading glasses propped on her nose to Katy.

"What's going on, girl?"

"Did you notice in that last class Parkhill Stables got dumped on again?"

Sally half rolled her eyes. "I don't know, Katy. It's hard to tell. That's why I'm a show secretary and he's a judge. I just enter the scores."

"But I know you want what's fair, too…like all of us."

Sally wore a rubber thimble on her finger to speed through papers and money. She leaned back in her chair and let out a big sigh.

"I don't want to get in the middle of a scandal. My husband and I need these jobs, even though they're not much pay."

Katy knew Sally and her husband Jimmy had been around horse shows forever. They were older now, on fixed incomes, and she remembered they worked extra jobs whenever possible. Sally drove a school bus and Jimmy mowed lawns as well as other odd jobs. He'd been complaining about his back and knees aching recently.

"We just want to keep our heads down, do the work, and go home."

Katy felt bad for her friends, but she couldn't keep quiet if Granger was cheating.

"Sally, I'm sorry. I do understand. And I won't get you involved. Can you help me with just one little thing?"

The older woman stared at her computer, then lifted her eyes and gave a slight nod.

"I'm looking for Judge Stone, the young woman. Can you tell me where to find her?"

"She might've gone back to the motel. Red Lodge. We usually provide judges' meals at the diner, but she had already left. You might catch her in the motel restaurant. Or, she might've grabbed fast food. She's kinda shy and doesn't hang out with all the show people."

"Thanks, Sally. Oh, do you have her room number in case I can't find her? The motel might not give it to me."

"Now you know I'm not supposed to give out personal information."

"This is important, Sally. I won't bother her. I just want to speak to her for a few minutes."

Sally wrote the room number, fifteen, on a small slip of paper and handed it to Katy.

"I said it before and I'll say it again. Be careful. Watch what you're getting into. I don't want to see you get hurt."

"I'll be fine, Sally. Thanks. I might go home tomorrow. I'm not sure yet. So, if I don't see you, please know, I value our friendship. And I hope you and your hubby take care. I'll probably see you at another show down the road."

The two women hugged, and Katy caught a glimpse of Sally's eyes misting over.

She jumped in her truck and was at the motel within minutes.

What did she plan to say to the girl? She went over it in her mind as she parked in front of her own room, which was close to room fifteen. She hoped that creepy Judge Granger wasn't staying here, or, if he was, his room wasn't close to theirs.

She decided to put her camera bag and notebook inside her room but locked it right away and came back out to find Stone's room.

Standing in front of the door she paused for a few seconds to listen and heard a low mumble of television voices. She gave a couple of quiet taps and heard the TV go dead.

After a long pause, a quiet woman's voice on the inside said, "Who is it?"

"I'm Katy McKim. Sorry to bother you. I'm writing a story about the horse show, and I'd like to talk to you, just for a few minutes."

Another quiet pause. Then, "I don't really talk to reporters. And I've had a long day, if you'll excuse me."

"Please, Ms. Stone, just a couple of questions. If you'd rather come out here or meet in the restaurant. I can show you my driver's license or you can call the desk to vouch for me. I'm staying here, in room ten, just down the hall."

Katy could almost feel eyes peering through the peephole and then she heard the chain scraping through the lock track.

The door opened a few inches slowly, then all the way. Judge Stone stood in the doorway wearing a long, oversized white T-shirt, black exercise leggings, and flip-flops.

"Come in." She wiped her mouth with a napkin, then scanned right and left outside the door obviously not wanting to be seen. "I was just finishing a chicken sandwich."

She pointed Katy to a chair at the half table near the window where the heavy drapes were tightly closed.

Stone sipped a cold soda through a straw from a fast-food place where she must have stopped after leaving the show.

"Thanks for seeing me. I'm sorry to interrupt your dinner."

Stone ate a few fries, then crumpled the food wrapper, and threw it in the trash can.

"Do you want a bottle of water?" she asked Katy and pointed. "I have a small cooler over there."

"No, thank you. I'm good. And thanks again for seeing me."

Stone appeared to be about eighteen or nineteen, but Sally had said she was twenty-five, the minimum age for a judge. She was so different without her navy-blue jacket and silverbelly cowboy hat. Her light brown hair was straight and long and a little wet. At the show it had been neatly braided and tucked up in her hat. She smelled fresh out of the shower and her face was clear of any makeup.

"Did you recently get your judge's card?"

"About five months ago. This is my third show."

"Sorry for asking," Katy said. "It's just you look so young."

Stone stared at Katy as she cleaned off the table.

"What did you want to ask me, Ms. McKim? I'm pretty tired."

"Please. Call me Katy. I just have a few questions. And rest assured, I won't quote you or anything. In fact, I might not even put this in the story. I'm just trying to find out the truth."

"What is this all about?"

Katy swallowed. She just had to get it out.

"In some of the classes today, it seemed obvious to me, and, frankly, to a good amount of the crowd...that the judges' results were really fluky."

Stone sipped on her soda and watched Katy. "Sometimes it comes down to a matter of opinion, Ms. McKim."

Katy nodded. "I know. It's just that...well, I'm sure

you noticed the horses from Parkhill Stables. Now I have no connection whatsoever. I'm just appreciative of excellent horses and how their owners care for them. They were by far number one horses, maybe number two, but certainly not sixth or however they placed in the various classes. They had no errors or flaws. The whole crowd was shocked. So, I just wondered why the judges ruled against them in so many classes."

Stone was quiet, cleared her throat, then spoke in a very professional manner.

"You must know that I can't really speak to every audience member who is unhappy with a judge's decision."

Katy wondered if the young woman was trying hard to maintain her judge's persona. She watched Stone wipe her hands with a paper napkin over and over again and couldn't help but think of Lady Macbeth trying to rid her hands of blood.

"Are you okay?" Katy asked.

"I tried to tell him." It was barely a whisper, but Katy heard the words.

"What did you say? Who did you try to tell…what?"

"Granger. I showed him my scores. But he threw them away."

"How long have you known him?"

"Not long. He told a friend of mine that he was instrumental in seeing that I passed the test for my judge's credentials. Which is not true at all. I judged with him at my first show a few months ago, but that's it."

Katy sat straight in her chair eager to hear more. "Why didn't he listen to you when you showed him your scores?"

"I think he just had his mind made up. He told me I'm

a novice and that he has a lot more experience judging horses. Said he could teach me a lot."

Katy stared at the girl a few seconds longer than normal in a conversation. She worried about her vulnerability. In Katy's mind she kept referring to Stone as "the girl," but Tara was almost Katy's age. The difference was Tara seemed young, like she needed protection. Although Katy didn't know anything about Tara's life or what she had been through. Her own, on the other hand, had demanded she grow up quick and harness and develop the strength within her.

"May I call you Tara?"

The girl nodded. "Sure."

"When I first arrived at the show, near the office, I saw you and Granger having a very heated exchange. Do you remember seeing me then?"

Again, a nod.

"Looked like he was being rough with you. Was he?"

After a very long pause, Tara said, "I don't think I want to talk about this anymore. I've had a long day and I'm tired. Would you please go now?"

Katy was surprised and didn't understand the quick shutdown. She must've hit some kind of nerve.

"Tara, I want to help you. I'm on your side. I'm thinking Granger is a bully and I don't want him to hurt you. I'll leave if you want. But please know, if you ever need me or want to talk, day or night, just give me a call."

Katy handed the girl a business card that had her cell phone number printed beneath her name. She didn't give them out to many people.

But Tara was different, and Katy had a feeling she'd be receiving a call soon.

"I can take care of myself, Ms. McKim." Stone stood straight as though she were mustering her strength, if only to hold on to her dignity. She held the motel door open.

Katy got up to leave the room and realized she'd better stay at the show another day, or at least half a day, until she could see Granger in action again.

"I know you can take care of yourself. But if you ever need a friend, Tara, I'm here."

# CHAPTER 13
## *Burglary*

KATY WALKED THE SHORT DISTANCE TO HER ROOM. SHE had decided to stay for the show the next day at least until the afternoon. She could always drive home early evening. It was only about an hour back to the ranch.

She thought about Tara. What was her story and how could Katy help? She wanted to try and put an end to Granger's blatant judging infractions. And how did Barker fit into all of this? What a day. She was tired and just wanted to relax.

As she opened the door, she was shocked to find a mild upheaval of her belongings. There would be no relaxing tonight.

*What the heck?*

Papers were strewn about the room along with clothes from her suitcase. The bag that normally carried her camera and notepad was flat on the floor. She was sure it was empty. Even without checking, she knew the judges' score sheets she had retrieved from the trash were missing. That was obviously the purpose of this break-in. Was Granger behind it?

Her phone vibrated in the back pocket of her jeans.

The screen showed handsome Matt's face wearing dark glasses like a sexy spy, his pearly white teeth filling a laughing smile.

"Hey." Her voice trailed downward.

"Katy, what is it? You okay?"

She wasn't sure she should tell him. Of course, he'd be worried.

"I just got back to my motel room, and it's been ransacked. I think my camera might be gone and some important papers."

"Did you call the police? And let the desk know?"

"Not yet. I just walked in."

"Be careful. The burglar might still be around. Call nine-one-one. I can be there in less than an hour."

"No, Matt. Stay there. Check on Cash for me. I'll call the police. Don't worry."

"Easy for you to say. I'll contact a friend there who's on the force."

"You seem to have more police friends in every county."

"The thin blue line. We're family. Now call nine-one-one and I'll call my friend. Keep me updated every hour. I'll be worrying about you, Katy."

"No need for that. I'll call you in a little while."

They hung up and she reported the break-in to the police and also to the motel desk. Within minutes blue lights strobed in the parking lot as two cruisers pulled up. It wasn't that late, but she hated the idea of disturbing other motel guests.

She greeted the officers, and they asked her to wait outside as they surveyed her room. As she waited in the glow of flashing lights, Tara walked up.

"Looks like you're the one in need of some help." The girl gave a slight smile.

"Someone broke into my room while I was with you."

"Anything of value taken?"

Katy leaned close. "My camera and maybe your original scoring sheets."

Tara's face went blank. "What were you doing with those?"

"Trying to find the truth."

A police officer came over to Katy. "Can you stay somewhere else tonight, Ms. McKim? We'd like to dust for prints."

"Uh...I don't know." She thought for a moment. "Maybe the motel could give me another room."

Tara intervened. "You can stay with me. No problem."

"I don't want to impose on your privacy."

"It's no imposition. No more discussion. Stay with me."

"Thanks. I appreciate that."

"I get up early."

"That's no problem. Me too."

A young dark-haired man in a jacket approached. "Ma'am? Katy McKim?"

"Yes?"

"I'm Detective Sanchez. I got a call from Matt Hartman." He showed his badge, then extended his hand and Katy shook it.

"Oh, yes. Matt said he had a friend here."

"Yes, ma'am. We've known each other for years. I told him I'd look in on you. Are you all right?"

"Yes, thanks. I'd just like to get in the room and see what's missing."

"They're dusting for prints, and we'll post a man

outside tonight. You may not be able to enter your room until sometime tomorrow. Do you have a place to stay?"

She nodded in Tara's direction. "Yes, Ms. Stone has been kind enough to invite me to bunk in with her."

Sanchez held his hand out to Tara who was still wearing the long T-shirt, leggings, and flip-flops. She could be mistaken for a teenager, fresh-faced and vulnerable. Katy thought some electricity may have passed between them.

"Ma'am," he said as he held Tara's hand and nodded.

Tara smiled but diverted her eyes elsewhere and slowly pulled her hand away.

He addressed Katy. "I'm sure the officers asked you some questions. I just have a few and then I'll let you ladies turn in for the night. Here's my card if either of you need to get a hold of me. Any time." He handed one to both women.

"All right." Katy was tired but would stand and listen to Sanchez's questions.

"Ms. McKim, you told the officers you were in Ms. Stone's room while this took place. And you left cash and your watch on the dresser, but they were not taken. Doesn't sound random to me. Who do you think did this?"

"I'm not sure. But I've got an idea."

"Care to share it with me?"

"Not yet."

His mouth smirked but his eyes narrowed. "Detective Hartman told me you like to play sleuth sometimes. I need to warn you that can be dangerous. He also told me to keep you safe. So, I hope you won't do anything to put yourself in danger. Can you give me your word?"

Katy's eyebrows raised. So, Matt talked about her to this detective. She wasn't sure whether to be miffed or flattered. It was one thing to call his friend for help. It was another to give Katy's personal "profile."

She held his business card. "Danger to one person might just be looking for answers to another. I can't give you my word for future situations that I don't even know about yet."

Sanchez took on a more serious tone. "Detective Hartman also said you might be difficult."

"I'm not trying to be difficult, Detective, just honest."

He smiled. "All right. We can talk more tomorrow. Hope you ladies get some rest. Don't open the door for anyone. Call me right away if you need anything."

"Thank you, Detective Sanchez." Katy knew he was just doing his job.

He noticed Tara one more time and nodded.

"Ma'am."

After about an hour the blue lights were gone, one cruiser was parked in front of Tara's room, and she and Katy were resting in their beds, not talking.

Then a quiet voice whispered.

"Katy? You asleep?"

"No. Are you?"

The two burst into giggles as though at a slumber party. Perhaps it was the release after hours of anxiety and being overtired.

"How can I be asleep and still ask you a question?"

Katy snorted a little. "How I can I be asleep and answer you?"

Tara cleared her throat and sounded serious now. "Do you know who broke in?"

"Everything points to Granger."

"Do you think he got what he wanted, or will he come after us?"

"Don't worry. There's an officer outside. Try and get some sleep. Morning comes early."

Tara made a grumble kind of sound. "Yeah, and I have to work with him again."

"Just do your job. I'll keep an eye on him."

When Katy awoke to a noise outside and a ray of sunshine peeking around the curtain, she could've sworn they had just closed their eyes for sleep. They must've really been tired. She didn't remember waking in the middle of the night as she sometimes did at home.

"What is it?" Tara groggily asked from her bed as she lifted herself to her elbows and ran her fingers through her long hair.

"Nothing. I thought I heard something. It's about six. Do you want to shower first?"

"No. Go ahead. I took mine last night. I'll just wash up in the sink, head to toe."

"Okay." Katy made her way to the bathroom.

"Hey," Tara called after her. "I put some clean undies and a T-shirt on the dresser for you. You probably don't have anything with you since they wouldn't let you back in your room. You can use my toothpaste and any makeup you want too. And the hair dryer I brought. I think the motel one is broken."

"Thanks a lot, but you don't have to do that."

"I want to."

After Katy showered and emerged in a cloud of steam, she saw Tara was already cleaned up, and wearing her judge's outfit.

"Wow, you're quick."

Tara spritzed hair spray on her pinned up tight braids. "Yeah, no muss, no fuss. Listen, I'm going to head out and see you at the show. I'll grab a little breakfast there. Lock the door. Be careful."

"You too." Katy smiled.

Tara peeked out the edge of the curtain before she opened the door. "Looks like the officer is still there and I think Detective Sanchez just drove up too."

"Ugh. I'm not ready to talk to anyone until I've had some coffee." Katy adjusted the towel around her body.

"See you later."

After the door was closed and locked, Katy carefully moved the corner of the drapes and saw Sanchez smiling at Tara.

"Uh, huh, just as I thought. He's interested in her."

# CHAPTER 14

# Groovy, Man

*Coffee. Need coffee.*

Although Katy slept through the night, which surprised her after having her motel room ransacked, she wasn't operating on all cylinders this morning. Maybe it was being away from home. She had never been too keen on traveling although she had done her fair share of it what with horse showing through the years. In desperate need of caffeine, her first destination would be the diner or food truck at the show, whichever was the quickest way to get her fix.

The food truck had no line, and she remembered the person serving the food had been nice the other day.

"One coffee, please." She kept her sunglasses on.

"How 'bout an egg sandwich?" The young guy smiled. Braids hung around his shoulders and the white paper hat with hairnet made him look a little goofy.

"No, thanks. I think I'll just start with coffee."

She lowered her glasses so he could see her eyes. She always appreciated when people did that with her, to make the human connection and not hide behind the darkened barrier.

"Okay. Coming right up. Cream 'n sugar's right over there."

He leaned his head down and pointed his finger out the truck's window toward a stainless-steel bowl on a table.

When he set her paper cup of coffee outside the truck's window, she noticed his vibrant colored tie-dyed T-shirt with words across his chest that read: "Make Someone's Day Groovy." Over his left pocket was the name Jeff. This young guy, probably around twenty years old, was enamored with the generation of her grandparents. That tickled her. And it dawned on her—she was only about eight years older than him. Maybe she was an old soul, she thought, or grew up quick by shouldering so much responsibility before her time, but she felt everyone was younger than her.

She gave him a big smile as she reached for her coffee.

"Be groovy, Jeff."

"Yeah, right on. You too, ma'am."

She stopped in her tracks and turned around to him. "Please don't call me ma'am. I'm not that old, Jeff."

His face flushed. "Oh, sorry! Peace."

He held up two fingers, and she wondered if he knew that originally was a victory sign during World War II before the hippie kids of the 1960s made it popular as the peace sign. Her dad told her that.

"We're cool," she said with a giggle to herself. She stirred a little cream and sugar into her coffee, then headed toward the show office to say hello to Sally.

Suddenly, from behind, a deep voice growled, "Hey,

hon" and a hand pulled roughly on her elbow, spilling coffee on her jeans and boots.

"Watch it!"

"Oops, my bad. Just wanted to introduce myself."

She turned sharply and nearly ran into the chest of... Granger. Or really, his belly would have hit her first. He was dressed in his judge's attire.

Leaning down to wipe her jeans with the napkin she had placed under her coffee cup, which now was only half full, she raised up to meet his eyes with a laser type of glare.

"Sorry about that, ma'am." He tapped his hat and nodded. "I just thought we should meet. I hear you bunked in with my protégé judge, Tara." He cleared his throat. "Uh, Ms. Stone, that is."

"How would you know that?"

His voice was low. "Word gets around a horse show. Plus, I'm staying at the Red Lodge, too, and I couldn't help but notice all the police presence last night. Someone said your room was broken into. Gosh, that's a shame. I hope nothing of value was taken. And, most importantly, are you and Tara okay? That must've been very scary for you ladies. You let me know if you need anything from me. Gordon Granger." His smile was repulsive to say the least. He extended his hand.

He sure had a lot to say about last night, Katy noted. Her eyes surveyed his hand as though it carried a most contagious plague, and she did not accept it.

"No, thank you. And we are *not* afraid. I've got my gun with me and have no qualms about putting some lead into the jackass who is stupid enough to come near us."

She turned her back to him and hurriedly walked to Sally's office, shaking all the way. She could not believe she had mustered the courage to say such things to him, but he deserved it.

A gun came in handy around her ranch, but she did not have one with her at the horse show. On second thought, yes, she did, in her truck. She sometimes forgot it was under the seat, but her dad had taught her to carry one when on the road alone. And, of course, her Army Ranger brother was another gun proponent, so he also wanted her to carry one to protect herself. Her father taught her at a young age how to safely use a gun, but could she really take someone else's life? That was a whole different matter. She never wanted to...but as she thought about it, in the worst-case scenario, if she or her family were threatened with bodily, life-threatening harm, she knew she would have to pull the trigger and ask God's forgiveness later.

As she rounded the corner to the show office, she noticed a large truck pulling to the back of the coliseum building. The logo across the side read *Fowler Feed*.

And although she wasn't sure she was seeing things clearly, who greeted the driver but Brett Barker? Why would the horse show need horse feed? Everyone brought their own special diet for their horses. What interest would Barker have in animal feed? It didn't make any sense.

Katy ducked next to a clump of high bushes so she could watch without being seen. Taking out her phone she was ready to take a photo of him with the driver. She also wanted to get a pic of the truck's license plate. She'd have to get closer.

Barker took the driver through the back door of the building, so she seized her chance and ran fast toward the rear of the truck. As she snapped, a voice from the passenger seat yelled, "Hey, what are you doing?" The man leaned out the window and scowled at her. He must have seen her approach in his side mirror.

She hadn't noticed a second person in the truck when they first drove up and didn't want to engage in case this was a criminal ring as Matt had alluded to. So, she about-faced and took off running toward the show office...not before she heard Barker come out to investigate. "Hey! What's going on?" He must've seen her, but she decided to deny, deny, deny if ever questioned.

Sally was in the show office getting her paperwork and computer ready before the first class as Katy dashed through the door.

"Hey, girl. Why are you so out of breath?"

"Let's just say I was getting my jogging in."

Sally frowned and gave her a quizzical look. "If you say so."

Barker must've been on her tail. He barged in right behind Katy.

"Were you taking pictures of me?"

Katy willed herself to stop panting and took time to gain her composure.

"What are you talking about?" Her brows knit together into an expression that inferred he was a lunatic.

"You were spying on me, weren't you?"

"I have no idea what this is about." She shrugged at him then shook her head in Sally's direction.

He came to face her and pointed his finger within a half inch of her nose.

"You listen to me. You had better stay out of my business. And that article of yours...I am this close to firing you." He held his thumb and index finger almost touching to paint the picture.

"If you don't want my article, Mr. Barker, I am sure a

competitor would be very interested. Maybe even the police."

"What competitor? There's no competitor for miles around."

"Did you ever hear of the Internet? We no longer need to be in the same geographic area."

"I'll say this one more time. Stay out of my business."

And he stormed out.

Sally's mouth hung open a little. "What have you gotten yourself into, Katy? You must've hit a nerve with that guy."

"Ever hear of Fowler Feed?" She smiled like the Cheshire cat.

"Actually, I have. They're new to the area."

"That's what I thought. Why would they be delivering feed to the horse show?"

"They wouldn't. Even if they did, they'd have to register with me. All vendors do. I collect the invoices and keep track of expenses. That's part of my job."

"Exactly."

Katy wasn't sure when she had gotten rid of her half-full coffee cup. She just knew she needed some more. So before going into the coliseum, she'd make another stop at Jeff's food truck.

"Hey, I'm empty."

"Black coffee, right?"

"To start with. Then I doctor it up some."

"Cool."

Jeff set a full cup of coffee on the ledge outside his window.

"Be groovy today." He gave her a smile.

"You too, man."

Again, she added a bit of cream and sugar to her java drink.

Entering the indoor arena, she saw Tara and Granger standing in the center of the ring back to back. Custom dictated that one judge scrutinize riders going around on the rail, while simultaneously the second judge covered the other side of the arena with the same horses reaching that point. That way, both judges saw all horses in the ring without their necks getting whiplash like at a tennis match and to avoid missing a beat in the performance. A Western pleasure class was in the ring now. Sometimes the schedule got switched around at shows. Usually, Western pleasure was in the afternoon, but if classes were large and had to be split, the other half of the class took place in the morning. That was the case today.

To Katy, Tara appeared rigid and uncomfortable, and seemed to refrain from making eye contact with Granger. Luckily, she was at his back. She diligently made notations on the form on her clipboard and precisely watched the horses' performances. Katy admired her work ethic and vowed to help her new friend however she could. She believed women should support and encourage one another as they strove for success.

Katy found a seat in the bleachers and decided to text Matt.

> Can't talk now – watching class. Things weird here. Can you check backgrounds – Brett Barker and Gordon Granger? I saw Fowler Feed truck. Barker talking to driver. Attaching photos of him and lic. tag. Barker said stay out of his biz. I'm suspicious of both guys. Staying at show this AM. Should be home tonight.

Immediately Matt texted back.

> Katy, don't get involved. I'm worried
> about you. Come home soon.

She replied.

> Don't worry. Will text or call before I get
> on the road. Gotta go.

She watched the horses go around and checked the roster Sally had given her to help with her article. Another Parkhill Stables entry. If things went south and Parkhill was left out of the running again, this would not be the first class she had witnessed firsthand where things seemed fishy and possibly rigged.

Walk. Trot. Lope. Both directions. Horses followed as though on a merry-go-round. They all displayed a good appearance. But Parkhill's horse was exceptional—gorgeously groomed, physically fit and attractive, and the horse was relaxed and listening to its rider who made everything look easy. Any command was invisible as though horse and rider had a telepathic bond. Katy could find no error to count off—a perfect score, in her estimation.

Others in the audience around her made various comments:

"Wow. That's the one to beat."

"Amazing."

"Number seven. It's a Parkhill."

Within minutes the class was over, and the announcer instructed the entries to line up. Places were called and first went to a horse that had missed its lead on the lope. Parkhill was fifth.

Katy wasn't at all surprised. She had expected it. But what could she do? Maybe she should just go home and let Matt and the authorities handle Granger. If the show association could prove wrongdoing by a judge, they could suspend. And law enforcement could arrest if Fowler Feed was found to be hiding drugs and the judge had a connection. Maybe Katy was in over her head. Even if she could find evidence, what then?

As the horses and riders left the ring, she saw Tara also leave. Where was she going? Didn't they need her for the next class?

Katy didn't want to abandon Tara if she needed help. And what about Melanie? If Barker turned out to be a crook, what would happen to his daughter?

Katy had to stay at the show. She'd let Matt know later.

## CHAPTER 15
### Retail Therapy

LEAVING THE BUILDING TO TRACK DOWN TARA, INSTEAD Katy ran into Melanie. The last time she'd seen the girl was when Barker had admonished his newfound daughter and made it pretty obvious for her to stay away from Katy.

"Oh, hey, Melanie. How are you?"

"Okay," she answered with a slight shrug.

"Just okay?"

Melanie carefully fingered show blouses on a rack outside a vendor truck that was parked close to the opening of the coliseum.

"I'm kinda bored. My dad's always busy. I'm not sure why I'm even here. I thought I'd get to talk to him."

The girl seemed pretty pathetic. So skinny. And probably uncomfortable in her high-heeled boots, as evidenced by her shifting back and forth from one foot to the other.

"Listen, I've got a little extra time. Do you want to do some real shopping instead of just hanging out?"

"What do you mean?"

"Well, you don't really seem that interested in the shirts. And your feet look kinda ouchy. How about a pair of real cowgirl boots?"

Melanie's face brightened as she checked out the boots Katy wore and pointed.

"Like yours?"

Katy didn't think her everyday boots were all that special, but she liked them. Comfy, good leather, with a few embossed flowers. Desert roses, they were called. When showing, she changed into tall English boots or polished Western boots depending on the class she entered.

"Sure. What do you think?"

A slight mischievous grin appeared, and Melanie said, "I've got my dad's credit card. He told me to go shopping." She patted the tiny purse hanging at her hip by a thin leather strap.

"Now you're talking. Why didn't you say that in the first place? Let's not disappoint him."

They both chuckled and climbed the fold-out metal steps into the vendor's trailer.

"Hey, Katy, how ya doin'?" The clothing vendor she saw at most shows in the area heartily greeted her.

"Just great, thanks. I brought you a new customer. This is Melanie. And she needs boots."

The woman's eyes examined Melanie's high-heeled patent leather boots and said with a smile, "I can see that she does."

"Something comfy and cowgirly."

"Gotcha. Coming right up. Over here, young lady. We've got lots of boots. I'm sure we can find a pair you'll love."

Melanie gave a big smile. And that warmed Katy's heart. Everyone needed to feel special and cared for.

The vendor pulled out boxes of boots in Melanie's size after the girl pointed to a few on display, aided by Katy's expert advice. She might've dressed functional around her ranch but with her horse show experience she knew good Western wear when she saw it.

While Melanie sat and tugged on boots, then checked them out in a mirror, Katy yay'd or nay'd her opinion. At the same time, she searched through stacks of blue jeans that would be more appropriate for a horse show than what the girl currently wore. At least the Western jeans didn't have any holes or jagged rips as though the wearer had been mauled by a bear. Katy hated those even if they supposedly were the latest trend. A friend had tried to get Katy to buy a pair, but she refused. Maybe she really was an old soul.

She smiled to herself about the way certain fashions took hold of a generation. In her younger years on the ranch, she wore standard blue jeans her mother ordered from a catalog or the feed store and helped her family with daily chores. Although she did go through a phase of rebellion with a girlfriend when they both poured bleach on their jeans to try for a tie-dye effect. Her dad shook his head and said, "This is not the sixties and you're just going to look like you flunked Laundry 101." He had laughed and said to his wife, "Everyone has to learn from their own mistakes."

Her mom wasn't as easygoing, and she and Katy sometimes butted heads. One contentious episode was the time she and her friend highlighted their hair together. When her mother discovered the result, she had a fit and the incident ended in tears for both.

"You'll ruin your beautiful auburn-colored hair."

Back then Katy wanted to be different from her family, be her own person. Now she would give anything to have her mom and dad back in her life. At least her brother, Shawn, had returned, which was a true miracle. She couldn't believe she actually had held a funeral service for him. But that was when she was in the depths of despair after her parents' death. When he went missing and she was deceived into thinking he was most likely dead, she just went through the motions and agreed zombie-like when a small memorial service was suggested.

"Ooh, Katy, look at this pair."

Katy fought to snap out of her detour into bad memories and pay attention to her young friend.

"They're pretty cool. Do you like 'em?"

Melanie pulled on the boots and her broad smile was infectious.

"Yeah. And they're really comfortable."

"Great. Are they the ones?"

The girl walked up and down a carpeted aisle and twisted and turned to view them in small mirrors that were propped on the floor. Her continuous big smile gave Katy the answer.

"I really like them."

"Well, get Dad's credit card fired up. Before you do, here, try on these jeans." Katy handed her a couple pairs of dark-washed denim.

"What's wrong with the ones I'm wearing?"

She couldn't help letting a laugh escape. "They might be okay for high school...or parties...or even a fashion show where the guys wear dresses and feathers...but not for a horse show."

"If you say so, Ms. Expert. Okay, let me have the cowgirl jeans. Yeehaw." Melanie rolled her eyes upward.

As she tried each one on, Katy was tasked with the difficult job of hunting for a smaller and smaller size.

And it worried her. The girl had previously mentioned having "food issues" and spending time in a rehab for an eating disorder. Katy hoped she was on the road to recovery, and wondered if she should bring up the subject with Melanie.

"Here, try these. They should be your size."

"Thanks for helping me, Katy. It's fun. Well, except that none of these fit."

"Sure thing. Us girls have to stick together, right? We'll find the right size. Not to worry."

Before Melanie turned back into the dressing room, she looked intently at Katy, her eyes glossing over with moisture.

"I didn't really have any girlfriends in school. They bullied me because I was so thin. My mom used to help me with clothes. Now she's gone."

Katy's heart nearly broke. "Melanie, how old are you? Do you have any other family?"

She rubbed her eyes. "I just turned eighteen. I thought my dad was going to be my family. Now I'm not so sure. I do have an aunt, my mom's sister. She's kinda nice."

"Well, that's good. Have you reached out to her? Do you have any plans for college?"

"My aunt lives near Redding and she said I could stay with her for a while. I'd like to go to college, learn about journalism, but I really can't afford it. I don't even have a job."

Again, her eyes filled with tears, but her fingers quickly moved over her face to prevent them from falling on her cheeks.

"Melanie, you've got to focus on the positive. That's great about your aunt. And college—maybe your dad could help with the cost, especially if you want to learn journalism. That's his business after all. Or you could apply for a scholarship. There are all kinds of ways to work things out. Don't give up."

"You're right. I guess."

Katy had so many thoughts and ideas for the girl. But first, she had to ask a burning question.

"Melanie, I don't want to intrude on your personal life…but, are you continuing counseling for the eating issues?"

She hesitated. "I was seeing a therapist right after I got out of rehab. But then stopped. I guess I should get back in it."

"Yes, I think that would be so helpful. As long as the counselor is good and 'gets you,' so to speak. Someone who is caring and knowledgeable about eating disorders. There's nothing to be ashamed about. It's like any other illness. I always say help is out there. Do it for yourself. For a better life."

Melanie nodded. "You're right, Katy. I will. And thanks again for caring. It means a lot to me."

"Okay, get in there and try those jeans on. We need to use your dad's credit card before he pulls the plug."

That generated a big snort and giggle from Melanie as she ducked behind the curtain.

Katy mindlessly glanced at silver jewelry and wondered what it would be like to have a daughter like Melanie. They were about ten years apart in age, but Katy felt like it was more like twenty just because she had been through so much. Would she ever marry and have children? She wasn't sure she could picture herself as a mother. Her own mother had been around until just two years ago, but even before, Katy was pretty independent. She had moved out of her parents' home into her own apartment with a friend and had a great work ethic from a young age. Her dad had instilled that in both his kids.

Despite all the tragedy she had experienced, deep in her heart she still wanted the fairy tale—a loving husband and loving kids. Her daydreaming wandered to Matt. Could he be the one? She made a mental note to call him. He must be worried about her. Plus, she had questions about Barker and Granger.

"This pair might work." Melanie called from the dressing room and pushed the curtain open.

She turned her thin hips this way and that to show off the dark indigo, straight-legged blue jeans.

"Those look great. I'd say they're keepers. What do you think?"

"I love them."

"Good. I hear your dad's credit card gasping now. Cha-ching! Let's go get some lunch. On him. I know a great food truck."

# CHAPTER 16
## *Young Love*

KATY THOUGHT MELANIE STRODE CONFIDENTLY CARRYING her purchases through the horse show crowd. Maybe she even felt like Katy's girlfriend even though there was the age difference.

"Lookin' good, girl." Katy smiled. "I'm glad you decided to wear your new outfit."

"Thanks. It is more comfortable."

"And you fit in with the horsey crowd now. People might think you're here showing your horse."

Melanie's brow furrowed and she shook her head. "I don't know about that since I have no clue about horses."

"Well, maybe someday you'll come visit me and I'll show you a few things. Horses are wonderful. They love us unconditionally."

"Thanks, Katy. That would be fun."

As they approached Jeff's food truck, he smiled at Katy. Today his T-shirt read "Love One Another. Give Peace a Chance." A red heart substituted for the word "love."

"Hey, Ms. Black Coffee, no ma'am."

"That's right, no ma'am. Are you having a groovy day, dude?"

Katy chuckled and Melanie screwed up her face in confusion.

"Always groovy. Is this your daughter?" He gave Melanie a nice smile.

"Oh, boy, you are treading on thin ice now, my friend. First, you call me ma'am. Now, you're saying I'm old enough to be Melanie's mother. That is no way to keep things groovy."

They both enjoyed a good laugh.

Then Jeff got serious. "Melanie. Hmmm. That's a pretty name. Like a soft whisper on the wind. When all the planets are aligned."

Melanie blushed and said nothing, but Katy offered, "Wow, you are a poet. That was beautiful. Yes, this is my friend Melanie. Melanie, this is groovy Jeff. If you ever need a good cup of coffee, Jeff's the man to see."

"I also make a yummy lunch taco. Today I have grilled chicken."

In a quiet voice, Melanie said, "I'm a vegetarian."

Jeff nearly did a little hop inside the truck and his braids swung back and forth. "Me too. I've got grilled veggies and a gluten-free taco. Would you like to try that?"

Melanie nodded. "Sure. Thanks."

Katy smiled. "I'll take the grilled chicken taco, please. I'm a carnivore."

"To each his own, I always say." Jeff grinned. "Or, *her* own."

"But," Katy added, "I've gotta tell you...the other day the taco was really skimpy. What happened?"

His face sank. "Oh, so very sorry. I wasn't here but

had a friend fill in for me. I'm afraid he is no chef. Today it's on the house."

"You don't have to do that, Jeff. I was just wondering what happened. It didn't seem like your normal menu item."

Jeff smiled, made the peace sign with his fingers, and went back to his food prep area to whip them up some lunch. They got settled on a picnic bench close by. Melanie propped her shopping bags next to her and Katy got out her phone and began texting Tara and Matt.

"Sorry but I need to touch base with a couple of people."

"No worries. Go ahead. I might text my dad."

As they both focused on their screens, Jeff approached with a tray.

"Wow." Katy raised up. "I never had such special treatment before. We would've picked this up at your window."

He beamed. "No problem for such lovely female beings. It's good karma for me."

Melanie couldn't help her muffled giggle hidden behind a palm to her mouth.

Katy's phone pinged back at her. "Oops, sorry, I've got to answer this. Thanks so much, Jeff."

"My pleasure." He displayed an elaborate bow to Melanie as though he were a prince vying for her hand before jumping on his steed at a jousting tournament, then returned to his food truck.

Katy watched some of this exchange from a side-glance, but she wanted to get back to her phone and communicate with Matt.

KATY

Anything on Barker's background?
Granger?

114

Matt replied.

MATT

Not much on Barker. Sued for breach of contract in past. Nothing criminal. He and Granger are partners in Fowler Feed through a bogus corp. Granger – prior arrest – sex harassment, got off. Watch out for him. When you coming home?

Dear, kind, sweet Matt. Always looking out for her.

KATY

Might stay another night. Home tomorrow. I've befriended Barker's daughter. Don't want to abandon her yet.

MATT

Be careful. Please. Should I come there?

Not necessary. Be home soon.

Okay. But I'm worried.

I know you are. And that warms my heart.

She added a heart emoji. She hadn't really said "I love you" to him yet, but if she were honest with herself, that's what she felt. And it consumed her thoughts.

So, Granger was a pervert. Her radar was on target. And Barker? She still didn't think he was squeaky clean. What about "actions speak louder than words?" He had acted like a bully around his daughter when Katy first met her. And spoke like a jerk to Katy on a few occasions. She couldn't give him a pass yet. Partners in Fowler Feed? That explained a little. She needed to know more about him.

But first she had to answer Tara.

Where are you? You okay? Can we meet?

About to go into class. Got news for you.

That was intriguing.

Jeff watched Melanie nibble on veggies, and she bestowed bashful grins upon him. Katy almost chuckled at this youthful flirtation but held it in.

"Hey, I've got to go watch the class that's in the coliseum now. Want to come? Or stay here?" She turned from Melanie to Jeff and thought she'd give Melanie an out. "Looks like you haven't quite finished your lunch."

"I think I'll stay."

"You sure you'll be okay?"

"Of course. I've got my kickin' cowgirl boots on." She extended her leg out straight from under the bench to show off her new footwear.

"That you do. All right. Have fun. I'll see you later." Then, because she couldn't resist, she called over to Jeff. "Hey, take care of my girlfriend. Okay, dude?"

"Of course. Not to worry. Everything's peace and love in my universe."

Melanie giggled and held two fingers in a peace sign as Katy got up to head to the coliseum.

Hunter under saddle was in the arena and Katy saw Granger and Tara slowly pacing in the middle, clipboards in hand, watching the horses go around on the rail. They did not talk or make eye contact with each other.

Katy found a low bleacher seat and smiled at the people around her. Her camera and notebook had been taken in the motel robbery so she relied on her cell phone for any pictures although she knew the quality wouldn't be that good.

The horses were judged on their walk, trot, and canter. Katy appreciated how it was now acceptable for them to have longer, freer strides than in a Western plea- sure class. Riders were dressed in English attire. Katy was quite familiar with this class as she often entered it when she showed.

No surprise to her, the favorite in her mind was from Parkhill Stables. Such a gorgeous example of well-bred, well-groomed, well-trained horseflesh. It was just a matter of time to see if Granger would blatantly ignore obvious rankings and continue his misdeeds.

The announcer asked the class to reverse direction and continue at the trot, which they all did but of course some performed better than others. When all was said and done, the class ended and exhibitors formed a line next to each other.

Then Katy witnessed the drama. Granger thrust his open palm to Tara, apparently asking for her scoresheet, to which she shook her head back and forth. She was not giving it up. Even from where Katy sat, she saw Granger's face redden. If this wasn't so serious, it would be comical.

The ring steward approached the two judges and a discussion ensued. No one could hear what was said but the tension in the stands was palpable with people on the edge of their seats. They knew what was going on when they saw Tara shaking her head again. She was deter- mined. And Katy was proud of her.

After what seemed like an eternity, the announcer spoke.

"Ladies and gentlemen, we have a unique decision for

this class. Instead of receiving double points as is normal when we have two judges in the ring who reach a consensus, this class will take into consideration individual placings by each judge. It's a little unusual but we've checked the rule book and it is entirely acceptable, and at our discretion, so we hope it does not cause any inconvenience for exhibitors trying to earn points.

"Having said that, we are pleased to announce that first place under Judge Stone is Parkhill's number one forty-seven. Under Judge Granger the same horse has placed eighth."

A rumble of discontent was heard throughout the audience as the announcer continued to call out such divergent placings, but it was hard to hear over the crowd's applause and enthusiasm. A few individuals were not shy about yelling out their displeasure with Granger's rulings. Things like, "Redo!" "Get another judge!" After all, the horse that placed first would lose points and be penalized for the eighth place that Granger gave him.

Granger finally showed himself to be the fool he was, or maybe cheater, and everyone in the coliseum knew it. He walked out...which left Tara to accept the applause and return it with a big smile on her face.

Katy could hardly believe this scene as she had never seen it happen in a show before. She stood with the rest of the audience and clapped. The moment was made even more special when Tara noticed her and nodded to which Katy gave a big thumbs-up.

## CHAPTER 17
# *Danger, Danger*

WHEN THE CLASS ENDED KATY MET UP WITH TARA WHO was in the show office on a short break.

"That was amazing." Katy almost felt tears forming, and they hugged one another tightly.

Sally organized some papers on her desk. "You can use that room if you need to talk privately." She winked and pointed to a small storage room with a table and chairs.

"I'm so proud of you." Katy took a seat next to Tara. "What happens now? Will you have to judge with him again?"

"No. I filed an appeal and we'll use another judge for the rest of the show. It'll be more work for me and the guy who is stepping in, maybe extra classes. Needless to say, Granger is majorly ticked."

"Should we be worried about him? Maybe call Detective Sanchez?"

"There's been no crime outside the show organization so Sanchez wouldn't be any help in this situation."

"Well, let's keep an eye on him. Oh, and I should tell

you...my...uh...friend, Matt, who is also a detective...he told me that Granger has a prior arrest for sexual harassment and that Granger and Barker have a business tie to Fowler Feed."

Tara grimaced. "That's creepy about the sex charge. I knew he made my skin crawl. What's that about Fowler Feed?"

"I thought I told you about it. Confidential of course. They might be transporting drugs in their feed tubs and bags. Do you know anything about Fowler Feed?"

Tara was quiet for a minute. "I only recently heard about them. They've been offering all kinds of discounts to barns in the area since they're new in town. Some are mega offers like over-the-top huge. At least that's what some friends have mentioned. However, a few horses have gotten sick, possibly after eating the feed. Gee, do you think the drugs could have leaked somehow? I'm not sure how that works."

"I have no idea, but thanks for telling me this. Do you mind if I share with Matt?"

"No, go ahead. And, Katy?"

"Yeah?"

"It's okay to call him your boyfriend."

They both broke out in laughter.

"It's just...I'm not a kid in high school. It sounds a little silly to say 'boyfriend.'"

"What else can you call him? 'Gentleman friend'? Or 'my man'?"

"Ew, those sound worse."

Hearty laughter filled the room until Sally knocked.

"Sorry to break up your party, but they need Tara for the next class."

Katy caught her breath. "Okay, thanks, Sally." Then to Tara, "You go do your thing. Let's catch up later."

"Sounds good, friend."

Katy decided to stay at the table and collect her thoughts. What would she do the rest of the day? Did she really need to stay at the show and watch any more classes? She had enough for her article and could always check online later for results of the rest of the show, if she needed them. Barker might not even want her article now, after all that had transpired. Maybe she should do her homework and look around for a competitor magazine.

For now, she wanted to find Melanie and see how she was getting along with Food Truck Jeff. Not sure why in her mind she put these labels on people, but she did. No one would ever hear them but her. And they weren't disparaging so she didn't feel guilty.

Meek Melanie, the daughter. Brash (and rude) Barker (who barked). Gross Granger. Sweet Sally. Tireless Tara (or Determined Tara because of her work ethic. Better yet, Tenacious Tara). She would never remember all of these, but it was fun coming up with them and it helped her with people's names like a memory game. And of course, Mild-Mannered Matt (she also wanted to add Kindhearted Matt) although he could be Militant-Matt if his job called for it.

Before she left the office, she decided to text him again.

KATY

> Judge Tara says Fowler Feed offers big discounts to barns to get new business. Some horses have gotten sick. Could tubs open and drugs "leak" into the feed? PS: I might come home tonight instead.

He answered quickly.

MATT

Interesting. I'll look into sick horses.
Good! Come on home. Let me know ETA
and I'll meet you at the ranch.

Katy got up to leave, then decided to text Detective Sanchez.

Hello, any news on my belongings taken
from the motel room? When can I get my
clothes, etc.? I'm leaving the horse show
before tonight.

He answered right away.

SANCHEZ

I have all your things at the PD. Will be
here till 6-7 PM. Text when you're
coming. If we find other belongings
(camera), I'll get in touch.

So, she'd find Melanie and visit awhile, head to the police department to get her things, and call Tara to explain she decided to leave rather than stay another night.

Sally was busy at her desk with an exhibitor, something about a mix-up in the fees he was charged, or so he said rather strongly. Looked like it was going to take a while to sort out and Katy didn't feel like waiting so she waved at Sally.

"Take care, Sally. Sorry to interrupt. I'm not staying tonight. I'll look for you at another show down the road."

"Okay, Katy. Sure thing. You too. Be careful." Sally waved.

The guy she was helping was obviously perturbed at the interruption, so Katy quickly opened the door and was on her way. There was a good bit of sunshine today, so she rummaged in her bag for sunglasses and placed them on her face.

Not paying attention, maybe that's why when she rounded the corner of the building, she bumped into the man who was on her right side. Or did he bump into her, on purpose?

"Oh, sorry. Excuse me," she told him.

They weren't facing, but she felt his lean, muscular arm when she tried not to fall, and thought he was a young guy, rather than older man.

"Yeah, you're sorry all right. Somebody ought to teach you a lesson. Bitch."

"What'd you say?" She was shocked at his language, not the word but the arrogance.

"You heard me. Better stop buttin' your nose in where it don't belong. Stop messing with people's reputations. Or you'll be sorry." He blocked her path. All she saw was a hoodie and sunglasses.

Now the hair on her arms stood up and she felt clammy. *Don't show any fear*, she told herself.

"Listen, I said I was sorry. Now, let me pass."

Before she could get another word out, he rammed into her with his shoulder like a football player against a tackling dummy, and she toppled to the ground hard in a face-plant move. They were at the side of the office shielded by a few trees and away from people's sight.

"Ow," she groaned when sharp pain pierced her cheek, knees, wrist, and shoulder upon landing.

To add to her misery, the guy launched a swift kick with his boot to her side. Such a stabbing pain, she clenched her eyes shut against the stars flickering there. No one had ever hurt her like this before.

*Lord, please help me.* It had been a long time since she had prayed, but she needed someone to rescue her. No telling what this guy might do next. Now she really wished Matt was with her.

As fast as the attack had begun, it was over. The guy had taken off, and she was immediately upset with herself for not getting a good look at his face. She had no description. She remembered his build seemed lean but with muscular arms. Maybe a body like Food Truck Jeff's—no extra fat, young, strong.

"Oh, no." A voice she recognized came close to her ear. "Are you okay, Katy?"

"Tara, help me up." Her voice came out like a scratchy whisper.

"I've got you. Take it slow."

Katy felt her friend's hands gripping under her arms. She first doubled over onto her painful knees but then was able to force herself to stand.

"I...uh...thought you had left to judge a class."

Tara hung on to her as they stood for a minute while Katy got her bearings.

"Don't try to talk if you can't," Tara told her. "There was a delay in the arena, so I hurried back for my cell phone. I left it on the table when we were talking."

"Thank God." Katy had muttered His name more times in the last hour than she had in the last few years.

"Who did this to you?"

"I didn't get a good look. He was wearing a hoodie and dark glasses. I think he might've been a young guy."

"Did he say anything to you or take anything?"

Katy held her cheek that was bruised. She must've hit it upon impact with the ground.

"Called me a name, told me to mind my own business, pushed me down and kicked me. Didn't steal my purse, though."

"Do you think it has anything to do with Granger? We should call the police."

"No. Let me figure this out."

Katy was wobbly on her feet, but Tara supported her. They stayed that way for a couple more minutes until Katy's breath stabilized.

Tara studied her. "You're not in the best shape right now to figure anything out. I could call for the EMTs that are on the showgrounds."

Katy shook her head. "No, don't. Please. I decided to head home instead of staying another night. There's no real reason for me to stay any longer. I was going to call you before I left."

"Well, we need to take you to urgent care. You said he kicked you when you were down? What a slimeball."

"I don't have time for urgent care. I want to get on the road. Besides, you need to get to your class. You're probably late."

"Don't worry about that. I don't want to leave you, Katy. And I'm worried for you to drive. What if you pass out on the road?"

"I think I'll just be sore. It's only about an hour to home. I'll contact you when I get there. Seriously. Don't worry."

"Will you promise you'll go to your doctor or urgent care and let me know what they say?"

"Yes, I promise. But I'm sure it'll be nothing, just some bruises. Haven't you fallen off a horse before? That's what it feels like. And you get back on."

Tara hesitated and scowled, obviously unsure about parting but Katy got her way. About to hug when they were ready to go in separate directions, Tara thought better of it and stepped back. She touched Katy's shoulders and held her hands up. "I don't want to hurt you."

"It's okay. Really."

"You be careful. I want updates."

Katy thanked her and watched Tara head to the arena to judge the next class, and then heard her say, "You're stubborn. You know that, Katy McKim?"

"I've been told that a time or two."

## CHAPTER 18
# *Wounded in Action*

WHEN TARA WAS OUT OF SIGHT, KATY HELD HER SIDE grunting in pain and slowly limped to Jeff's food truck. She hoped Melanie was there.

Jeff was outside his food truck wiping off a couple of card tables he had set up next to a picnic table that belonged to the horse show grounds. He raised his head as Katy got closer and smiled, then frowned when he saw a bruise on her cheek and that her walk was more of a shuffle.

"Oh, my gosh. What happened to you?"

"It's nothing. Had a little spill."

He quickly pulled out a chair at one of the card tables. "Here, sit, sit. Do you want a cold drink?"

"That would be nice, Jeff, thanks. Is Melanie around?"

"She should be back soon. Said she wanted to take the packages to her car."

"Okay. I'll just wait if that's okay with you."

"Sure thing." Then he winked at her. "Melanie and I had a nice visit. I wanted to thank you for introducing us. Hey, can I call you Miss Katy instead of that nick-name I made up?"

"Katy is just fine. And I'm glad you both enjoyed getting to know each other. I thought you might hit it off."

"I'll get your drink." He shook his head and muttered, "What a bummer. You sure you're okay?"

"Yes. I'll be all right."

Katy gingerly sat and exhaled as though she had run a marathon. She shifted off the sore hip and wondered if she'd be okay to drive. But she had to get out of this place and was determined to make it home.

She checked her phone. That's what people did nowadays, whether waiting in a doctor's office or at the DMV or waiting for a friend. No one picked up a magazine, they might be germy. No one looked around at another person, wary of making eye contact. Everyone stayed in their own bubble. She didn't want to join the masses in this strange behavior and at times she tried to break the habit. Popular culture just happened like an addiction. She had read articles about how humans received an endorphin high from the act of swiping on their devices. She had read that on a digital device.

"Katy, you're back." Melanie sat next to her with a big smile that quickly faded to worry. "What happened? Your face is bruised. And you're hunched over."

"It's nothing. Just a little accident."

"You fell? Off a horse?" The girl put her hand on Katy's arm.

"No. I must've tripped. Hey, listen, I came to tell you, I'm heading home now. I have enough for my article, and I need to check on my horse."

The girl's face was downright pitiful. "Oh, gosh, I'm

missing you already. We had so much fun together. You rescued me."

That warmed Katy's heart and brought a sweet smile to her face.

"I was serious about you coming to visit, Mel. I'll send my contact info to your phone. Please keep in touch."

"Absolutely. I totally want to. Our time together has meant a lot to me."

Jeff appeared carrying two fruity-looking drinks.

"Me too, no ma'am. Here's a groovy soothing drink for you...uh, Katy...and one for my princess that the universe has graciously bestowed upon me."

"Wow," Katy said. "Princess? That's an amazing title. I guess I've missed some things in my absence."

The young couple chuckled.

"Let's just say, Jeff and I are on the same streaming channel. I think the older generation calls it wavelength." Melanie blushed.

"Totally. I feel we are about to embark upon the most amazing friendship the world has ever known." Jeff put a hand on Melanie's shoulder.

Katy's eyes widened. "You sure have a way with words, dude. And I hate to break this up, but I really need to get on the road now." She stood and leaned close to Jeff. "Thanks, man, for being so cool. And for the drink." She held it up and smiled.

"You too, ma'am. Oops, no ma'am. Don't be a stranger."

And then to Melanie she said, "Take care of yourself. Call me anytime about anything. Promise?"

"I promise."

As Melanie hugged her, Katy groaned a bit.

"Are you sure you're all right?"

"Yes, just sore. Now, I am going and don't want to say 'goodbye' so it's 'see ya soon.'"

In case they were watching her go, Katy tried her best to walk straight and disguise her limp which only resulted in a slower gait than normal, but she finally made it to her truck. It was a little tough climbing up to the driver's seat. Her body just wanted a strong pill and a soak in Epsom salts. But that would have to wait. She needed to stay alert for the drive ahead.

First a quick stop at the police department to pick up her clothes and toiletries that Detective Sanchez no longer needed. She hoped her camera and notebook would turn up soon.

The minute he saw her enter his office he openly showed his surprise.

"What happened to you? You look like you fell off a horse or something."

"It's nothing. I'm fine." She felt she had said those words at least ten times in the last half hour.

"I'm serious, Ms. McKim. You have a bruise on your cheek, and you look like you're in pain. Don't make me call your boyfriend, Hartman."

"Please don't. I'll talk to him when I get home. I'm on my way now. I just wanted to get my things from you."

He reached behind to a credenza and handed her a couple of plastic bags containing clothes and bathroom items, also her overnight tote.

"So, let's hear it and I'd appreciate the truth please."

She didn't want to tell him anything, but his intense stare cut right through her.

"Some kid ran into me. I think he wanted my purse. But a friend came along in the nick of time and the kid took off. I'm sure it was just a random thing. I'm all right, really."

She avoided his eyes. "I need to get on the road now, Detective. I appreciate your help. Thanks very much."

He stared at her. "You know I don't believe you, right?"

"Detective, I can't change what you believe. I just know I've got to get going. I have an hour's drive. And I'm anxious to get home."

"All right. Please be safe, Ms. McKim. I'll contact you if I find your camera."

"Thank you."

"Give my regards to Hartman."

She gave a half smile and exited his office.

## CHAPTER 19
### *Attack*

CLIMBING INTO HER TRUCK WAS SOMEWHAT OF A challenge. The pain in her side stabbed when she reached for the grab handle to hoist herself up. Her knees hurt from when she hit the ground. Her bruised face hurt from who knows when or where, probably the face-plant. Everything hurt.

But she made it into the driver's seat and was determined to get home. Rummaging in her bag she found a bottle of everyday pain medication, not the kind that would make her sleepy but one that hopefully would relieve some of her aches and pains and help her concentrate to drive. She gulped three tablets and took a swig of water from her metal bottle.

Then she decided to call Matt, not text. What should she tell him? If she said she had been mugged, he'd freak. Maybe he'd start driving to her. But she had to tell him something. And she sure hoped Detective Sanchez wouldn't contact him and spill the beans.

She started the truck, maneuvered it out of the parking area, and once on the road, pushed the hands-free button and spoke his name into the microphone on the ceiling. She meant to leave earlier but her stop at Detective Sanchez's office had delayed her, and now it was nearly dark.

"Hey, babe, you coming home?"

"Yeah. I just left the showgrounds. Should be home in an hour. I can't believe it's dark already."

"Good. I'm looking forward to seeing you. I'll get to the ranch around the same time. Maybe we can have a nice dinner. I'll cook for you."

"Well, that sounds like a deal. I haven't really eaten the best, just horse-show food. I'll take you up on it, sir."

"My pleasure. I've missed you, Katy."

She didn't say anything when headlights behind her appeared to gain ground rapidly. She squinted into the rearview mirror to see if she could identify the vehicle. They were nearly right on her tail. What jerks. Why did people have to drive so fast and recklessly?

"Katy? Are you there? Can you hear me?"

"Yes. I'm sorry. Somebody's on my bumper. I was trying to see who it was."

"Be careful. Maybe pull over and let them go around. They might be drunk."

She tried to watch in the mirror, but the headlights were blinding so she had to pay attention to what was ahead instead of the other vehicle.

"Oh, never mind them. What have you and the guys been up to? Any news on Fowler Feed?"

"Not much more than what I told you last time. Barker and Granger are on the partnership papers. Well, not their names but a bogus company is listed. After some digging, we found their names. One of our informants tipped us about drug trafficking, but it takes a while to gather hard evidence and witnesses to a crime."

"I hope Barker's daughter won't get hurt if he goes down. She's a sweet girl. I invited her to the ranch sometime."

"That's nice of you."

"How's Cash? And the neighbor horses? Everybody okay?"

"Yeah, I saw your neighbors. They're such nice people. Shawn and I checked on the horses."

She was uncomfortable in the seat because of her bruises and wanted to move around, maybe even grunt or whine but she had to continue her act with Matt that all was well. Unfortunately, she figured he would discover her pain when she arrived home.

"Thanks for doing that. Lily and Stan are great. I'll have to get them a nice gift—uh, oh no." The breath went out of her.

Suddenly the truck tailing her ran up on her bumper with such force she lurched forward toward the windshield. Her shoulder hit the inside wall of the cab when her truck leaned to the left. Grabbing the steering wheel tight she tried to control the truck and keep it on the road.

Matt's voice came through the speaker. "Katy, what's the matter? You all right? Talk to me."

But she couldn't. Too much was happening. Rocking and swaying. Brakes squealing. Gravel spitting. The vibration from the rumble strip on the shoulder of the road sounded like a machine gun when her truck darted out of the lane she was trying so desperately to stay within.

Everything around her was awash and blurry in the glare from headlights. It was as though an unwanted spotlight was blasting on her.

Ugh! Another loud hit from behind. The other driver was ramming her, forcing her off the road.

She knew it was bad. Try as she might, she was losing control of her vehicle. Quickly her panicky voice sounded although she felt it didn't belong to her.

"Matt! Help me. He's wrecking my—"

Her mind wanted to say "call 9-1-1" but her mouth couldn't form the words. It was too busy screaming and fixed in a frantic expression. She wasn't sure she would make it out of this alive and was bracing herself for when the airbag exploded. She knew it would.

"Katy! Katy!"

She held on as her truck tumbled off the road, down a gradual embankment, and aimed for a tree. Boom! Before she could steer it to the right or left, hard impact. The white airbag burst with a pop and expelled dust throughout the cab. Katy's hands had flown up to cover her face and eyes.

Surprised that the bag felt hard when it hit her, she recalled a memory of a child she knew whose arms were broken in a similar situation when he and his mother were in a vehicular accident. He had put his hands up to cover his face. Unfortunately, the airbag, and seatbelt, gave him worse injuries than the crash itself. Katy knew those devices also kept him safe and most likely saved his life.

She was helpless and all she could do was hang on. She was hardly aware that inside her thoughts she was asking God to be with her.

And then all was quiet. The airbag dust floated around her, and it seemed surreal like snow falling lightly in a dream.

Opening her eyes, she pushed the remnants of the bag away. Gradually she was able to unhook her seatbelt.

She had seen movies where the belt got stuck and had to be cut away. Grateful that hers came undone easily, and that her arms or hands were not broken, she let out a breath. The truck was upright. It had not rolled over.

In no hurry to move around because pain was setting in, she laid back and steadied her breathing. In and out, rhythmically. She willed herself to stay conscious.

Rustling grass and muffled voices broke her reverie.

"Is she moving?" A man's voice grumbled from a short distance away. She didn't recognize it and couldn't move much to look around.

For some reason she didn't think he was there to help her. She was able to turn slightly but couldn't see his face, only two arms covered in colorful tattoos. She froze and her eyes squeezed shut. Was he the driver that had rammed her truck?

Suddenly a siren screamed in the distance, but soon sounded closer and closer.

Another voice said, "Let's get the heck outta here."

Katy wanted to see who they were but when she tried to raise her body from the seatback and turn her neck to the left, a jolt of pain seared upward and forced her to lie back.

A loud motor roared, and she was sure it was the other driver making his getaway.

Her head started to throb, and her throat was so parched. She couldn't imagine getting out of the truck and climbing up the embankment to the asphalt road. But if she stayed where she was, would her truck blow up as she had seen in too many movies? She didn't smell any fuel and had planned on filling it up when she got farther down the road. A memory came to the forefront of her mind about an article reporting that only about five percent of vehicles in an accident catch fire. No matter what the movies portray.

As she thought of various scenarios and listened to the wailing sirens, she felt herself drifting, floating with the airbag dust particles like tiny Tinker Bell fairies. Where was Matt?

And then she was out. In dreamland.

And that day

# CHAPTER 20
## *Déjà vu*

"MATT. THANK GOD YOU'RE HERE. I THINK I LOVE YOU."

It was so good to see him. They were having a picnic, and their horses were grazing nearby. He had spread a blanket in the very green grass, almost artificial turf green, and was filling small plates with meat, cheese, and crackers for them. Gosh, she was hungry and so thirsty.

"Katy, Katy, wake up."

She felt a hand on her shoulder rocking her gently. If this was a dream, why in the world would someone wake her? She wanted to stay on the blanket surrounded by wildflowers and blue skies, and Matt.

What was that awful sound? That incessant *whoop-whoop*, blaring *hee-haw*. Someone's car alarm? *Make it stop, please.*

"Katy. The paramedics are going to take a look at you. You're going to be okay."

That wasn't Matt. But it was a familiar voice.

"Katy. Stay with us. They don't want you to go to sleep."

It took all her effort, but she forced her eyes open for

a few seconds and stared squarely at him but couldn't quite place his face. Where had she seen him before?

"It's Detective Sanchez. You're going to be okay. Stay with us."

She drifted in and out, so sleepy, and thirsty.

When she woke again, she was inside a vehicle, on a bed or cot, and it was bumpy. That infuriating siren. Why wouldn't someone shut the darn thing off? It was hurting her head. Something annoying was on her face covering her nose and mouth, smelled like a plastic beachball. She wanted it off so she swiped at her face, but someone held her hand down against her chest.

"Leave it alone, please. It'll help you breathe."

Two strange men in starched white shirts and gold pins on their pockets were poking and prodding, taking her blood pressure, placing an ice pack on her head. One had a stethoscope in his ears, and he reached inside her shirt and placed the round metal end against her skin. It was cold. She wished they would back off and leave her alone.

Another man leaned toward her. That familiar voice again. He touched her arm.

"Katy, it's Detective Sanchez. Do you recognize me?"

She stared at him and frowned.

"I contacted Matt. He's on his way. He'll meet us at the hospital."

"Matt..." Her eyes opened wide and she tried to get up, but the men pushed her back down.

"You're going to be okay. Nothing's broken."

"My truck..."

"Don't worry. We'll get it for you later. Just relax."

Katy leaned her head back against the pillow and her mind drifted. She wanted to get back to that picnic... Matt...and the horses...the flowers.

Sanchez interrupted her thoughts. "Katy, I'm sorry for the bad timing, but I've got to ask. Do you know who did this to you? It appears you were run off the road."

Her thoughts were a jumble. She stared into his eyes and frowned. "Dunno" was all she could muster.

~

EVERYTHING WAS A BLUR. The next thing she remembered was waking in a hospital room. She was trying to piece things together, what happened before her truck went off the road. She had said goodbye to Melanie and Food Truck Jeff, then collected her things at the police station, and called Matt. She also remembered the headlights from the truck behind her and the forceful rams on her bumper as they literally pushed her off the road.

And then she remembered, when the accident had occurred and she was stuck in her truck, she heard a man ask his partner, "Is she moving?" It didn't sound like a compassionate query.

But who were they? She didn't recognize their voices. It wasn't Barker or Granger.

Fear mixed with anger tingled through her body. Were they trying to kill her? Why?

Her body ached. She remembered saying to Tara about how it was to fall off a horse. This felt like that but coupled with some trampling and maybe a beating, too, like she had been run over by a truck...literally. She carefully moved in the bed trying to find a comfortable position.

"Ms. McKim, would you like some water?" A pretty nurse with dark hair and a friendly smile came to the side of her bed.

"Yes, thank you. I'm thirsty."

The nurse filled a little water cup on the bedside table and winked. "You also have a handsome visitor who's been waiting."

Katy moved her head toward the door opening and felt her heart might burst.

"Matt." A tear threatened to form in the corner of her eye.

The nurse moved out of the way, and he came right to Katy's side. He leaned toward her, gently but firmly held her shoulders, and planted a kiss on her forehead.

"Are you okay?"

"Yeah. Just sore."

The nurse moved to the foot of the bed. "Sorry to interrupt. I just wanted to say the doctor will be in soon. I think he wants you to stay overnight, but he'll give you the final word."

"Thank you." Katy carefully raised up and Matt helped prop pillows behind her.

"I got here as fast as I could."

"How did you know I was in an accident?"

"When I heard what you were going through on the phone, I called Sanchez. He sent the rescue crew and kept in touch with me. Said it appeared you were run off the road. Do you remember anything?"

"Yeah. Bits and pieces. But I don't know who did it."

"How's your head?"

"Sore." Her hand went up to her forehead. "Ow."

He came close and placed his hand on her shoulder.

"Remember when we first met at the Golden horse show? You got a concussion in the show-ring. Wish you could be more careful, Katy. You're scaring me."

She frowned a little at him. "I didn't do this on purpose, Matt. They ran me off the road."

"Were you playing detective again?"

Did he just smirk?

"Oh, Matt."

She rolled her eyes. She didn't need someone chastising her right now.

"I'm sorry, Katy. I'm just concerned about you. You could get hurt. I mean, even more seriously than this latest incident."

She'd been taking care of herself for a while now. It had been two years since her parents died and during that time, her brother went missing. Even before all that tragedy she was used to calling the shots in her own life. Her parents had taught her to be strong. She wasn't used to someone else trying to control or direct her actions. Part of her liked his concern but another part bristled at the threat to her independence.

"Matt, what about Fowler Feed? Anything new? And does Shawn know about the accident?"

"Yes, I called your brother as soon as I heard. He wanted to get here right away but I told him I thought we'd be home soon. Hope that's okay with you."

"Sure. No sense in him driving an hour or so and then me not being here. Thanks for calling him. What about Fowler?"

"We've been looking into it. Turns out at least four horses got sick, and the owners have been trying to pinpoint the cause. They all have Fowler Feed in common."

"What else have you guys done?"

"We obtained a few bags and tubs and they're being analyzed to see if they were opened and resealed. Also, to see if the feed contains any remnants or particles from drugs. We're waiting to hear back from the lab."

"Are you going to question Barker and Granger?"

"We don't have any evidence against them. Katy, you

should be taking it easy, not worrying about all this stuff."

She pretty much ignored that comment.

"Matt, I'm just lying here in a bed. It doesn't hurt me to ask questions." She could tell he was frustrated, but she continued. "You said they own Fowler Feed."

"These things take time, to piece together a case. Besides, owners can be far removed from their drivers."

A man in a white coat came into the room.

"Hello Ms. McKim. I'm Doctor Hollar. Looks like you're feeling better."

"Somewhat."

He nodded to Matt, then focused back on Katy. "Is it okay to review your chart with you now or do we need some privacy?"

"It's okay. This is my...uh...boyfriend." She was never sure what to call him.

"Okay. Well, I wanted to ask about a couple of previous injuries you have unrelated to the recent accident."

"Previous?" Matt asked, but Katy remained silent.

"There's a bruised rib and your cheek also. They are not consistent with the auto accident, but still look very recent. They are on the right side of your body and, from what we've determined happened in the truck, the new injuries are on your left. Do you know when and how the older ones occurred?"

Her eyes darted to Matt.

"Maybe I do need some privacy." She quietly said to the doctor.

"All right." He started to put his electronic pad away.

The two of them looked at Matt but he didn't seem to be budging.

"Now wait a minute. Even if I'm not technically

family, *yet*, I'm a detective who is working on the investigation of this case. Katy, were you hurt before?" His neck displayed a quick flush of scarlet.

She took in a big breath and let it out slowly pursing her lips.

"Fine. He can stay. At the horse show a young guy ran into me, knocked me down. Probably just after my purse. It was nothing really. I got a couple of bruises. End of story."

She could tell by Matt's stare he was a little upset with her.

"Why didn't you tell me that before? It could all be connected. What did the guy look like?" Matt touched her forearm.

The doctor cleared his throat. "Not to interrupt your spat, but let me continue, please. No concussion from the auto accident. Nothing broken. Mostly jostled around and bruised. How does your neck feel? Any whiplash?"

"Just stiff and sore." She winced as she shrugged her shoulders up and down.

The doctor set his electronic device containing her chart down on the bedside table, came closer, and felt her neck. He placed his fingertips on her jaws and moved her head gently back and forth.

"Any pain? Turn to the right, then left." As she did, he asked again, "Any pain?"

"Some. Just sore. I'm sore all over."

The doctor made a note on his device.

"You live near Redding. Is that correct?"

"Yes. Libertyville."

"It's getting late. No sense in your getting on the road now. I'd like you to stay overnight just as a precaution. I'll write the order for discharge. You can leave in the morning. How's that sound?"

"Thank you, Doctor." She gave a small smile.

When he left the room, Katy sheepishly avoided Matt's eyes.

"Maybe you can find a motel close by and get some sleep," she suggested.

"No way." He pointed to the recliner in the corner. "We've done this before, haven't we? I know all about sleeping in the chair."

He was referring to the past incident where her horse was drugged at a show, she fell off, hit her head on a jump standard, resulting in a concussion and stay in the hospital. Matt had bunked overnight with her then also...in a recliner.

She let out a bit of a giggle. "It can't be very comfortable. You might wake up with whiplash."

He smirked. "I've slept in worse places. Besides, I'm not letting you out of my sight."

"By the way...what did you mean before about 'not family *yet*'?"

That produced a huge grin on his face. "Well, you never know, right?" He hesitated, and his expression changed to serious. "I think you know how I feel about you, Katy. I hope you feel the same way about me."

"I care a lot about you, Matt."

He came closer and planted a passionate kiss on her mouth that she felt all the way down to her toes.

When she opened her eyes and took in a breath she gently pushed on his shoulders with her fingertips.

"But for now, sir, you'd best retreat to your side of the room, in that recliner, or else we'll get in trouble with the medical staff."

"Well, aren't you the killjoy. I was just getting started. And this recliner is déjà vu, isn't it? I'm becoming an expert at watching over you in hospital rooms."

Just then the cell phone on his hip buzzed.

"Hey, Shawn. She's doing better. She's right here." He handed the phone to Katy.

"Hi...yeah, I'm all right...no, you don't need to come here...we're heading home in the morning...no, I'm not sure who ran me off the road...have you and Andre found anything more on Fowler Feed? Okay, keep us posted...yes, Matt is staying with me the night...I will...love you, Brother...take care of yourself."

She handed the phone back to Matt who was adjusting a pillow in the recliner. He came back to retrieve his phone and gave her a kiss on the cheek.

She rested her head against the pillow. What a day. She was so tired. But grateful. Grateful to be alive, grateful to have her brother back in her life. Especially grateful for Matt.

As she drifted off, she heard the words repeating in her head. "Not family...*yet*..."

## CHAPTER 21

### Fang

THE NEXT MORNING THE NURSE HELPED KATY DRESS IN the jeans and shirt she had been wearing the day before at the horse show. Even though she'd given herself a sponge bath in her hospital room's bathroom, she couldn't wait to get home and take a nice, long, hot shower.

"The doctor has signed the discharge order so you're good to go," the pretty nurse said. "He also sent a prescription to your pharmacy for pain medication if you need it."

"Thanks to you and everyone for taking care of me. I appreciate the work you do."

"Of course. You're very welcome. Now where's that handsome friend of yours? Will he be driving you home?"

Katy watched the pretty, young nurse's face light up when talking about Matt and thought it cute, but not very professional. She couldn't fault her, though. Everyone liked Matt and he was attractive. She was glad he wasn't a flirt or womanizer. Their relationship would be short-lived if he were. Some men in her past, mostly acquaintances except for one boyfriend, flirted with every lady who fluttered her eyelashes. Katy was embarrassed for them and thought they acted like teenage boys. She didn't need that drama.

"Yes. My truck will be in the shop here for a while. Maybe Matt went to the cafeteria for coffee or something."

His deep voice sounded in the doorway at that moment. "Here I am. And yes, I've got coffee. One for me and one for you." He handed a cup to Katy. She was glad he focused on her and didn't pay the nurse much attention.

"My hero."

"That is so sweet. Do you have a brother?" The nurse winked.

Katy was sure the young nurse was flirting with Matt, but she let it go. And she was glad he did too.

"I'll get someone to bring the wheelchair," the nurse said. "It's right outside. You know she must ride in one out to your vehicle, don't you? Hospital policy."

The nurse's voice took on a sultry lilt and her eyes focused on Matt with such an intensity that Katy thought it might have trouble unlocking any time soon unless they hightailed it out of there.

Matt held up his hands in surrender. "I have no problem with that, ma'am. She's the one you need to corral."

Katy pulled the sheet across the bed and got ready to leave. "Just put me in it and get me home. No offense, but I'm not wild about hospitals."

She thought of her parents even though they had died in their bed at home and never made it to a hospital.

Still, this place conjured up thoughts of sick and dying people.

After goodbyes and well-wishes from the nurse, which included a tug on Matt's forearm and a lengthy invite to take care and visit whenever they were…rather, whenever *he* was…back in the vicinity, they were off.

He helped Katy up into his truck and even clicked her seat belt snugly in place around her. She thought about telling him she could do it herself but decided not to spoil his role as her protector. And she kind of enjoyed it too. She had always believed in the complementary differences between the genders and thought they should be embraced and applauded, not erased, or blurred. Which didn't mean she had to be a "damn damsel" as her brother used to tease when they were kids. She could be a strong woman, independent, able to take care of herself, while still appreciating the masculine qualities a man offered.

"You comfortable? Want a water?" He steered his truck out of the hospital parking lot and headed for the freeway toward Libertyville.

"No, thanks." She settled in her seat and glanced out the window. She couldn't resist a tease and let out a giggle. "That nurse sure was taken with you."

"She was just being friendly."

"Yeah right. 'Come visit when you're in town.' I think she totally forgot I was the patient." Katy singsonged the part of the vixen and giggled.

"You have a wild imagination, Ms. McKim." Although his voice was serious sounding, she caught a slight smirk he let escape. He squeezed her hand and they both shared a pleasant chuckle. Katy admired his tanned forearm against the rolled-up shirtsleeve, then his strong jaw, and thought how comfortable it was to be with him.

And…if she were honest with herself…how passionate she felt for him.

Zooming along the highway, she made conversation. "I totally forgot it was Sunday. My days are kind of mixed up."

"Yeah, I guess the family is in church."

She knew that was important to Matt. "Oh, gosh, I'm sorry you're missing it on account of me. Did you have plans to see them?"

He held her hand again. "No worries. I'm right where I want to be. I had thought about seeing my sister, but maybe you and I can visit her next Sunday."

"I'd like that. Angel is really sweet. And that baby of theirs is so adorable."

"Yeah, my little man, J.L." His warm smile conveyed the love he held for his nephew and whole family.

"I think your sister wants you to call him Jon-Luis."

"We'll see about that. Maybe I could call him Picard like Jean-Luc."

"Ooh, I think that might really frost Angel. You'd better not try that."

They laughed.

"Hey, I didn't ask about Rocky. Is your cousin the pet sitter taking care of him? What's her name again?"

He gave her a side-glance remembering when Katy had first met her and commented on her tank top.

"Gina. Yeah, it's easy since she's in the same apartment complex. Plus, she loves Rocky."

"Now don't make me jealous. I thought I was his number one fan."

"He loves you too."

"I think that dog loves everyone."

"That's what goldens do. It's their job to love everyone."

A melodic ring like an old-timey landline phone interrupted their conversation and Matt hit the hands-free button on his steering column.

"Matt Hartman."

Katy wondered why he didn't just say "hello." Was he always on the job?

The speaker sounded. "Hey, Hartman. It's Sanchez. How's Katy doin'?"

"She's right here. We just left the hospital. I'm driving her home."

"Oh, good, you both can listen. I've got some news and a couple questions for Katy."

"Hello, Detective Sanchez. I'm here." Katy leaned a little closer to Matt and presumably toward the microphone in the ceiling although it really wasn't necessary.

"Hey, Katy. Hope you're feeling better."

"I'm doing okay. What have you got?"

"Well, we picked up a young guy on drug charges, dealing. Goes by the name of Fang. He's got jagged teeth. His legal name is Max Cooper. Did you, by any chance, see him around the horse show? Dresses all in black, kind of sleazy-looking. Dark glasses, chains on his jean pockets. I never understood what those were for."

She was quiet a little longer than normal as she thought of her young friend Melanie. Could she be in danger?

"Katy?" the detective asked to make sure she was still there.

"I'm here. I might have seen him around the food truck."

"Do you think he could be the young guy who mugged you? Maybe even one of the guys who ran you off the road?"

She hesitated and thought of Food Truck Jeff. Gosh,

she hoped he wasn't involved. He seemed so nice. But sometimes those were the ones who surprised you the most.

"I guess it's possible. Although I thought the voices I heard after the truck accident sounded like older men. I can't be sure. I was kind of out of it."

"Of course. Well, we're going to question him and see who he's involved with."

Matt interjected. "Do you think he could be working for Barker and Granger?"

"Why would you say that?"

"Just something I'm working on."

"Why don't we all share information? It'll make our work a whole lot easier."

Katy placed her hand on Matt's and shook her head. She had a nagging feeling and wasn't sure what it meant. Seemed there were already a lot of people involved—her and Matt, Tara and her brother, Shawn. And she had confided in Melanie, Barker's daughter, and Sally, the show secretary. Maybe they should wait before sharing everything with Sanchez.

"We're not sure what we've got yet," Matt said. "How 'bout we call you when we get home and situated?"

"Sure. No problem. Safe driving," Sanchez said in closing.

Matt clicked the call off and crinkled his brow at Katy. "Why the hesitation with Sanchez? What's on your mind?"

"I'm not sure. Just a feeling. I don't think we should open up about everything. Not just yet."

He frowned. "Okay. I don't quite get it, but I'll go with your gut."

"Thanks." And then another thought hit her that might make Matt happy. "Hey, you know we could probably make the late church service with Angel and Luis if you want."

"That's sweet of you, but I think I should get you home to rest. I mean, you did just get out of the hospital. Duh."

She smirked at him and had to admit she was tired. "All right. You make a pretty good nurse, Detective Hartman. Not as cute as that young lady at the hospital."

He glared, playfully.

Right as they pulled into her ranch driveway, her cell phone buzzed.

"Hello? Oh, Melanie. How are—" She could hardly get a word in edgewise and shrugged as she looked over at Matt. "Wait, slow down Melanie, what's the matter? Are you okay? I'm sure your dad didn't mean that... listen, why don't you come to the ranch, and we can talk about it. You can spend the night if you want. I'll text the directions. Be careful driving."

Matt put the truck in park. "What was that all about?"

"Melanie said her dad went ballistic. He was upset she was hanging around with Food Truck Jeff. And with me. Said he wasn't even sure if he was her father. Can you believe that jerk? She's such a sweet girl. I invited her to stay tonight."

Matt was quiet as he helped Katy out of the truck.

"Are you okay with that?"

"Of course. I'm just thinking...there go my romantic dinner plans." He winked.

"I'm sure we can make up for it in some other way, Romeo. Besides, this stuff with Barker is important. Right? I'd like to figure out what's really going on, and who's responsible. Don't you?"

"For sure. I was just teasing you, Katy. Although I'd still like to have a romantic dinner...whenever we can."

"Okay. It's a date, Detective."

"You haven't called me that in a while. It's so…uh… endearing?"

She swatted his arm a little and they both joined in a chuckle when he nudged her side.

"Ow, easy, remember I was just a hospital patient. My body is sore from head to toe."

Matt made a pouty face and silently mouthed "sorry."

"Hey, you know what would really be endearing? A cold drink, a visit with my horse, and maybe a nap. I have a feeling I'll need my energy when Melanie arrives."

"Coming right up, m'lady. I am at your beck and call." He bowed and gestured flamboyantly.

She grabbed his shoulders. "You are one silly man."

Their closeness gave him the opening to wrap his hands around her waist and pull her to his chest.

"I'm glad you're safe, Katy. Don't scare me like that again."

He moved close to her face and kissed her lips gently, then ardently.

"Well, when you put it that way, how can I refuse?" They both grinned and stayed in their embrace longer than they had ever done so before.

# CHAPTER 22

## *Melanie*

MATT CARRIED KATY'S OVERNIGHT BAG IN, POURED FRUIT juice from the fridge, and they both slumped on the soft living room sectional. He was about to click on the television when she held her finger to her mouth, "shhh," then stretched her legs out on the cushions and laid her head on his lap.

Before he knew it, she was out. After a while her breathing sounded like a whispering, gentle snore.

She was right to say no to the television. He loved quiet times like this, just the two of them, especially after all the drama they had experienced lately. If only he could protect her from it all. But he knew that wasn't possible. Long ago he had accepted that life on earth was a constant struggle and he sincerely believed in the powers of darkness. He had learned about it growing up in his mother's church but sometimes he thought of that as his childhood faith. He was a man now and his police training taught him to search for the facts. He also had come across people in life who blamed God for injustices and losses in their lives. In fact, he had been one of them.

That was until the day he met a soldier during his time of military service who had shared his faith with Matt in such a real and passionate way that Matt couldn't write him off as a nutjob. His comrade-in-arms conveyed to Matt how many people believed life was like a fairy tale and that they were entitled to a happy life and if they didn't get one, they figured it must be the fault of their imagined figure of God—the white bearded one in the sky. So, they were angry with Him for not bestowing upon them everything easy and good and fun. The fellow soldier even gave Scripture to back up his claim. It touched Matt's heart and made perfect sense to him, and he held it close all these years. We weren't on this earth to live out fairy-tale lives. There was actually spiritual warfare around us and we were being duped if we pointed the finger of blame at God who loved us when, in fact, it was the Enemy who hated us and wanted more than anything to kill, steal, and destroy. It was easy for Matt to remember John 10:10.

So, he watched Katy sleep and stroked her auburn hair. She looked like an angel. Beautiful. Delicate. But strong. And he loved her. He would do everything in his power to protect her, physically of course. But also, spiritually. He would pray that God and His angels would protect her too. And he added a very personal prayer. He prayed that one day she would be his wife and that they would be blessed with a family and children of their own.

Katy's eyes fluttered open and she gave him a smile. "Were you talking to yourself? I saw your lips moving."

"No, I was talking to someone else." He kissed her forehead.

A knock at the door interrupted and Katy roused herself from the couch. "I'll get it."

"Katy, wait, let me—" He didn't want to scare her but he worried about the people who had run her off the road, and also the guy who had mugged her. Enemies were out there.

But she was too quick. Independent and at times, headstrong.

"Melanie! Come on in. I'm so glad you came. Welcome to the ranch."

Katy hugged the girl and led her into the living room. "This is Matt."

He stood quickly to shake her hand. "Hi Melanie, nice to meet you. Can I get you a cold drink?"

The girl was so thin and frail and Matt thought he had even felt her shaking when he grasped her hand.

"No...uh...thank you. I've been drinking my water in the car."

She was like a skittish deer to him. He turned to Katy hoping for a cue as to how to handle the situation.

"Matt, do you think you could check on the horses? Melanie and I might need a little girl talk."

"Sure thing. I need to stretch my legs anyway. You ladies take your time."

AFTER MATT LEFT, Katy sipped her drink but realized it had gotten lukewarm and diluted while she had napped. She went to the kitchen to make a fresh one.

"Melanie, make yourself at home. Have a seat." She pointed to the couch. "You sure you don't want a juice drink or something?"

"No. Thank you, though."

Katy brought her drink to the living room and joined Melanie who suddenly broke into a flood of tears.

"Oh, Katy, he said some awful things." She bent forward, elbows on her knees, and buried her face in her hands.

"Your dad?"

"Yes. He said maybe he's not even my dad. How could he say that? Katy, he screamed at me. Told me to stay away from Jeff…and his friends."

"Maybe he's just concerned for you. You know, I wanted to ask you about that guy that hung around the food truck. With the teeth. What's his name?"

"He calls himself Fang." Melanie wiped at the tears on her face.

"Did you ever talk with him? He seemed a little rough to me."

"I tried being nice to him, but he was rude. Told me to ditch Jeff and go off with him for a little fun. What a creep. He gave me the willies. I don't think Jeff likes him either."

"Why do you think Jeff lets him hang around?"

"I think Jeff was doing some work with him or something. I never got it straight. Jeff used to get all serious whenever Fang came around. And he'd tell me to go for a walk. He didn't want me around Fang."

"Do you think Jeff was doing anything illegal?"

Melanie's brows pushed together. "Gosh, no. Jeff isn't like that. You know what a gentle spirit he is."

"Sometimes the gentlest people get involved in something beyond their control. They get pushed into it and have a hard time getting out. Did your dad know Fang?"

Katy realized Melanie didn't know what had transpired after Katy had left the horse show. It was time to tell her, but first, Katy wanted to know more about why Barker was so upset.

"I saw my dad talking to Fang, right before he blew up at me. I think Fang worked for him, drove one of his trucks or something."

"I heard your dad has gotten into the feed business. Fowler Feed."

"That's right. He's always doing new business ventures. Says it's good to be involved in a lot of things. That's the way to make money."

"I guess he might be right." Katy viewed the girl on the couch. She was so sweet, and Katy hated to see her mixed up with these unsavory people. "Melanie, did you tell me you like to write, to journal?"

"Yes. It's one of the only things that makes me happy. And sane."

"Maybe one day you could write for your father's publication, *Pegasus*."

"I dunno. I mentioned it to him before and he said I have a lot more to learn."

"Well, things can change. Just keep at it. I can help you if you like, take a look at your writings."

"Really? That would be so great. Thank you."

Katy watched her new friend and thought back to her younger years when she wrote short stories about her horse, about growing up on the ranch, and about a boy at school who she thought might be her Prince Charming. Turned out he didn't even know what her name was or that she was in love with him, at least what she thought was love at that young age.

She hid her stories away so that her brother couldn't find them, because if he had, he would surely tease the living daylights out of her. Knowing him, back then, he would probably tell all his guy friends and anybody else at school about her rambling writings.

Her parents knew she liked to write but her father always told her she needed "real work" to make a living. Or else, get married and her husband would support her as she raised babies just like his livestock broodmares. She would always be his little girl. He gave her a mixture of a dash of coddling with a megadose of tough work ethic. And she didn't fault him now when she thought about the generation her dad grew up in. It might've been more limiting for women in certain areas of life, but it also had a lot of good points.

As much as her mother dreamed of her daughter marrying and having children someday, she encouraged Katy's independent spirit. "Learn to take care of yourself also, Katy. Sometimes in this world the fairy tale tarnishes. The man may not always be there to take care of you. You've got to be strong too."

Katy wanted to help Melanie to be strong, to make wise decisions, and to cultivate and improve her writing skills.

But there was also the business of sorting out who her father really was—not just biologically, but morally. Was he a sleazeball who didn't care much for her? Did he even possess the right tools to be a good father?

And bottom line—was he a criminal? Katy had to find that out, first and foremost.

## CHAPTER 23
# Welcome to the Ranch

MATT CAME IN FROM THE BARN, HIS FOREHEAD AND NECK glistening with sweat. He washed his hands and forearms in the farmhouse kitchen sink and dried them with paper towels. He whisked the towel over his face and neck too.

"You girls been catching up?"

Katy uncurled her legs to sit up straight on the edge of the couch.

"We have. How 'bout you? The horses doin' okay?"

"Oh, yeah. I mucked the stalls. They weren't bad. Looks like the neighbors had turned them out today."

"Thanks for doing that."

"Of course. Now they're all set for the night. I think I need a shower. Do you mind?" He pointed in the direction of the guest bathroom.

"No, go ahead. I may actually rustle up some dinner for us."

"Really? You can cook?" He grinned mischievously.

Matt headed off to the guest bath where he sometimes showered when he came for a visit. He mostly

161

slept in the loft bedroom of the barn but since the fire the shower there hadn't been remodeled yet. There was only a small bathroom downstairs next to the horse stalls.

From the very beginning when they had first met, Katy knew he would respect their boundaries. People might not believe it and she had to admit, sometimes she was tempted by her physical feelings, and could only imagine he was, too, but so far it had worked for their relationship. Plus, he wasn't there all the time. He had his own apartment about an hour away. Sometimes she daydreamed about what it would be like to have a more intimate relationship with him and even let her mind drift to what marriage might be like. But for now, this would have to do. There were so many other things going on in her life. How could she juggle one more? And she knew if they crossed that line, things would get complicated.

With Matt gone, she told Melanie who he was. Her boyfriend...she had to admit...and a detective. She hesitated, though, telling the girl he was working on the investigation into her father and Granger. First, she wanted to see if Melanie knew anything.

"Mel, did you say Fang was a driver for the feed company your dad owns?"

"Yes, I think so. I heard my dad talking to him and Jeff. Actually, chewing them out."

"For what?"

"He said some of the feed bags appear to have been opened. Fang denied it of course."

"How is Jeff involved? Is he a driver too?"

"No. He got Fang the job after asking that creepy Judge Granger."

"Why do you say 'creepy'?"

162

Melanie avoided Katy's stare and instead fidgeted with her hands. She toyed with a thread at the knee of her jeans, a blown-out hole which was the current style Katy didn't quite like but she knew each generation had to spread their wings in some way. Her dad would have shaken his head and laughed while saying, "Humans will fall for anything." It seemed Melanie was back to wearing her comfy, torn up jeans although Katy had helped her buy the new Wranglers at the show. Maybe she was saving those for another day.

Finally, Melanie whispered, "He came on to me."

Katy was shocked. "What do you mean? Granger made a pass at you?"

"I guess that's what the older generation calls it." She immediately realized her insult. "Oh, sorry, I didn't mean you, Katy. You're still young. But yeah, it's the same thing. He's a perve. I heard another girl say the same thing at the horse show, one of the exhibitors."

"I'm so sorry, Mel. Did you tell anyone? Your dad or Jeff?"

"I wasn't sure who to tell. I didn't want either of them getting into a fight with Granger. You know how guys can be. All jacked up with their macho stuff."

Katy noticed the girl's hand shake a little. "Mel, you don't have to be alone in this. Now you've got me. And please know, none of this is your fault. That man has a real problem. And he should be reported."

"Well, I just steer clear of him. I don't want things to get blown out of proportion. My dad already yelled at me for being friends with Jeff. If he found out about Granger, he might not even believe me. He might say I led the old guy on."

Katy wasn't sure what to do. She already had information from Matt that Granger had past dealings with the law about sexual harassment. Then there was Tara who had run-ins with him. And now Melanie. Katy almost wished Mel wasn't eighteen yet. If she were underage instead, things might go that much worse for Granger. She would certainly share this information with Matt.

"You hungry, Mel?" she asked as she got up from the couch and headed around the granite island to the kitchen.

"I'm starving. I could eat a horse." The girl quickly put her palm to her mouth. "Oh, gosh, sorry. Bad joke."

"No worries. How 'bout pasta, grilled salmon, and salad?"

"Yum. You know how to cook that?"

"It's easy. You can help."

Matt came into the room wearing gray sweatpants and a black T-shirt emblazoned with a bucking horse and the words "Redding Rodeo 1943." His dark hair was damp from the shower and curled at the nape of his neck. His tan feet were in slip-on sneakers.

Gosh, did he look sexy, Katy thought. She desperately wanted to kiss his neck, but of course she refrained because of Melanie. Maybe that was a good thing or else things might get out of hand.

He set his phone down on the counter and touched Katy's hand. "Shawn just texted. He has some news and wants to come over. How're you feeling?"

"I'm okay. Melanie's going to help me with dinner. We can always make extra. Is he bringing Andre?"

"No. I think Andre's working on another case."

"Could you please text Shawn and tell him about dinner if he wants to join us. But I want to make it an early night. Mel and I still have some visiting to do, plus I think we both need a good night's sleep."

"Sure thing, boss." He saluted which had become an inside joke with them.

"C'mon, Mel. Can you chop up this tomato for the salad?"

"Sure thing, boss." She copied Matt's salute and they all laughed.

As each got busy with their own task in the dinner-making process, Katy stole a glance at Matt and Melanie. He washed and dried lettuce. She chopped tomato, scallions, and other items as Katy lightly seasoned the salmon fillets.

Her mother had been a good cook and Katy could almost imagine her now moving about the kitchen, the one her father had arranged to have remodeled shortly before their joint death. Of course, he couldn't predict their future fate. Katy thought of them most every day and remembered how sweet her life had been prior to that tragedy. Maybe the way they had passed—next to each other in their bed, asleep, unaware of the evil that preyed upon them—maybe that was the least cruel way to go. They did not experience any moments of stark fear. They did not clutch at each other and scream and cry. They just drifted…together…asleep toward heaven.

Why did it have to happen? They were such good people and never hurt another soul. She asked this of God nearly every day. She knew the churchy answers. They lived in a fallen world where sin and evil roamed. It wasn't a perfect Garden of Eden. It wasn't a fairy tale where everything was supposed to be rainbows and unicorns. And she knew it wasn't God's fault. He didn't cause the tragedy. In fact, His heart broke as hers did that two of His creations had met an untimely death.

And she knew the evil had come in the form of someone she had known, one she hadn't seen, or recognized, in many years. One who had harbored jealousies against her and her brother and acted out on those resentments by killing and destroying the two people they held most dearly in their hearts. What better way to hurt them and exact revenge?

A heavy knock at the door yanked Katy from her musings. She clutched her heart and drew in a sharp breath. "Oh, my gosh! That scared me." She dropped the fork she had been using to arrange the salmon on a pan.

"You okay?" Matt asked. "It's probably just Shawn."

In the next second her brother's auburn-colored hair flashed past the front door as he opened it widely. His toothy grin and hearty laugh lit up the room.

"Hey, you guys. When do we eat? I'm starving."

# CHAPTER 24
## *Shawn*

HER BROTHER HAD ALWAYS BEEN AN ENIGMA TO HER.

Quiet and thoughtful, kind, loved his family, a bit of a prankster and fun-loving, but since his time with the military he also possessed strength, cunning, and suspicion. And those were only the things Katy knew about. What he actually worked on—during his time in the armed services or since with Andre at the Kleos company—was anyone's guess, and frankly, something she didn't want to think about.

When he seemed out of touch to her, she remembered childhood times of racing their ponies across the pasture and how he used to wake her on a Saturday morning to watch television together. He'd lightly glide his index finger across the tips of her sleep-laden eyelashes until they fluttered open. He shushed her so they wouldn't wake their parents and they watched Westerns and science fiction shows with the volume on the TV turned down low. Sometimes they'd sneak to the barn, get the ponies or horses out, and go on wild adventures. Years later their dad confessed that he knew about their escapades and sometimes heard the television, but he never disciplined them or ruined their fun.

She loved those memories, and she loved her brother.

And now she had him back. She didn't really want to think about how she had almost lost him. In a bizarre way she was grateful for her "zombie phase" after her parents passed away and some months later when she was told that Shawn was missing on a private mission for Kleos. She had been in such a state of trauma that when she was told he was most likely dead and was encouraged to have a memorial service for him, she went along with it. Of course, she regretted it now. Should she have fought harder for more accurate information? Why had she allowed herself to be so duped?

And then she met Matt at the Golden horse show and the truth started to unfold and, unbelievably, she and Shawn were reunited. Every day she told herself it was a wonder her head didn't explode during that time. So now she just wanted to be grateful for what she did have —her brother back, a relationship with Matt, and daily life settling down into some sort of "normalcy," if you could call it that.

After giving her brother a hug, Katy told him, "It'll be ready soon. Salmon, pasta, and salad." Then extending her hand toward the girl, she said, "This is my friend, Melanie."

He flashed his smile. "I'm Shawn, the big brother. Smart brother. Handsome brother." He winked and Katy rolled her eyes.

"Nice to meet you." Melanie took his hand to shake but also lowered her eyelids. She still was pretty timid around new people.

Matt opened a beer and placed it on the counter in front of Shawn who had climbed onto a barstool.

"So, what's this news you couldn't wait to tell us about?"

Shawn took a swig. "Well, we followed Fowler Feed and, sure enough, some of the tubs contained drugs. We're working with Detective Sanchez and—"

Katy frantically made hand gestures behind Melanie's back as though she were cutting at her throat. Gosh, would he stop talking?

"What?" Shawn frowned and shrugged.

"Let's not talk shop now." Matt shook his head back and forth.

But there was no pulling the words back once they were out of his mouth.

Melanie looked around at all of them. "What are you talking about? Fowler Feed and drugs?"

Katy had to tell him. "Shawn, this is Melanie Barker. Her father is Brett Barker."

He coughed and abruptly set his beer down. "Oh...uh...I am so sorry."

Everyone saw tears forming in the girl's eyes. "Tell me what you're talking about. Is my dad in trouble? Is he doing something illegal? Please."

Katy stepped next to her and put a hand on her shoulder. "We don't know anything yet, Mel." And then she shot daggers to her brother. "Isn't that right, Shawn?"

He sputtered. "Uh, totally right. We're just investigating."

"But you said you found drugs." Melanie stared at him.

"We don't know who they belong to. It could mean a lot of different things. Maybe someone planted them."

"Please don't lie to me. I'm not a kid."

But she was still a kid, Katy thought. And she was trying to love her dad and have a relationship with him.

Katy wanted to protect her, but she also didn't want the investigation to blow up and have the guilty parties walk free. She had to enlist Melanie's help.

"Mel, we want your dad to be innocent, but we also need to know the truth. You want to know the truth, don't you?"

"Yes."

"Will you help us by not saying anything to anyone about what you heard here today? We need to know you can keep a confidence and in return we'll promise to find the real truth and reserve judgment about your father until the facts are known. Can you keep this to yourself?"

Melanie's innocent face displayed all her honesty and goodwill toward others, but also the agony of fear and pain her young life had endured so far.

"Katy, I trust you and thank you for being my friend. Yes, I will wait and not say anything. Please keep me posted whenever you find out any information. I hope my father won't go to jail."

"And Mel, I know this might be awkward since you just met Matt and Shawn. If you don't want to talk about it, that's okay. But I wanted to give you the opportunity. Do you want to tell them about Granger?"

Matt was quick to spring. "What about Granger?"

Katy held up her hands and frowned slightly as though to tell him to slow down.

Then Melanie quietly spoke as she seemed to avoid eye contact with the men in the room. "I think he's a slimeball. He tried to get very hands on with me, if you know what I mean. I pushed him away and ran. I try never to be alone with him."

"Did you tell your father?" Shawn asked. "They're partners, aren't they?"

"No. I didn't want to make a big thing about it. Yes, I believe they're partners."

Matt's voice took on his law enforcement persona. "Do you want to file a report against him? If you were under the age of eighteen when this occurred, it could have very serious consequences for him. You could help put a stop to him so that he doesn't harass or assault another woman."

She clammed up for almost a full minute. Everyone could see the turmoil bubbling within her. It was obvious.

Finally, she spoke. "I don't know. I'll have to think about it. I just want to forget it even happened."

Katy touched her friend's forearm. "Let's stay away from him. You know, someone like that...he could try to bother you again."

A look of sheer terror transformed Melanie's face, which Katy was sorry for. She didn't mean to frighten the girl any more than she already was. And coupled with worrying about her father, Katy could just imagine what was going on in her head and the heavy burden she carried. Katy wasn't quite sure yet how she could help Melanie...the word "pray" seemed to nudge her thoughts repeatedly.

The guys suggested that Melanie join them at the barn to see the horses...if she wanted. Katy said she'd finish cleaning the kitchen and then catch up. But she could tell that Melanie was a little reluctant and needed some reassurance. "It's okay. I'll be right there."

No sooner had the three left the house when Katy's phone buzzed. She was shocked to read the caller ID. It was Barker.

"Hello?"

"Katy! Have you seen my daughter with that food truck guy? What's his name?

"Jeff?"

"I'm afraid she's run off with him since the horse show. Have you seen him?"

"No. I haven't seen Jeff." She wasn't lying.

"What about that other sleazy guy? Fang. Have you seen him?"

"No." She decided to go out on a limb, maybe taunt him a little. "Doesn't he work for you?"

"What do you mean?"

"I heard he drives for your feed company."

Silence on the phone. She waited.

"That's not my company. Listen, why don't you come to the office tomorrow? Bring your article."

Click.

That was weird.

Did he even know she was just in the hospital after getting run off the road? Did he have anything to do with that?

She thought of how Barker's voice had changed, from almost frantic about his daughter...did he really care? To steely and frigid as though he were tricking her and trying to entice her into a trap. She wasn't at all sure she should go to his office the next day.

## CHAPTER 25
### *Pegasus Publications*

THE FOUR OF THEM ENJOYED A SIMPLE BUT DELICIOUS dinner—grilled salmon, corkscrew pasta, and a giant salad. Matt opened a light rosé wine for everyone except Melanie who was under the legal drinking age. She was fine with water.

"Even if I was old enough, I don't like the taste." She scrunched her nose.

Katy smiled. "Maybe you'll like the raspberry sherbet after dinner."

"Now you're talking. I like every kind of dessert."

When they had first met, Melanie shared with Katy about her eating issues and having spent time in a program. Katy was grateful for whatever food Melanie put in her mouth.

The guys—Matt and Shawn—refrained from talking shop which they would have done freely if Melanie had not been present. It was obvious to Katy they were trying to be on their best behavior and not upset the girl with news of her father's possible involvement in crimes with Granger.

Katy talked about her horse, Cash, and how she might enter him in an upcoming horse show to which Melanie shared that her new friend, Jeff, was scheduled to be there with his food truck. She said she really liked him but that her father was trying to keep the two apart.

"A real Romeo and Juliet story," Melanie said.

After dinner and the kitchen clean up, the two women walked to the barn where Katy did the final check on her horse and the neighbors' two. All was well.

They sat in a couple of canvas chairs outside Cash's stall as he munched on a small bedtime snack of hay that Katy had tossed into his feeder.

"You know, Mel, I hope you think about what Matt said. You could file a complaint against Granger. I heard a few other women have had similar experiences with him. Your testimony could help put a stop to his behavior."

"Yeah, then I'm labeled as 'that girl,' one of those he hit on. I'd rather not get involved."

"Wonder if everyone said that? They don't want to 'get involved.' If we don't stand up for our rights of privacy, it's like we're giving free rein to the perves, as you call them, to do whatever they darn well please."

"I know, Katy. It's just that I'm not strong or outspoken like you and other women."

"You can be, Mel. You've heard of strength in numbers? Well, there's me, and the others, to stand beside you. Just think about it. That's all I ask. Don't try to handle this alone."

"I'll think about it. I'm not much of a feminist. I'm more low-key."

"It's not about being a feminist. Just a human being with rights to privacy, to not being touched or talked about in a sexual manner against your will. A man has these rights also."

Cash reached over the stall door and sniffed Melanie's hair. "Maybe it's easier being an animal," she said and smirked at Katy.

"Sometimes they get picked on too. Especially in a herd situation. They call it the pecking order."

"Katy, what was your brother talking about that maybe my dad is involved in some kind of crime with his feed company?"

If Katy could protect the girl, she would do her best. "We don't really know yet. Please don't say anything to your father or anybody else."

"But is it true? Has he been hiding drugs inside feed bags?"

"Maybe he's not even involved. Let's wait to hear before we jump to conclusions. Okay?"

"Will you tell me the minute you find out something?"

"Yes, Mel, if I hear what's going on, who's involved, and if it's the truth, I'll be sure to contact you."

That seemed to satisfy the girl for now.

"Now let's turn the light off and let Cash and his horsey friends get some sleep. And we should do the same. The guest room is ready and waiting for you."

SHAWN THREW a sheet and blanket on the living room sectional where he decided to bunk for the night. Matt gave Katy a kiss as he made his way to the barn's loft bedroom. And the ladies went upstairs and got ready for bed.

In the morning, they were all like ships passing in the

night. Shawn had gotten up and vanished early, bedding neatly folded on the couch, a note of thanks near the coffee machine.

Matt came in to share a quick cup of coffee with Katy and said he'd be meeting with Detective Sanchez soon. She had already told him about her appointment at Pegasus Publications and he advised her to be careful with Barker. He kept his voice low in case Melanie could hear.

Melanie came downstairs, greeted them, but declined coffee. She said that she, too, needed to get going.

"Thanks so much for the nice dinner. It was really nice to be with all of you."

"Take care, Mel, and come back anytime." Katy gave the girl a big hug and walked her out to her car.

After a kiss and hug from Matt, Katy got in the rental car for the thirty-minute drive to town. He watched her put her seat belt on and chuckled when she said, "I can't wait to get my truck back. This sardine can is for the birds."

"Well, you be careful. I'll make a call and check on when your truck will be ready."

"Thanks. You're my knight in shining armor." She gave him a big smile and steered the little car down the gravel driveway.

KATY WALKED into the offices of Pegasus Publications and smiled at the receptionist. She remembered the girl from the first time she had come to meet Barker—college age, pretty, and bubbly. Although this time the girl wasn't. In fact, her eyes were red as though she'd been crying.

"Hi." Katy scanned the desk for a name plate sign but found none. "Sorry, I don't know your name."

The girl snuffled. "Candy."

"Nice to meet you. I'm Katy McKim."

"I remember."

"Are you okay, Candy?"

The girl scanned all around to make sure no one could hear her.

"I'll be okay. My mom says I'm too sensitive. I just don't like people raising their voice at me, especially when I'm pretty sure I did nothing wrong."

"I tend to agree with you, Candy. There's no reason to yell and blame others."

Before they could utter another word in their conversation, Barker's office door flew open and he shouted, "Candy! Announce my visitor and wipe your face. No one wants to see a blubbering receptionist."

Katy touched the girl's arm and leaned close to her ear. "Don't worry. I've got this. He's a royal pain in the ass."

That made the girl giggle as she wiped her eyes with a tissue.

Barker didn't say a word and flew back inside his office. He yelled from there, "McKim! I don't have all day."

Katy rolled her eyes in Candy's direction and took her time sauntering back to his office.

Once there, she sat in the chair across from his desk and exhaled a big sigh.

He thrust his pointy-toed boots up on his side of the desk. She was determined to not let that bother her.

"I don't have all day either, Barker." She enunciated his last name and noticed his eyes widened at the sound. Determined to stay professional and not sink to his low level, she also told herself not to bend or fold under his dictatorial behavior. "And may I say, that was quite the rude display of histrionics out there."

"First of all, you may *not* say. This is my office. I am the boss; you are the employee." His face was getting super red.

Oh boy. He did not just say that. Katy filled her lungs with a big breath and every ounce of courage she could muster. She would not roll over and quietly accept his derogatory treatment. Her parents had raised her to stand up to bullies.

"Now look, Barker..." She almost laughed to herself calling him by his last name again. "...If we're going to work together, we're going to have to learn how to get along. And this behavior of yours makes it difficult for anyone who comes in contact with you. Why don't you tell me what's really bothering you?"

"What's bothering me is *you*. I did not like your behavior at the horse show, and I did not like you hanging around my daughter."

"That's ridiculous. Did you know that I was attacked at the horse show? I sure hope, for your daughter's sake, that the investigation does not reveal the guy who mugged me is an employee of yours. Is that how you run your businesses? With violence and threats."

"What are you talking about?"

"That guy, Fang. He might be the one who pushed me down and kicked me. He's one of your drivers, isn't he? For Fowler Feed."

Barker appeared uncomfortable, as though this was news to him. Katy wondered whether she should say anything about the other attacks, when her truck was run off the road, or when her motel room was broken into. She was sure he knew about both incidents. Matt would probably tell her to keep things "close to the vest."

He was quiet for a minute, and just stared at her. She didn't like him yelling but she also didn't like him being silent. Goosebumps crept up her arms.

"I don't know anything about that. Sorry you were hurt."

She didn't know what to make of him, and didn't know whether to believe him or not, about anything. And that morsel of sympathy was no more genuine than the idea that his flashy boots could make him into a cowboy. She decided to change the subject.

"I finished my article. It's a little different from the usual. I did report on some of the horse show placings but there was also controversy with that judge, Granger. I mentioned that in the article. Judge Tara Stone had to take over and Granger might end up getting suspended, or worse."

Barker's booted feet came swinging off the desk and planted firmly on the floor as he sat straight up in his chair.

"You know that he's my partner in another business, don't you? I can't publish defamation about him. He'll sue me."

"It's objective reporting. It happened. I just reported on the facts of the horse show. Do you want me to email the article to you?"

He gave a sarcastic chuckle and picked up a letter opener and proceeded to clean his nails. "If you do, I think you know where it's going to end up."

"Well, then I'll see if one of your competitors is interested in the story."

"Are you trying to get yourself fired, McKim?"

"I told you from the very beginning. I'm a freelancer,

not your employee. If you don't want to buy my article, I'll find someone else who does."

She got up to walk out when he said, "You must really like trouble, don't you, McKim? You seem to attract it. Let me just emphasize one more thing. Stay away from my daughter."

She glared at him with every bit of distaste she could conjure up, even though an inner voice told her to turn the other cheek. "I think you'd better take your own advice, Mr. Barker. That sweet girl is too good for the likes of you. And as a matter of fact, so is the one at your front desk."

Exiting his office before he could get out another word, she couldn't resist closing the door strongly, almost to the point of slamming it.

To Candy at the front desk, Katy leaned close again. "You don't have to put up with him. I know you could get a better job somewhere else. Take care of yourself and don't settle for this kind of abuse."

Candy whispered her thanks, then her eyes quickly darted back to Barker's door, which remained closed.

CHAPTER 26

# May the Force Be with You

WHILE KATY WAS MEETING WITH BARKER AT PEGASUS Publications, Matt and Detective Sanchez agreed to meet halfway between Katy's ranch and Sanchez's office at the police station in Corning. That way neither would have to drive too far. Along Interstate 5, Big Haul truck stop was known for its hearty breakfast and endless pots of strong coffee, so that's where Sanchez suggested they meet.

Sanchez had already laid claim to a booth in the back of the restaurant and stood to shake hands when Matt found him.

"How're you doing?" Matt removed his aviator sunglasses and took Sanchez's hand with a strong grasp. "Directions were good. I've never been here before."

"Good to see you." Sanchez returned the tight grip, then sat back down. "Yeah, they've got a good breakfast. Sometimes work takes me all over so I get to know where the best food is. By the way, hope you don't mind, I went ahead and ordered two breakfasts and a pot of coffee. Thought it would speed things up."

"Thanks," Matt said. "I'm hungry. And have a full schedule too."

Sanchez grinned at the reference to the common line of work they shared. "Well, you know how it is then, don't you?"

"Yep. You go where the lead takes you. And you eat on the run."

"Speaking of which, thanks to you and Shawn and... uh...I can never remember the other guy's name..."

"Andre. But he hasn't been working on this one as much as Shawn and I have. Andre's busy on another case."

"Oh, well, anyway...thanks to you and Shawn for the lead to Granger's cronies. It panned out."

Matt could tell Sanchez had his eyes out for anyone in the restaurant who might be listening to their business, obvious by the booth he selected far away from the breakfast crowd. He told Matt he always sat with his back to the wall so he could view other patrons or wait-staff approaching.

"I try to do the same. Tell me more about the case," Matt said.

Sanchez reached into a tote bag on the bench seat and pulled out a fancy camera with a long lens.

"I believe this belongs to your girlfriend. We found it in the vehicle of two men who work for Granger. Looks like all the photos have been deleted, but it has the option to save images to the cloud so maybe Katy can still pull them up from there."

"Thanks. She'll be glad to get this back." Matt grabbed the tote and put it next to him.

"Ask her to let me know if she finds any incriminating photos. And I don't mean of you and her hugging." He chuckled.

"Very funny. So, what else about those guys?"

Sanchez drank his coffee. "Well, we're pretty sure they were the ones who broke into her motel room. Their prints were on the camera but not much inside the room. Although one guy must've taken his glove off. We found a print on the dresser."

Matt cleared his throat and his voice took on a deep, serious tone. "Were they the ones who ran her off the road?"

"Their vehicle has damage to the right front and there's paint that matches Katy's truck."

"That's pretty substantial evidence."

"Can't be positive yet and she said she didn't see their faces. But she heard their voices. We might consider conducting some kind of lineup and get them to say the phrases she heard. She might be able to identify them that way."

Matt shook his head. "You know that probably wouldn't hold up in court, don't you? I don't want to put her through that for nothing."

"It might help the case."

"What about that kid, Fang, or whatever his name is? Katy thought maybe he's the one who mugged her at the horse show. He works for Granger too. Anything on him?"

Sanchez pulled a notebook from his jacket and began reading.

"Fang. Max Cooper. Twenty-one. Looks younger than he is. Juvie trouble in the past, petty crimes on his adult record. Has one dealing charge for a small amount of pot. Now a second one, dealing at the horse show. He's the kind of punk who's working his way up to the big stuff. Also was charged with beating up a girl but she changed her mind about testifying. Or maybe he changed it for her. Leads me to believe he's a bad one and could be dangerous, especially if he's under the tutelage of Granger."

Matt drank his coffee, took a bite of eggs and toast, and looked toward the windows at the front of the restaurant. "I'll tell Katy to be sure to steer clear of him."

Sanchez glanced at his vibrating phone but ignored it for now. "Have you got anything new for me? I'm going to have to go pretty soon. Sorry I don't have more time."

"I met Barker's daughter, Melanie. Katy has befriended her. Skittish girl. Keep this info confidential, for now, but she shared that Granger made a pass at her. She didn't elaborate. Katy advised her to make a police report, but she's not ready to do that yet."

"Thanks for telling me. It's one more piece in the puzzle we're building to take him down."

Matt sipped his coffee. "I understand he also harassed Tara Stone, the horse show judge. And maybe another female exhibitor."

"That guy is just racking up the charges against him, isn't he? We heard about the scandal kicked up at that horse show and I've got people working on it. I'm not positive yet about Barker but that Granger is definitely a scumbag."

"Keep me informed. I'm going to touch base with Shawn as soon as we're done here, see if he has anything new."

Sanchez's phone buzzed again. He glanced at it quickly and texted a short message.

"I'd better eat quick. Then I've got to get going. No rest for the weary."

"Yep, I hear ya. Thanks for helping watch over Katy for me."

"No problem, man. I know you'd do the same."

# CHAPTER 27
## Wes Stevens

At first when Katy stormed out of the Pegasus offices, she was so angry she could nearly spit. And when she had to squat down to climb into that stupid rental car, she felt even more upset at the world she was sure was trying to conspire to ruin her day, maybe even her life.

She sat in the car for a few minutes, getting control of her breathing and vowing to herself not to cry. No way would she let Barker push her buttons to trigger that emotion.

Maybe she should pray. That would be Matt's method for dealing with chaos. Even though he hadn't really discussed this with her in depth, she saw him, on occasion, pause and appear to be talking to himself...but she knew he was praying, talking to God. It endeared him to her, and she wouldn't change anything about him or his faith.

Maybe she should give it a try. She was raised with prayer but had been silent on the practice the last few years since her parents had died.

"Lord…it's Katy…okay, you know that. Geesh. If you could just, please help me with all this stuff. I don't know how much more I can handle. Um…thanks. Amen."

It wasn't an A-plus pretty prayer or one her parents might have approved of, but it was something at least. It would have to do. She noticed her breath was calmer and she felt she could take her time and think about her next move.

Before she could touch the ignition button of this toy car, her phone buzzed. The screenshot face that appeared shocked her as she hadn't spoken with him in some time but was just thinking of him.

"Wes? I can't believe it's you. I was just about to call you. How weird is that?"

"Hi, Katy. I was wondering if we could get together. I need to talk to you about something. It's important."

Wes Stevens, former publisher she worked with for a lot of years before the current maniac, Barker. Or was that megalomaniac?

"Well, sure. I'd love that. I'm in town. Where do you want to meet? The coffee shop?"

"Can you come to my house instead? I'd rather not meet in town."

"Sure thing. I'll be there in a few minutes."

Wes and his wife lived outside of town in an old ranch-style house that had been in his family, and hers, for generations. She had been the girl next door and years later when they were married the two properties were combined. The Stevens Ranch was well known for quality livestock as well as organic vegetables, goat's milk, and honey.

Hundreds of acres of land once made up the homestead, but little by little, over the years, parcels had been sold off to pay the taxes, or buy out relatives, as well as take care of medical bills for various family members including Wes's wife. They were both older now and could no longer take care of such a big spread. A few acres around the house still sported a big vegetable garden and there was plenty of room for some chickens, horses, and goats. Beyond that they still owned more land, and hoped they could hold on to it, but didn't work it like before.

Wes was waiting on the porch sipping iced tea when Katy drove up in the little rental car she was growing to despise.

"Welcome, Katy girl." It struck her funny how he had always said that, reminding her of an Irish uncle...or maybe a leprechaun.

"Hey, Wes. How are you?"

She came up onto the porch and gave him a big hug including arms around his neck. He had been good friends with her father and Katy could never think of a day in her life when she didn't know Wes and his family.

"Good, good, we're all doin' pretty good."

"Is Miss Marjorie here?"

"No, my Margie is out with the girls...her church group. They get together for lunch at least once a month."

Katy remembered how he had always called his wife "my Margie." She hoped one day she would have someone who would love her as much as Mr. Wes loved Miss Marjorie.

"Aww, darn, wish I hadn't missed her. Please tell her I said hello."

"Well, if you stay long enough, you might be here when she gets home. Then you can tell her yourself."

He chuckled and his belly moved up and down just like a jolly Saint Nick.

"Meanwhile, have a seat and some iced tea. And look, I raided my Margie's cookie jar. Chocolate chip. You can't say no to that."

She giggled. "I can't stay too long. Gotta get back to the ranch. I do want to talk to you about something, but you go first. On the phone it sounded like something was on your mind."

He stared into his glass of tea, then set it on a small end table next to him.

"How are you getting along with Brett Barker? Any problems?"

Katy nearly choked on the gulp of tea she had just taken.

"Wes, I don't even know where to start. He's arrogant, rude, a narcissist, a misogynist, and for all I know, a criminal to boot. I wouldn't say these things to just anyone, but you and I go way back. You're like a second father to me. Why do you ask? Are you having problems with him?"

Wes leaned back in his chair and Katy thought he had gained some weight since she had last seen him.

"A lot of people are. But just speaking from my perspective, I regret selling the magazine to him. Margie and I thought we had no choice. We're getting older and medical and other bills were mounting up. He approached me. Sent an email, then called me from Portland. He's very charming and promised us the moon. I think it's only been...what? ...two months or so since he's taken over. And do you know what? He hasn't paid us one penny yet, not one red cent."

"You're kidding! What does he say about that?"

"That's just it, Katy girl. He ignores my phone calls, emails. I even started texting, and you know me. I do not text. I went in person a few times. He kept me waiting, sometimes more than an hour! He shut his office door so I couldn't just walk right in on him. The receptionist said he was busy. So, I ended up leaving. I think the young people call it ghosting or something."

"Wes, that's horrible. What about the bank? Or a lawyer. Can anyone help you?"

"The bank's no help because it was supposed to be an all-cash deal, broken up into monthly payments to me. I was too trustworthy. I do have a promissory document he signed, though. That's gotta count for something."

She hated to see her old friends taken advantage of like this. Her father would do something about it...if he were here.

"Listen, Wes. I'm going to get you some help. Put that document in a safe place, not your house, a safe-deposit box at the bank. I have a couple of friends who are detectives. Please keep this confidential, but they're watching Barker about something else. Have you heard of Fowler Feed? Or Gordon Granger?"

He had a surprised look on his face.

"Funny you should mention those names. I got a call and a letter offering me big discounts with Fowler Feed. But we don't have a large number of livestock like we used to, so I ignored it. Then that guy Granger came by here when I was out one day. He kind of scared my Margie. Actually, wanted to come in the house and she told him no. He left discount coupons, but she said we weren't interested. He insisted on leaving them so she could show me. She said he was nice and charming at first, then got pretty rude. When I got home, I called the phone number on his coupon but it was out of order, or no such number existed. A scam if you ask me."

"Stay away from him, Wes, and tell Miss Margie to do the same. He could be dangerous."

"What do you mean?"

"Just trust me about this. Again, it's confidential, but he's being investigated. Promise me."

"All right. I promise." He stared at her for a long minute.

"There's something you're not telling me. I noticed it the minute you walked up on this porch. Katy, were you hurt recently?"

She had hoped she wouldn't have to tell him about that, but he always saw right through her...from the time she was ten years old and she and Shawn had skipped school to ride the horses and go fishing. Wes had stumbled upon them when he was checking things on his ranch, and Katy told him they were out of school due to a teacher's workday. He was so disappointed in her when he found out the truth that she hadn't told such a bold-faced lie since then.

"I'm okay. My truck was run off the road after that horse show I was covering for the magazine. We're not sure, but maybe Barker and Granger had something to do with it. Remember, keep all this confidential. Please. And if you tell Miss Marjorie, tell her not to say anything to her friends about it."

"Oh, Katy. That's awful. Now I know I won't stop worrying about you."

"I'll keep you posted when I find out more from my detective friends. And Wes, I wanted to ask you about the magazine. Do you think you'd ever get back in the business? It hasn't been that long."

He sipped his tea and gazed at the sky. "I don't know, Katy. Why do you ask?"

"I wrote an article on the horse show over in Rolling Hills. Things were pretty suspicious. Granger was a judge and he kept placing horses that everyone knew were inferior to the obvious winner. He never placed one from Parkhill Stables. You know how good they are. He was actually kicked out of the show, and another judge I know filed a complaint against him."

"Wow, that's pretty crazy stuff."

"Yeah, it is. Barker was all upset with my article because Granger is his partner in Fowler Feed. He was super rude to me. I'd like to find another publisher for my story."

He took a bite of one of the cookies. "I have some contacts in surrounding towns who have papers or magazines. Maybe one of them would want to run it."

"I was thinking…maybe you and I could run our own publication. It would be like old times."

He tilted his head back and forth in thought.

"Oh, I'm not sure, Katy girl. I need to talk with my Margie. We had hoped to start our retirement, maybe go on a few trips, but then this financial stuff happened with Barker. Now we're worried about being able to stay in our home and pay the bills. Things are so up in the air, I'm not sure about starting a new venture. I'm sorry."

Katy reached over and gently touched his arm. "That's okay. I'm just putting it out there so you know what's on my mind. I'll either search for other publishers or…who knows? I may start my own blog…or a podcast…whatever the latest thing is…then my own digital and print publication. That way I don't have to answer to anyone. If you decide to come in on it later, we can talk."

Wes nodded. "All right, Katy girl. You always were full of ideas with the gumption and hard work to back them up. I know you'll be successful at whatever you do."

"And don't you worry, Wes. We'll get this thing with Barker sorted out."

As she started to leave, he called after her. "Katy? I'm sorry."

"For what? You haven't done anything wrong."

"For trusting Barker. For taking his offer in the first place. If I hadn't agreed to his idea of purchasing the magazine, he would never have come to town. You would never have been hurt. Miss Margie and I would not be in the fix we're in now. It's really all my fault."

She loved him like her own father. How could she make him understand, lessen the burden he had imposed on himself?

"Wes, none of this is your fault. My mom and dad taught me a long time ago that there is evil in this world. Bad things happen to good people. Look at what happened to them in the end. I may have forgotten some things they taught me when I was younger, but lately it's all coming back. You made a business deal with Barker. In the beginning, it sounded good. He sounded good. And honest. If you hadn't taken his deal, maybe another person would have come along instead. We can't blame ourselves for the junk that happens in life. We can only try to do what is right and help others. We can choose to be kind and honest. So, I want you to forget all that other stuff and release yourself from any self-blame. You hear me?"

He stared at her with glistening eyes. "When did you get so smart? And bossy too?"

They walked toward each other and he embraced her in a bear hug, like a father and his daughter.

"You know what gets me even more than Barker not paying us anything?" Wes looked sadder than she'd ever seen him.

"What's that, Wes?"

His eyes lowered. "He supposedly bought the name of

my business—Pegasus Publications—that I'd had for years. That was our corporation's name. When you and I worked together we called the magazine *Cali Horse Shows*. But Pegasus was always dear to my heart. I feel Barker has tarnished our name."

Katy put her hand on his shoulder. "We'll get it back, Wes. Pegasus will fly again. Don't you worry. I won't rest until we make everything right."

# CHAPTER 28
## War

KATY LEFT WES'S HOUSE AND STARTED TO HEAD HOME TO her ranch. She had a lot to think about and wanted to talk with Matt. She tried him several times, but his phone went straight to voice mail. She left a short message after her third try.

"Hey, Matt. I'm heading home. Just saw my old publisher, Wes, and I've got a lot to tell you about Barker. Give me a call back when you can. I should be home in about thirty minutes."

As her rental car glided down the road emitting a quiet hum she despised more and more, she turned her head to see a broken-down van on the side of the street... no, it was a food truck, Jeff's truck. She wasn't sure if a tire was flat or what the problem was. She immediately stepped on the brakes of her toy car a few lengths beyond the food truck and proceeded to back closer to its nose.

Checking the rearview mirror for guidance as well as the backup camera, suddenly she saw a human fly out from inside the truck.

What the heck? She wasn't sure what was happening. Was that Jeff being thrown from the truck, flailing around on the ground? And then Melanie on his heels? Crying, screaming, hitting whoever was punching Jeff.

Katy felt as though she was watching television on her little car's camera rather than real life. She had to help them. She should call Matt...or 9-1-1. Just then Melanie screamed again.

Katy jammed the car into park, turned it off, and sprang out. No time to call anyone.

She ran back toward the truck. A black-hooded person was punching Jeff.

"Hey! Stop it. Leave him alone," she yelled.

The figure turned to face her. Fang.

"Get outta here, lady. This is none of your damn business."

He punched Jeff again, knocking him back to the ground. Melanie screamed and tried to pull Fang away, but he shoved her hard to the ground.

"Now it *is* my business," Katy yelled. She wasn't sure what she'd be able to do against him, but she couldn't stand by and let him hurt Melanie.

"No, Katy, no!" Melanie screamed.

Fang faced Katy, but suddenly a man jumped between them. "It's her."

His voice was deep, and Katy thought it was familiar somehow but she didn't recognize his face.

The man extended his arm onto Fang's shoulder to keep him at bay. Another man came forth and restrained Melanie who fought to squirm out of his grasp. He covered her mouth to keep her from screaming and causing more of a scene on the street. It was one of the back roads out of town, not very populated, but still, they couldn't have a brawl in broad daylight without attracting unwanted attention.

"I don't know what you guys are doing, but I've already called the police. They're on their way." Katy hoped they wouldn't be able to discern her fib. She had meant to call the police. But things were happening so fast.

The first thug stepped closer to her. "I think you're lying, Ms. McKim."

"How do you know my name?" That voice of his saturated her brain like an eerie fog.

He just grinned, two inches from her face. She could smell his bad breath. Onions.

Inwardly she tried saying silent prayers, asking God to help them out of this mess. But she was angry. And a little afraid.

Fang asked the one who seemed to be the leader, "What should we do with them?"

"Put them all in the food truck."

Melanie whimpered as she was forced to climb up through the back entrance of the truck.

Jeff, whose face was bloodied and bruised, mustered his last ounce of courage. "Hey, leave her alone."

But he was only shoved harder and told to follow her without argument.

Katy hadn't been harmed...*yet*, she thought. As she was pushed inside the truck, she was determined to keep her wits about her and fight these guys however she could. The doors slammed behind her, and she listened to the sounds of metal clanging. Chains? Or what?

"They're locking us in! They're going to kill us," Melanie screamed. Jeff hugged her close.

"It's okay, Mel." Katy tried to reassure the girl all the

while her mind was whirring with ideas of how to escape.

It dawned on her. Her cell phone was still in her pocket. What dopey criminals to not even search her. She dialed 9-1-1 but kept it on silent in case their captors came inside the truck and heard the operator answer, or maybe they'd be able to hear her from the outside. She wasn't sure.

Jeff and Melanie watched her in apparent disbelief and held onto each other. Katy held up a finger to her mouth to convey silence.

When the operator answered, Katy quickly stated her name, mentioned Matt's name, and gave their location and the predicament they were in. She was told help was on its way, and to keep the call open in case the bad guys came through the door. At least the authorities would have a recording of what happened. Katy didn't want to think about that in case it turned into a life-threatening situation.

The strange thing was they could no longer hear their captors. Were they still outside? Had they fled? Why didn't they come through the door to hurt Katy and her friends?

She took a chance and rattled the back door. It sounded like a chain or something was in place. The door partially opened a bit but the apparatus holding it closed was too tight. She couldn't budge it open all the way.

All kinds of terrible thoughts ricocheted through her mind. The criminals could start a fire under the food truck and its occupants would be burned alive. She shook her head trying to rid the negative scenario. And she certainly couldn't share any of this with her friends.

Melanie already gave indications that she might head over a psychological cliff soon.

"Jeff!" She jostled him out of his protector mode with Melanie.

"What?"

"Those windows on the side...can we get one open and go through it?"

"They've pulled the shutters down. If they didn't lock or chain them, we could try to push them up."

"Let's do it."

Thank goodness for Jeff. Even though he was lean, he had some strong muscles. He huffed and heaved the shutter up, with Katy's help.

She quickly turned around to Melanie. "Go through it, quick. We'll drop you to the ground."

"No, I can't." The girl's face was awash with tears. Jeff consoled her.

He said, "You go, Katy. They might come back at any minute. Hurry!" He grabbed her arms and pushed her toward the opening.

Against her better judgment, she went through the window, not before saying, "Help is coming."

She landed on the ground hard and the air was knocked out of her for a few seconds, but she grappled to stand. Not before hands grabbed around her waist.

"Where do you think you're going?"

Standing face to face with Fang again, she was surprised at the thought that sprang into her head. *Lord, give me strength.*

She punched his nose hard, then kneed him where it counted. He screamed an obscenity and crumpled to the ground.

She ran like an Olympic sprinter to her roller skate of a car and jumped in.

Fang had gotten to his feet, and she saw a gun in his hand, leveled at her windshield.

"Lord, forgive me. I've got to stop him."

Then she aimed her car for him, but turned the wheel slightly at the last second. She didn't want to kill him, but hopefully wound him, stop him from hurting her or anyone else.

Her car clipped him in the legs, and he went flying into the air. She watched his body make an arc in the sky as though she were watching a cartoon with that silly roadrunner—up, up he went, then splat, landing like a sack of rocks. She truly hoped Fang was not dead. Maybe he could still turn his life around if he got the proper help. Or, if he was determined to lead a life of crime, she was afraid that would mean years of jail time for him.

Sirens blared the arrival of rescue personnel, and she turned in that direction. At least two police cars, a couple of unmarked ones, and one ambulance. Thank God help had finally come. She let out a long breath, maybe her first one in an hour.

The familiar smell and dust from her car's airbag engulfed her. She'd been through this before, but nothing about it was something she wanted to repeat.

Stiffly and slow, she opened the driver's door and climbed out. How much more could her body take? She was so sore, but she had to get to Melanie and Jeff. Were they okay?

She found them next to a police officer who held bolt cutters at the back of the food truck. They held each other tight, Jeff wiping Melanie's tears with his hand and she gently touching his battered face.

"Are you guys okay?"

Melanie grabbed her in a hug. "Oh, Katy. I was so scared. I thought maybe they got you."

"No," a deep voice cut in. "More like, she got them."

Katy turned. "Matt! I am so glad to see you."

"Likewise. I got your message from the nine-one-one dispatcher and got here as soon as I could."

The annoying trill of the ambulance nearby pierced their conversation and Katy heard a banging on the back door signaling the driver to take off with its patient to the nearest hospital.

She asked Matt, "Is that Fang in there?"

"Yep, I believe so."

"Is he dead?"

"No. I understand he's banged up but hanging on."

"He pointed a gun at me."

"I heard that. He also fired. There's a bullet hole in your windshield."

"Can I please get rid of that car now?"

Melanie, Jeff, and Matt all looked at her, silent at first, then everyone broke into a big laugh. It was like a release from a balloon after all the air had whooshed out.

Police and other responders milled about them, rapidly asking questions but also reassuring the victims' safety. Is that what they were, victims? Katy had never wanted to be one again, not after her parents' death and then Shawn's disappearance. She refused with every fiber of her being.

## CHAPTER 29

# *Strength in Numbers*

It was late and everyone was exhausted after the food truck attack and subsequent police discussions. Matt was able to garner some favors from detectives on the scene so that Katy and the others were not required to stay for any extra time into the wee hours answering additional questions. His colleagues trusted him to have it under control, so everyone was turned loose to get some sleep.

Katy invited Melanie and Jeff back to her ranch. Jeff couldn't stay in his truck as it had been impounded for evidence. After receiving medical attention for the beating Fang gave him, he said he'd love to come to the ranch.

And Melanie didn't want to be alone. Her dad had called on her way to the ranch asking how she was, which was kind of mysterious. He didn't really say whether he knew about the incident with Fang and the other men, so she guarded her words. She told Katy she wasn't sure if she could trust him now. So, she blew him off, said she was fine, and that she'd talk with him tomorrow.

Everyone gathered in the living room and Matt handled drink orders—water, tea, hot chocolate, sodas, anything they wanted. Katy watched him. He had such a calming effect on everyone, especially in a crisis situation, and was always so helpful and caring.

"I'm sorry, Katy."

"What do you have to be sorry for, Mel?" She tilted her head in confusion toward the girl.

"I fell apart in the food truck. When you needed me to jump out the window, I was weak and totally lost it. I froze."

"You'll get stronger. I remember years ago not being very strong. Then after all I'd been through, I toughened up. You will too. I'll help you." Katy hesitated and added, "Not that I wish hard times on you...the strength just comes with experience and maturity."

Melanie smiled and Matt softly winked at Katy as though she was doing a good job mentoring her young friend.

Katy called out sleeping assignments. "Mel, the guest room is for you. Jeff, you stay in the barn loft with Matt. There's a pullout couch in addition to the bed. Plenty of space. You guys okay with that? Hope no one snores too much." She grinned.

They both bobbed their heads up and down.

Of course, Matt had come back to the ranch, too, after the food truck attack. He told her he didn't want to leave her side which nearly reduced her to tears. It was a great feeling to have someone care so much.

Heading to the kitchen for water, she didn't want Melanie to hear and get upset so she whispered close to his ear. "What about those other men? I'm pretty sure they were the ones who ran me off the road. I recognized their voices."

"We'll find them. They disappeared when Fang went after you and the police showed up. We've got an APB out on them."

"And Fang? Will he be all right?"

"The hospital is supposed to update me. I'll call again before turning in. It wasn't your fault, Katy. He was trying to kill you."

She held her arms across the front of her body in a self-hug. "Don't remind me. He's a creepy guy. But I feel sorry for him nonetheless."

Jeff cleared his throat and came over to them. "Sorry to interrupt. I just wanted to apologize also, Katy."

"What for?" She wrinkled her brow and chuckled a little. "Why is everyone apologizing to me?"

When he started, she noticed his flowery hippie-dippie speech was gone. He sounded like a normal twenty-something-year-old kid, but also serious like a grown man.

"I just didn't want you to think that Fang was a friend of mine."

"Why were you hanging around with him then?" Matt asked, his strong voice leaving no room for frivolous banter.

Katy gave him a bit of a stern look and a tiny shake of her head as though to ask him to back off his interrogation routine. Jeff was their friend and she wanted to allow him time to talk. Matt gave a little nod to confirm he got her message.

"It was more like he was hanging around with me. I was just trying to be nice. You know, peace and love and all that. I guess it doesn't work on everyone."

Katy smiled. "You're a kind person, Jeff, but you're right. Not everyone else is."

"So, what happened?" Matt was still all business getting right to the point.

"My finances were messed up and I had loans to pay off. The food truck needed some repairs and...well... Fang said his boss could lend me the money, so I took him up on it. Then I had a hard time repaying it. The interest was so high, and they tacked on late fees upon late fees. They wanted me to drive one of their feed trucks to take care of my debt, but I refused. Fang kept coming around threatening me."

Matt asked, "Who is his boss?"

Katy knew that Matt was already aware of the answer. He obviously wanted to hear Jeff confirm it.

"Gordon Granger."

Katy and Matt's eyes locked.

Almost inaudibly Melanie spoke. "And then Granger threatened me."

Jeff's head whipped around. "What? When? What are you talking about?" He placed a hand on her shoulder.

Her head tilted up to him. "I didn't want to tell you. Katy knows a little about it."

"What did Granger do?" Jeff's eyes pleaded, full of caring and protection for his new girlfriend.

"He said if I'd be friendly with him...uh...he would reduce your loan, maybe even forgive it altogether."

Jeff's face changed colors to something resembling a red rash overtaking his face and neck. "I'll kill that old creep."

So much for peace and love, Katy thought.

Matt stepped toward him. "Be careful with your threats. They could be used against you later if anything were to happen to him."

"I don't care. He's a monster." Jeff was furious.

Katy intervened, but gently. She didn't want Jeff to explode or go after Granger and get himself in trouble, or worse...killed.

"I'm sorry for all of this," she said, "but hopefully Granger will be arrested soon and sent away to jail for a long time."

She glanced at Matt for support, but he was silent.

"Do you really think so?" Jeff asked. "What can we do to make sure that happens?"

Katy didn't want to put Melanie on the spot or say anything out of turn about Matt's investigation.

But she did say, "There are some other women he has harassed. If they were all to come forward, it would build a strong case against him. He might also be involved in some other crimes."

Matt frowned as though he didn't want her to go on and divulge too much, so she stopped short.

Jeff hugged Melanie from the side. "You should totally go to the police. Join the other women. Stand up against him. Don't let him get away with this."

"I don't know." She shook her head back and forth. "If the others speak out, why would I have to?"

"Strength in numbers," he blurted out. "Don't worry, sweetie. I'll be with you. Every step of the way."

Katy gently placed her hand on Melanie's back. "We'll all be with you."

Then to Matt she said, "You're the expert with law enforcement. Do you think it would help put Granger away if more women came forward?"

"Most definitely. It always helps a case if there is more evidence, or more witnesses to a crime. And you could be anonymous," he said to Melanie. "Pick him out of a lineup. He wouldn't see you."

Melanie trembled. "Yeah, but when he goes to court, he'd see me. And would I have to testify against him? I don't think I could do that...up there on the stand, him staring at me." Jeff kept his arm around her.

Katy felt motherly toward the girl and stepped close. "Mel, remember we were just talking about being a strong woman? This is one of those times. Don't let people take advantage of you. Don't let them silence your voice. You have every right to speak up. And your 'no' means 'no.' This is your moment to be a strong woman. Look around. You've got all of us by your side."

Melanie smiled sweetly. "Thanks, everyone. I really appreciate your support. Let me think about it."

"All right," Katy said. "We've all had one heck of a day. Why don't we turn in?"

"Sounds good to me. I'm exhausted." Melanie's face was drawn and her eyes bloodshot.

Jeff hugged her tight and planted a kiss on her forehead. "Good night, sweetie. Sleep well. I'll head to the barn with the other animals." He let out a howl, then a loud, snort-like laugh which made her giggle.

## CHAPTER 30

# *Independent Streak*

THE NEXT MORNING KATY WAS GLAD TO HAVE MATT alone over a cup of coffee before the others arose and joined them.

"Melanie must be exhausted. I didn't hear a peep from her room this morning," Katy said.

"Jeff too. Although I did hear a peep. A very loud peep. For your information, *he's* the snorer. Sounds like a sawmill. I was able to tiptoe out of the loft and he's still deep in dreamland." Matt chuckled.

"I'm glad to have this time with you."

He snuggled next to her on a barstool at the kitchen island. "Oh, yeah? Me too." He kissed her neck.

"Okay, okay. As much as I like that, too, I have something to tell you." She kissed his cheek but moved away to grab her coffee. "Remember I left you a voice mail yesterday before all the craziness with the food truck? I wanted to tell you about my meeting with Wes."

"All right, Miss Buzz Kill. I remember." He was teasing her, and they both hugged.

"So, listen to this. Wes told me that since he made the

deal with Barker to sell him the magazine, which was a few months ago, that Barker has not made any payments. It was a cash deal to be paid monthly to Wes. He and his wife were making retirement plans, to go on trips and all that, but now…"

Matt listened intently. "Can't he get a lawyer and take him to court?"

"I don't think Wes can afford that. Here's the other thing. Barker is avoiding him like the plague. He doesn't return Wes's phone calls, or emails, *and* he has kept him waiting an hour or more at his office. He locks his door and tells the receptionist to say he's busy. Poor Wes waits and waits. Isn't that rude?"

"Yes, it is. But it's not against the law, sweetie, to act like a jerk."

"Maybe it's a clue."

"What do you mean? A clue to what?"

"Why Barker acts like a jerk. He's hurting for money. He's stressed. Maybe that's why he teamed up with Granger. Because he needs money."

Matt ran his hand over his whiskers. "I don't know, Katy. There's something missing. We just don't have the whole story yet."

"Well, we need to find out what it is."

"Now listen, missy…" He tapped her nose. "You've already had your tangle with some very dangerous men and have been injured more than once. I really would rather you leave the detective work to the professionals. And that would be me, or Sanchez, even your brother."

She let out a grunt. "What is Shawn up to anyway? I haven't heard from him in a while. Not since he popped in for dinner when Melanie was here."

"I believe he's working a case with Andre." He sounded noncommittal like he knew more.

"By the way, don't call me 'missy' and you know I don't like being told what to do."

Even though she smirked and turned back to toy with his shirt buttons, she was serious. She also figured he knew that since this wasn't their first go-round about her stubbornness and independent streak.

"Roger that, Ms. McKim." Matt poured his coffee into a travel mug and saw her eyes roll upward. "Just promise me you'll be careful and not put yourself in harm's way."

"I'll do my best. Same goes for you in your job." She winked.

"Ka—ty. I mean it."

"Aye, aye, Capitán." She saluted. "Hey listen, I got a message that my truck is ready. I'm so glad they transferred it from Corning closer to home. Can you drop me off at the dealership?"

"Sure. What about your little roller skate of a hybrid car?" He made the biggest toothy grin.

"I think it's safe to say that ridiculous excuse for a car died a necessary death, shot in the windshield and all. I never want to see it again. I'll call the rental company and give them the info to have it picked up. They can repair it...or have an official cremation for it."

"Ooh, you are one harsh lady. I am really surprised at you, Ms. McKim."

"Well, sometimes life is harsh. Only the strong survive. And that hybrid had it coming. It was like driving a sewing machine down the road. I know it could never pull a horse trailer. So what good is it?"

"Easy, easy. The poor little car. And what about the environment? A lot of people think they're great." He was definitely egging her on now, with a twinkle in his eye.

"Why don't we just table this discussion for another time? I've got things to do today and people to see."

"Oh yeah? What people? Should I put a tail on you so you don't get into any more trouble?"

She was feeling playful and partially turned her back to him a little. "I don't think I need a tail, sir."

Since they had been dating, they both had tried their best not to get too provocative with each other in case it was to lead too quickly to intimacy, which they had discussed could be a slippery slope. It's not like they were total prudes or ready to join a religious order, and they both had some experience with past relationships. They just wanted this one to be different —based on respect and their faith. If the rest of the world thought they were silly or strange, so be it. It was their decision and what they felt was right for them.

Matt seemed to be pondering his reaction. She was cute and was being flirty. There were different directions he could go with this. It appeared the one he decided on was to also be a little playful but to shut it down.

"If you turn that thing to me again you might just get a spanking…or a tickle fest. Which do you want?" He held his fingers out like bear claws and started toward her.

Like a young girl…which she had no qualms about being right then…she squealed and took off running around the long kitchen island. "You wouldn't dare."

He made the claw hands again and started toward her slowly.

"Stop! Stop! You'd better not."

Through gales of squeals and laughter, Melanie and Jeff both entered the kitchen looking a little worse for the wear. Jeff's hair was sticking up on end and Melanie's eyes were still bloodshot. Maybe she hadn't slept very well.

Before Katy could say anything to them about her and Matt's chase around the kitchen, her phone played a horse whinny ringtone that she had recently downloaded when she was toying around with apps.

"Hey, Tara...how have you been?"

She didn't put it on speaker so the three people in the room couldn't hear what Tara was saying. They tried to be quiet and polite as Matt offered Melanie and Jeff juice or coffee.

"Tara...wait...slow down...are you okay? Sure, I can meet you...I know where it is...we just need to swing by the dealer and pick up my truck real quick. That's not too far from where you are. You sure you're okay? All right. I'll see you soon."

The call ended and Katy just stared at Matt with a blank expression.

"She didn't sound good. I think she's in trouble. Let's go. I need to get my truck. Fast."

Matt's phone buzzed with a text. "It's Shawn. He wants me to meet him. Says it's important."

Melanie stepped forward. "I can take you to the dealer and follow you to where Tara is."

"I dunno." Matt shook his head. "I'm not sure I feel comfortable letting you both go on your own."

"*Letting us?*" Katy frowned. "We are grown women, you know."

"Katy, you know what I mean. After all that's happened. I'm worried about you."

"Yeah," Jeff chimed in. "Maybe I should go."

Melanie touched his hand. "But you've got that appointment today with the bank."

"I can change it."

"No. Keep it. We'll be fine."

"Sorry." Katy's face softened toward Matt. "I know what you mean. And I appreciate your concern. Both of you. But we've got to go now. How 'bout I call you the minute things look out of the norm? If that even happens."

Matt pondered a few seconds. "I do have to meet Shawn. Just stay in touch. Or else I'll send out reinforcements."

"Gotcha. C'mon, Mel, let's go." She gave Matt a kiss.

Melanie followed suit with Jeff although she looked a little embarrassed about the PDA.

# CHAPTER 31

## *Tara*

MELANIE GAVE KATY A RIDE TO THE DEALERSHIP TO PICK up her truck. She followed inside as Katy signed the paperwork and chatted for a quick minute with the Service and Body Repair department personnel.

Before Katy was ready to hop in, she patted the truck's door.

"Good to have you back, girl."

Melanie walked beside her. "You haven't named her?"

"What?"

"Like Bonnie, or Blaze, or Wildfire, or Jolene or..." The girl smiled.

"You're kidding, right?"

Melanie chuckled and shrugged a shoulder. "Well, some people do."

"Not me. It's a truck. Hey, listen, let's get going. Tara's waiting."

"Where is she?"

"Off the interstate. That parallel road outside of town, not too far. It's a deserted stretch."

"All right. I'll follow you."

When they pulled up near Tara's sport-utility vehicle, it was at a funny angle off the shoulder of the road, flat tire, and nose awkwardly pointing down toward the dirt. The driver's door was open and Tara was inside, her head in her hands on the steering wheel.

Katy rushed to her along with Melanie.

"Are you okay? What happened?"

Tara's face was flushed and her eyes wet. She told Katy, "It was Granger."

"Did he force you off the road? Are you hurt?"

"No, just shook-up. He and his goon were chasing me. Their truck got so close and hit my bumper. When we stopped, suddenly he was out of his truck and came up to my window, said for me to withdraw my appeal against him, or else."

"What did the man with him look like?"

"Tall. Arms covered with tats. Deep voice. I think he had a gun under his vest. I'm not sure."

"I'm calling the police. And Matt."

"I don't know," Tara said. But then she realized Katy's determination was as thick as quicksand and just as serious. "You're right. We can't let him get away with this stuff."

Katy dialed 9-1-1, gave their location and situation, then called Matt.

"We're okay," she told him. "But that sleazeball is getting bolder and more dangerous. He needs to be stopped. Now."

As Matt was telling her that he was on his way, a black truck appeared seemingly out of thin air and was speeding in their direction.

"I think that's them, coming back again." Tara's voice trembled.

Katy hated seeing her like this, scared. In the horse-show ring, Tara was all business, in control, and had worked hard for her position. Now, she appeared to be at Granger's mercy, drowning in fear.

"Hurry! Get on the other side of my truck. Duck down when they come by. The cops should be here soon."

The black truck had a menacing loud sound, whether it was from the engine or exhaust—Katy couldn't remember all the parts and names her brother used to talk about, or their meanings—headers to speed up the flow of the exhaust, forced induction, pipes, cat backs. She had no clue what those were. Whatever this truck had in the way of modifications, it sounded like the devil himself roaring down the road hell-bent on devouring them.

The girls ran around Katy's truck and crouched down close to the dirt, holding on to each other. The truck rumbled as it slowly approached, but they didn't dare peek around their hiding place for a look.

Voices sounded as a second vehicle pulled up.

Was it Matt or the police already? Katy crept along the dirt to get a better look. She turned back to Melanie. "I think it's your father."

"Granger, what are you doing? Scaring women? I didn't agree to any of this." His voice was raised.

From the black truck came a menacing message from Granger. "Mind your own business if you know what's good for you. Now I've got to clean up this mess. If you don't agree with my methods, get the hell out of here."

Katy crawled around her truck's bumper and tried to get a better look. She saw Barker's vehicle. He was now out of it standing in the middle of the deserted road, hollering at Granger who was in the backseat of the scary truck, window down as though he were being chauffeured by the tattooed driver. There was a front passenger Katy couldn't make out.

"I will not," Barker said. "You're taking things too far. First the thing with the drugs in the feed, and now this. I don't want any part of your crime ring."

Granger laughed an evil, guttural sound. "You're in it as much as I am now. And if you want out, well, we can take you out. No problem."

Katy watched the driver's arm extend out the window of the black truck, then a shot flew over Barker's head. She ducked. He ducked.

But Melanie darted out. "Dad!" she screamed.

"Mel, get down!" Katy called.

It was too late. Melanie was out in the open and Barker turned around toward her.

"Melanie, what are you doing here?"

"Helping my friend. Dad, what's going on?"

Barker moved quickly and tried to push her back behind Katy's truck. "Get down."

But Melanie stood fast. Until Katy grabbed her and pulled her to the ground behind the truck and held her tight. "Mel, stay down. Please."

Another shot whizzed by, this time connecting with flesh—Barker's upper arm. He grabbed it and went down in the street. "Uh!"

"Dad!" Melanie screamed again.

Tara was behind the truck and Katy saw her slowly crawling toward the front. Before anything could be said, Tara was holding a pistol, arms extended and hands cupped together, standing straight, legs apart, like a soldier. She fired twice toward the black truck, hitting the tires and glancing off the driver's door, enough to make him duck and not fire back at her. A *thwap* sound echoed, then hissing.

"Dammit! Drive!" Granger's voice bellowed his curses.

The tattooed driver hit the gas but when the truck moved it thumped and couldn't quite grab traction.

Sirens fractured the air.

Melanie ran to her father who had slumped to the ground, her eyes clouded with tears.

"Dad, are you all right?"

He held his upper arm as blood trickled through his fingers and blotched his pale-colored shirt.

"I'm okay." He grunted. "What in the world were you doing in the middle of all this?" His face conveyed anger, or maybe it was pain.

"They were after Tara. Katy and I had to help her."

He touched her cheek with his clean hand. "They're dangerous men."

Two police cars stopped, along with an ambulance. Soon medical personnel rushed to help Barker, checking his vitals, and readying him for transport to the closest hospital.

"Melanie, come with me?"

She looked at her father, then to Katy who nodded for her to go.

"I'll find you, Mel. And I'll let Jeff know where you are."

Katy eyed Tara. "I didn't know you had a gun. Where did you learn to shoot like that?"

"I grew up in the country. My dad taught all us kids to shoot. Snakes, other critters. I didn't want to kill Granger, just stop him."

The two women hugged each other. "I'm glad you're

okay." Katy held her friend tight. "I hope they catch those guys."

More police arrived on scene, including Matt who parked his truck on the side of the road and jumped out and ran toward Katy.

"Are you all right?"

She quickly let go of Tara and nearly collapsed into his arms.

"I'm so glad to see you." She tried her best not to lose it in front of everyone but a few tears trickled out, and her body trembled as though she was cold.

"It's okay. I've got you." He wrapped his arms around her.

Katy eyed her truck. "There had better not be any bullet holes in her."

Matt shook his head and held her tight.

He was warm and his chest and arms were strong. She wanted to stay in his safe embrace forever. But someone clearing their throat broke the spell. She turned and saw it was Shawn.

"Hey, Sis. You okay?"

He held out his arms and she hugged him too. She was silent and just let him hold her.

She had a quick vision of when they were kids. Before age seven or eight they teased, hugged, even kissed on the cheek. At around age ten or twelve they didn't hug at all upon threat of being punched or tickled. Girls had cooties and all that. As young teens they certainly didn't hug. "Sisters, yuck," Shawn had said back then more than once.

But later, closer to their early twenties when Shawn had been in the military a couple of years already, they started hugging again, knowing that they could lose one another any second due to something out of their control. And now...she was so glad to hug him, and she felt the reciprocal emotion from him.

"Yes, I'm okay. Haven't seen you in a while. Where've you been?"

"Just busy. Working." He and Matt shared a look.

Shawn released her and she saw him glancing at Tara, even detected a smirk, smile, or glimmer of something. Tara returned a shy, girlish look of interest toward him.

"Oh, this is Tara. I don't think you've met yet." Katy placed her hand on Tara's shoulder and nudged her closer.

Shawn held his hand out and Tara took it. They seemed to hold that touch for a longer than normal time, both locking eyes and grinning like high schoolers.

Katy and Matt shared a knowing look. This was interesting, she thought. She hadn't seen her brother with a girl in a long time. Then again, it wasn't that long ago when she hadn't seen Shawn at all for that matter.

One of the police officers snapped them out of the moment as he addressed Matt.

"We stopped them down the road. Tires shot out." He surveyed the small group. "Whose handiwork was that?"

Everyone turned to Tara. "I guess that would be me." She held her palm up a little and waved it back and forth, almost playful.

"Well, good work, ma'am," the officer said. "I guess you've got a permit for that?"

"Yes, sir. I do."

Katy watched Shawn smiling big as though he was watching a video game where the hero is a woman in tight pants and carrying an automatic weapon. He obviously found Tara very appealing.

"Okay. We can confirm all that at the station. Was

anyone hurt?" His head swiveled from Katy, then back to Tara.

"We're fine," Katy said.

The officer asked Matt, "I assume you want to be in on the questioning of those guys?"

"Definitely." He and Shawn both nodded their heads.

# CHAPTER 32
## Cemetery

FANG HAD BEEN IN THE PASSENGER SEAT AND GRANGER IN the back seat of the truck that had come after Katy and her friends. One of Granger's goons was the driver who shot at Barker. Thanks to Tara's sharp shooting of the tires, the cops were able to pick them up down the road.

"What happens next?" Katy asked Matt.

"Well, Tara's going to the station to answer some questions. Shawn is driving her, by the way."

They smirked at one another, and Matt raised his eyebrows playfully.

He continued. "And you know, Mel went to the hospital with Barker. It'll be interesting to see how that plays out, if he's going to mend his ways and stand up to be a real father."

"Will he get jail time?" She so hoped Melanie wouldn't get hurt anymore by that man.

"I'm not sure. But it does sound like he was in on some of the crimes, so he deserves some kind of punishment."

"What about me? Do I need to go to the police station? Gosh, I wonder what will happen to Pegasus Publications now. Wish I could get Wes back in on it."

Thoughts bounced around in her head. What if Barker went to jail? What would happen to Melanie? What would happen to the magazine? Her job? But why should she care about that? Her last encounter with Barker had pretty much solidified the fact that she couldn't stand working with him. She wanted to talk to Wes again.

Matt touched Katy's arm. "I thought you should get home and rest. It's been pretty stressful for you lately. I arranged for you to answer questions at the station in a few days or so. Hope that's okay with you. They agreed since I vouched for you." He smiled that smile she had grown to love and added a little wink.

"Always looking out for me. How lucky can a girl get?"

He conjured up a mischievous look and tilted his head. "I'm not gonna answer that. I could get myself into some trouble." He nudged her side lightly and she squirmed. Then he added, "I'll send a tow truck for Tara's vehicle. You okay to drive your truck?"

"For sure. I'm not leaving her here." Then she stopped abruptly in her tracks. "What about Melanie? I told her I'd find her. Maybe I should go to the hospital?"

"We can call and check on her and Barker, let her know you need to get home."

She continued walking alongside him. "I guess so. She'll tell me if anything is critical. Maybe they need private time anyway. I'm not exactly Barker's favorite person."

It was a relatively short drive to her ranch and when

they parked both trucks in front, she couldn't help exhaling an audible sigh. She was so glad to be home and was relieved to have the "bad guys" in custody. Maybe now her life could get back to some kind of normalcy. Whatever that meant.

Matt opened the front door of the house for her, and immediately they were greeted by a jumping, fluffy Rocky dog.

"Whoa, fella. I didn't know you were in here." Katy bent down and patted his head and sides while his whirligig tail kept time to his panting tongue.

"Oh, forgot to tell you. I left him here when I got the call to get to you. Thought he'd be okay by himself for a while."

"No worries. He probably took a nap on the couch." And then to the dog as she scrunched his ears and accepted his wet kisses, "Didn't you, boy?" He followed her to the kitchen. "Who wants a treat? C'mon, Rocky."

Matt smiled and went to the fridge. "Do you want a water or something?"

"Sure."

"I'll bet *you'd* probably like a nap on the couch too," he said to Katy.

She was still caught up in Rocky's exuberant greeting. "Whoa, wait, you're gonna knock me down, boy. Take it easy."

Matt gave one stern command. "Rocky, down."

And the dog obeyed, although not before giving his master a look that could be interpreted as, "Aww, gee, Dad."

Katy got up and went to the sink to wash her hands. "Uh, what were you saying? Before I was attacked by the beast."

"I said you'd probably like a nap too."

"I am pretty exhausted. Mentally, I think. I'm kind of wound up from all that has transpired. I'd like to visit the horses. They always calm me down. And you know what else?"

"What's that, sweetie?" He opened a bag of pretzels to munch on.

"I'd like to visit my parents."

There was a small cemetery on the ranch property some distance from the house. In the two years since her parents had been gone, she had visited the spot a handful of times. Maybe fewer. She knew they weren't there, but also believed humans sometimes needed a tangible, physical place to sit and reminisce. And if she were honest with herself, she knew she avoided the place because it made her downright sad. It brought the reality of their loss right in front of her face, no hiding from reading their names carved on the stone markers.

*Howard and Dorothy McKim,*
*Devoted Husband and Wife,*
*Best Parents in the World,*
*Gone Too Soon, Loved Forever.*

"Do you want me to go with you?" Matt asked.

"Not this time. I think I need some alone time with them. You understand, don't you?"

"Of course. Take Rocky with you. I can do things around here. I've got my laptop. I'll check in with the station, and see what Shawn and Andre are up to."

"All right. If you're okay with that."

"For sure I am, sweetie. Do you want something to eat first? I think we missed breakfast."

"No. Thanks. You know I've gained a few pounds since knowing you, Detective."

He smiled and pulled her close grabbing the tail end of her long, auburn-colored ponytail. "And I love every ounce of you."

They kissed for a minute while Rocky tried to wedge between them. Katy couldn't help her giggles. "You big goof, Rocky. Can't ya see we're busy?"

"I tell you, he's jealous of me. He wants you all to himself. You've stolen my dog, Ms. McKim."

She held her hands up. "Guilty as charged, sir."

"I might have to get the cuffs and restrain you."

"Settle down, Detective. You and Rocky are so rambunctious since we got home. Maybe I should go visit the horses and my parents while you jump into a cold shower. And take that wild beast with you. He could probably use a bath anyway."

"Aww, Rocky, she hurt our feelings, didn't she? C'mon with me, boy."

"Wait just a minute. I think we said he was coming with me."

"Well, you'd better get going then. Make up your mind. Rocky won't know whether he's coming or going." He grinned.

She always enjoyed the banter and teasing with Matt. He had a gift of taking her mind off the dreadful things of her life. But where was it leading? Were they really a couple now? Was he "the one"? The one to cleave to and no other, as the Bible taught. She wondered about that word "cleave." Reminded her of a meat cleaver. Her silly writer brain. She remembered her mom and dad had taught her it meant to stick to one another's spouse, one flesh, for ever and ever.

Could she make such a big decision about Matt? A lifelong, forever choice? She sure wished her parents were here to advise her...all the more reason to get on with her trek to their gravesites. She had some important matters to discuss with them.

# CHAPTER 33
## Monster

"C'MON, ROCKY." AFTER SADDLING HER HORSE IN A JIFFY, she called to the dog to keep up with her and Cash.

He obliged and bounded through tall weeds alongside them. Picking up a super long stick along the way to hold between his teeth, it appeared he was smiling and showing off his treasure, happy to tag along on this grand adventure.

"You goofball. Don't hit us with that stick."

He lost his hold on it, dropped it, and rearranged it in his mouth, then journeyed on ahead of her as if in a race. She always wondered what a dog's life must be like, or a horse's for that matter. For a dog it must be so freeing, full of excitement and happy feelings, no gloom and doom or regrets. If there were any sad feelings, she was sure they could be chased away in an instant. They only had to pick up a stick or sit beside their master and receive ear scrunches or belly rubs. What a life. God must've had fun creating and injecting them with such unconditional love and abandon, kind of like facets of His own personality. She didn't mean to be sacrilegious in any way comparing the dog to God, but she was sure He'd be okay with her illustration.

They had arrived at the small family cemetery which was over a small hill away from the main house and barn. It was near a country road toward the back part of the property. Katy immediately felt rather guilty for not taking better care of the gravesites. Weeds could wreak havoc and start a junglelike growth in such a short time, and she only visited every three or four months.

She switched Cash's bridle for a halter and let him graze. Kneeling, she yanked the intruding vines away from the concrete markers, then brushed her hand across the names. Her parents were buried there, and her father's parents. Her mother's parents were in another state. Baby Emily Ann, her grandparent's baby who died right after she was born in the same house Katy lived in now, was also laid to rest there. Katy grieved for her grandmother. How awful to carry a child for nine months only to lose it on what should have been the happiest day. If Emily Ann had lived, she would have been sister to Katy's father. She imagined he must have thought about her his whole life.

Her musings veered off to her own brother, Shawn, and she was grateful for their childhood together. She wondered what it would have been like if they had had more siblings, maybe a sister to grow up with. She imagined more pony rides and wild adventures most likely. And someone to lean on in the hard times. Maybe play dress-up with and giggle about teenage dating if there had been another girl.

Gosh, she was so glad not to be looking at a marker with her brother, Shawn's name spelled out on it. Although, during that bizarre time when he went missing, she let people around her convince her to have a small memorial service. Luckily, she did not take their advice to add his tombstone to the graveyard and bury an empty casket. Thank God.

The area was cordoned off with a white picket fence that was in need of a coat of paint and some repair to keep it from leaning. She made a mental note to attend to that...one of these days. Surveying the area, she was glad it was situated beneath a grand oak tree as though it would protect those buried there...even though she knew they were gone.

She had to chuckle when she saw three small graves away from the big ones, tucked next to the tree. Peter, the bunny. Callie, the cat. Bellow, the frog. Childhood animals that she and her brother had begged their parents to bury in the family cemetery. How could her father refuse when she came to him, her big eyes awash with tears over Peter, her favorite? She couldn't abide the frog—that was her brother's. They both liked Callie who was easy to get along with as she weaved in and out of human legs purring as she went.

Rocky was somewhat tuckered out, or maybe just getting his second wind, from all his antics running at full tilt and carrying the gargantuan stick. He dropped it and plopped down next to Katy as she continued to spruce up the tombstones and began her conversation.

"Oh, Mom and Dad, I'm sorry I haven't been here much. I promise I'll try to do better. That fence needs painting, I know. I hope you're doing well..." Her eyes went skyward. "You're probably dancing and singing with Jesus. I know you are, Mom. Dad, you're probably building or planting something for Him." She smiled to herself.

"This is Rocky. I don't think he was here the last time I visited. He's Matt's dog. You probably know that, right?

That's what I wanted to talk to you about. No, not Rocky. Matt." She shook her head and chuckled.

"What do you think of him? Pretty great, isn't he? He's been so kind to me. We really get along, like we're meant to be together. Shawn likes him. They work on cases sometimes. Matt's really smart. And, Dad? He goes to church. Thought you'd like that. He has a nice sister and family. His dad is gone, and his mom is getting older. I just wish you were here. I mean, wonder if I decide he's 'the one'? Wonder if we get married? Who will walk me down the aisle? Yeah, I know Shawn would do it. But, Dad, I wanted it to be you...Wonder if we have kids one day? Mom, I wanted them to have you to teach them things. You'd be the best grandma ever..."

And then she teared up. In fact, once she started it was hard to stop. Rocky reached to her face with his snout as if to comfort her, and then his long pink tongue lapped over her cheek. Good thing she liked dogs.

Resting her face in her hands, she relished the darkness when she closed her eyes. It was peaceful and her breath became calm and rhythmic. She believed in allowing herself a small pity party, then get a hold of herself and back to work.

Rocky surprised her with a guttural growl before letting out an alerting bark. The hair on the back of his neck and down his spine stood up on end. A rustle in the bushes beckoned her to look up from her prayerful meditative state. She hoped there wasn't a snake nearby.

"What is it, boy?" She held his collar to prevent him from bolting after something until she knew what it was. "Stay."

A human voice startled her. It began slowly from behind a tree, then grew louder as the form walked toward her.

"What a touching scene. A girl and her dog talking to the dead parents. Just like *Little House on the Prairie.*"

She couldn't believe it was Granger. Why wasn't he in jail?

"What are *you* doing here?"

"Thought we should meet face to face. You've been causing me a lot of trouble lately. Just wanted to ask you kindly to stop."

He reached in his pocket, and she shivered thinking it might be a gun. Instead, it was a roll of cash. He was a chunky guy and when his shirt lifted some, she noticed his puffy stomach which matched his double-chin. She knew sometimes food wasn't the only culprit in the war against unfitness. Sometimes it was alcohol, medication, poor diet, lack of exercise, or a combination.

"I'm prepared to put you on my payroll, Ms. McKim. Or, give you a gift payment. Whichever you prefer. You name it and I'll see how I can accommodate."

A shiver went up her back. She was standing now and he evaluated her up and down, which gave her the creeps. He was more of a slimeball than Barker.

She felt like her parents were standing beside her, though, as she mustered the courage to ask, "What would you want in return?"

He let out a dirty-sounding laugh. "Well, I'm trying to keep this all business and not be crass. Unless you want me to be." He laughed again, then got serious. "I would ask you to look the other way. To stay out of my business. Whatever you see or hear, just mind your own business, and leave mine alone. That's all. Easy-peasy. Win-win."

She kind of hated those expressions. They were so… lacking in substance…stupid. As though the person couldn't think of anything better to say.

She glared. "Why don't we start with this? Get off my property."

"Ooh, aren't you the fierce one? I actually find it very attractive when women are tough. Sexy even."

What a creep. She felt like throwing up right then and there. Maybe she should. That would sure surprise him. But she had to stay in control.

"Listen. I asked politely. Get off my property." She reached in her pocket and brought out her cell phone and held it up. "Do you want me to call the police and have them take you right back to jail? In fact, how are you even out so quickly after what happened earlier?"

She saw his expression change from playful sicko to serious anger. He reached to the small of his back and produced a gun which he pointed upward, almost cavalier like he was waving a toy. Most likely his hired thugs took care of the real dirty work he assigned to them, and he wasn't in the habit of gunplay.

"Let's just say I hired good attorneys. I think this trumps that cell phone. Throw it to the ground."

Rocky pulled and gave a few angry barks at the threatening stranger.

"Hold that dog or I'll take care of him for you. For good." His mouth took on an ugly snarl.

She tossed her phone gently into the grass, but not too far. She was hoping to get it back soon and call for help.

"Leave him alone." She held tight to Rocky while the wheels in her brain spun at breakneck speed. How was she going to get out of this situation with her and Rocky unscathed? She glanced behind Granger and saw his truck parked on the normally unused country road. It didn't look like anyone was with him. Maybe a neighbor or delivery person would come by and see she was in trouble. What about Matt? Would he hear Rocky's barks, and come to check on them? Or were they too far from the house? Immediately she changed her mind and hoped Matt would not come so Granger couldn't hurt him. She'd have to do this on her own. Maybe she could keep him talking, take his mind off the gun he held.

"So, you liked Tara? Did you know she was single?" She made her voice friendly.

"What? Who?" His face crinkled.

"You know who I mean. You judged that horse show with her."

"Oh, her. She's all right. Thinks too much of herself, though. Men don't like high-and-mighty women who want to wear the pants. We want to wear our own pants." He laughed that disgusting laugh, like a hyena.

Katy was careful to look to the road again. Too much and she thought Granger would get suspicious. She inwardly prayed someone would pass by and see her.

"Maybe she was just nervous around you. She told me she thought you were kind of tough, a little too aggressive, but said she liked strong men."

"Did she now?"

He squinted and stared at her like he was unsure whether to believe her or not, trying to figure out if she had a motive to trick him. Or maybe he was considering if it was true about Tara.

# CHAPTER 34
## Rocky Makes Three

KATY HAD TO KEEP HIS ATTENTION. "I'M JUST TELLING YOU what she told me. She talked about you quite a bit actually."

His eyes squinted at her. "Then why did she file an appeal with the horse show association to get me thrown out?"

"Oh, that wasn't personal. Tara told me. She had to protect her position. She didn't want to get in trouble for rigging a class or taking a bribe from an exhibitor. Someone hinted that maybe Tara was showing favorites. She wanted to explain to you that she didn't have a choice. She hoped you would forgive her."

He nearly growled his next words. "Is that why she shot at me? Because she likes me?"

"I don't think she knew you were in that truck. She was trying to protect the young girl we were with. Barker's daughter."

How could she get the gun away from him? He was the kind who would shoot her in a minute, no qualms, Rocky also. Katy couldn't have that.

234

Nestled on the short grass, her phone began to buzz and she and Granger both saw Matt's smiling face displayed on the home screen.

"Don't even think about answering that." Granger pointed the gun upward. Thank goodness he had not pointed it at her yet. "How sweet. The boyfriend is checking up on you. I guess we'd better get on with our business before he starts nosing around."

What could she say to him to stall? She'd have to lie.

"He's at work. Uh...in town."

Granger laughed again. "Do you think I'm stupid? Don't you think I watched your house...saw his vehicle? I know he's in there."

"Maybe he came back early. I'm sure you could talk to him if you want. He might be able to help you."

"Why would I need any help from him?"

"Uh...well...aren't there still charges pending against you? Because of the shooting earlier. You're going to have to face those at some point."

His face reddened again. "I *told* you. I have lawyers. They're working on it. Why would I need your detective boyfriend? Besides, I didn't shoot anyone."

She wasn't sure what to do now. And Matt would worry when she didn't answer his call.

Right as she thought that, her phone vibrated again. She tried to pray for help.

"That guy just doesn't quit, does he? I'll take care of him."

Before she had another thought...*BLAM!* Granger fired his gun at the cell phone and blew it to a bunch of pieces that flew all over. She turned away and covered her eyes with one hand as she desperately tried to hold on to Rocky. The loud noise scared the dog at first. He hunched down and scampered closer to Katy. But when

Granger raised his other hand to point at her...Rocky lunged at Granger's ankle and clamped on tight with his teeth, growling all the while.

"Get him off me! I'll shoot him. I swear I will."

Granger punched and shoved the dog who whimpered slightly, then continued his attack.

Katy had to do something. She had been kneeling beside a big rock, the size of her hand, and had been contemplating her plan and fingering it all during their conversation as she pretended to pet the dog. But Granger never paid any attention.

She stood and aggressively went for Granger's head with the rock. The blow made contact, but it only made him mad. He raised his arm and pointed the gun directly at her. She decided she had to take a chance and push his arm so that any shot would go in another direction. The two of them struggled.

"You bitch! I'll kill both of you."

But before he could, another shot rang out. *BLAM!* And Granger dropped to the ground.

First thing she thought to do was move his gun away from him. He might still be alive. She was confused and looked around.

"Oh, Matt, you came."

"Are you all right?"

"Yes. I was worried for Rocky."

"Of course you were." He came close and held her tight. "Katy, that was a dangerous move to confront him like that. I was so afraid I'd lose you."

She looked up and stared into his eyes. "Never."

And they kissed. But stopped when they heard movement. And Rocky's growl.

Granger was moaning and stirring.

"Rocky, watch him." The dog complied like the good

partner he was complete with a fierce open-mouthed growl.

Matt immediately got on his phone and called the authorities, also asking for medics for Granger. He noticed the scattered pieces of Katy's phone in the grass.

"I guess you'll need a new one of those." He pointed.

"Yeah, I will. And it had such a nice screenshot of a handsome detective."

"Was he blasting at my pic?"

"You could say that."

"Gee, that hurts my feelings."

"You'll just have to get over it. Besides, I think I'll use a new pic of my current hero."

"Oh, really? And who might that be?"

"He's very handsome. Kind of furry, though. He has a golden personality. And he's so protective of me. I mean he would bite anyone's ankles who tried to mess with me." She grinned.

Matt took hold of her sides and kissed her neck, which made her shriek and struggle to get away, alerting Rocky to jump in between them.

The sun was planning its ritual descent and bathed the group in a rosy peach glow.

They were a silly threesome, a little family, full of young love. Katy hoped they'd always be that way. She could imagine building a good life with Matt.

But those were her heart feelings. She just wasn't ready to speak them out loud to him yet.

THE FIRST RESPONDERS had arrived quickly—an ambulance for Granger and police to investigate the shooting. Mixed with the peaceful glow of a descending sun, now the chaotic flickering of red-and-blue lights added to the surreal scene as they all parked on the country road near the family cemetery.

Of course, the authorities all knew Matt and recorded the pertinent information he provided. The police had been keeping up with Granger's escapades and knew his lawyer had arranged his release earlier in the day.

In all the excitement two figures approached nearly running through the haze. Katy could not discern their identity at first and only saw shapes.

"Are you all right?" When she heard the voice and his face became recognizable, she realized it was Shawn. His hand was holding Tara's who tried to keep up with him.

He let go of Tara and wrapped both arms around Katy. "I was so worried when we heard what was going down."

"I'm okay. You're choking me." She coughed and pushed him away but smiled at her brother's concern for her.

"Oh, sorry." Shawn pulled back, still holding her shoulders. She watched his eyes as he surveyed her body for any injuries.

Tara came near, smirked at Shawn, then hugged her too. "We're so glad you guys are okay. That Granger's a real nutcase."

"Thanks. I had a great protector." Katy reached down to pet Rocky who seemed to be loving all the attention.

Matt grinned. "I guess I'm chopped liver, not to mention I think she's stolen my dog. I mean, I am the one who shot Granger. Don't I get any accolades?"

Katy leaned up and kissed his cheek. "You will always be my hero, Matthew Hartman."

"Aww…yuck. Don't make me gag." Shawn teased, to which Matt shoved him a bit.

"You guys are like kids." Katy winked at Tara and the two women nodded in partnership.

"Hey listen, if you're really okay and no one needs us, I'm gonna take Tara home. She's without a car since hers got messed up." Shawn reached for her hand again.

"Uh-huh…" Katy made a schoolteacher-like judgmental expression which broke into a smile. She loved teasing her brother, and he, her.

"Fast work, bro…" from Matt.

"Shut up, both of you. C'mon, Tara, let's leave these two…uh, sorry Rocky…three…amigos."

As they walked away, Katy said, "Shawn?" He turned back to her.

"I love you, Brother. Thanks for checking on me."

He grinned big. "I love you, too, Sis. Try to stay out of trouble. At least for an hour or two. You sure are racking up too many scary incidents."

Low and to himself, Matt said, "Fat chance of that."

Katy heard him, pushed on his arm, and poked his stomach. "Hey, you, watch it. I'll sic my dog on you."

Katy called after her brother again. "Shawn, why don't you two come for dinner tomorrow?"

Tara answered for him. "We'd love to!"

# CHAPTER 35
## Meeting the Parents

THEY WERE AT THE BARN EARLY THE NEXT MORNING AND after the horses were fed, they tied them in the center aisle to be brushed and tacked up.

"I know you have work, Matt, but thanks for coming with me for a quick ride. I think it'll clear our heads and lighten our moods."

He smiled. "My mood has been fine. I'm just hoping the lunatics will all settle down and leave us alone."

"I heard you on the phone earlier. How are Granger and Barker doing?" She brushed Cash. She hadn't had much quality time with her horse lately.

"They'll both be okay. I shot Granger in the leg so he might have a future limp, or not, but he'll survive. They'll transport him from the hospital to the jail in maybe a week, then to court sometime later. I don't have a date yet. Barker's getting out today or tomorrow, with his arm in a sling, also heading to jail to await trial. Sounds like he'll get lesser time. He was just stupid, thought he was a big shot, and wanted to get ahead by bending the law. He got involved with the wrong people. Granger *is* the wrong people. Thief, liar, drug trafficker, ringleader, attempted murderer, probably a sexual predator too. He needs to go away for a long time."

"I sure hope so. He's a scary guy."

Matt had positioned a saddle blanket on the horse he'd be riding, then hefted a Western saddle off a rack to place on top of that.

"It was nice of your neighbor to let me ride his horse."

"Stan would literally give you the shirt off his back if you needed it. And his wife Lily...well, you know, you met them...she's just a saint. I couldn't ask for better neighbors."

"They are sweet, that's for sure."

"When the crazies aren't stalking or trying to shoot us, this is a nice place to live, isn't it?"

He gazed at her with kind of a dreamy expression. "Yeah, I could get used to it."

That sure warmed her heart. She smiled and thought of the implications. Did that mean marriage? She envisioned Matt as her husband, living together on the ranch, just like her neighbors. They were such a kind couple, helped everyone they could, and obviously were in love with each other. Katy wanted that life.

But maybe she was getting ahead of things. How long had she and Matt really known each other, been dating? A friend of hers once told her to date a man for one thousand hours before considering marriage. She tried to do the math while she was saddling Cash. If you got together for dinner and hung out for three hours at a time...divide one thousand hours by three...that would equal three hundred and thirty-three...what? Not days... dates? What about a four-hour date? Two hundred fifty dates? What? Three hundred sixty-five days in a year. You'd have to see them almost every day.

While she frowned trying to contemplate how many times she and Matt had been together...on an outing...at her house for a meal...or even in a shootout...a rambunctious fluff of dog bounded around to the front of the horses. He knew not to get in the way. Matt had already scolded and schooled Rocky about that.

"Did you hear me, Katy? I said I could get used to living here. Looks like Rocky could too. He wants to go with us on our ride."

She shook her head and blinked to break out of the mathematical quiz her brain had been wrestling with.

"Yeah, sure. C'mon, Rocky, let's go."

They both mounted their horses and settled into the saddles at a walk. Rocky took off ahead of them, but not too far, always keeping his people in sight. The morning air was cool but not cold. She loved this time of day and to be on horseback with someone she loved just made it perfect. Their horses were side by side and Matt reached out to take her hand just like in a romance movie. Her heart was near to bursting.

"You doing okay, sweetie? You seem a little preoccupied. Are you all right after our scary incident with Granger?"

"Yes. Just thinking. You know, I was talking with my parents before Granger came along. And I was imagining that Shawn could've been buried there too. I can't believe I had a memorial service for him. That was such a weird time when he was missing."

"Oh, hon, that's a lot for anyone to deal with. Was it good to talk to your parents?"

She gazed at him under her brows, head low. "You don't think I'm a wack job, do you? I know they're not really there."

"You are not a wack job. For centuries, it has helped

people to go to one location and speak from their heart to loved ones who have gone on ahead. Did you talk to them about anything specific?" He squeezed her hand but then let go so they could hold their reins.

She wasn't sure she could be totally honest with him but decided to take a chance.

"I told them about you."

"Me?"

"Yeah. Told them I liked you and wanted to know what they thought."

"Did they answer? I'm just teasing."

"They didn't speak audibly of course. But I did feel an inner peace. And when confronted with Granger I felt they were standing next to me, no matter what was about to happen."

"Well, I'm glad. And I hope I met with their approval. Wish I could have known them."

"Me too. And yes, I'm sure they would approve wholeheartedly of you."

"I guess I'll have to accept that since I won't be able to talk to your dad, man to man."

She halted her horse and snapped her head quickly toward him. "What about?"

"Well, you know...I'd like to tell him that I love his daughter...that I'd like to more than just date, be more than her boyfriend..." He winked but it flustered her.

This might've been the second or third time she heard the *L* word come out of his mouth. She couldn't help but stutter a little. "Uh, well, I...uh...I'm sure that'd be okay with Dad...I...uh..."

He chuckled. "Settle down, Katy. Maybe I'll talk to Shawn about it."

She knew her face was rosy. "Uh, sure. By the way, what's happening with him and Tara?"

"You know he went with her for questioning. It worked out okay, he told me. They looked up her gun permit and asked about her horse-show appeal against Granger. I understand she and Shawn went for coffee afterward."

"I saw them making goo-goo eyes at each other," she said.

"What exactly do those look like? Have you ever made them at me?"

She tilted her head, rolled her eyes skyward, and fluttered her lashes. "All the time, mister. Now c'mon, let's trot at least. Rocky's getting bored. And we're burning daylight."

"Do you have a date or something later, Ms. McKim?"

"I just might." She took off from a quick trot into a lope, leaving him behind as she giggled.

"You know that's cheating, don't ya?" He clucked to his horse, and they sped up to catch her.

After an invigorating lope, Katy slowed her horse and felt her new phone vibrating in her pocket.

"Hello? Oh, hey, Mel. How are you? And your dad. I'm glad, good to hear. Sure, come over. I've got a few things to do today. Hey, you wanna come for dinner tonight? My brother and Tara will be here. Bring Jeff. You sure you're doing okay? All right, good. Take care. See ya later."

Before she could get a word out, Matt said, "Mel's coming for dinner. We'd better take some meat out. Or is she a vegan? I can never keep track of everyone's dietary preferences."

"She eats like a bird no matter what she is. Let's go. I'd say I'll race you, but we'd better take it a little slow heading back to the barn."

"I know. Your dad taught you that."

She smiled and imagined how it would've been if Matt had known her dad. She could see the two of them grilling while she helped her mother in the kitchen. But she knew she couldn't control life. She just had to embrace whatever came next.

# CHAPTER 36

# Feels like Home

AT THE BARN THEY REMOVED THE TACK AND BRUSHED THE horses. Katy then led Cash back out to a large pasture and turned him out. Matt followed with the neighbor's horses.

Walking together back from the gate, she said, "They'll be happy in the pasture. I'll tell Stan and Lily when I call to invite them to dinner. We'd better make sure we have enough food or else we'll have to make a grocery run. How many people did we talk about?"

Matt counted as he unfolded his fingers. "You, me, Shawn, Tara, Melanie, Jeff, Stan, Lily. I think Andre might come too. That's nine. Anyone else?"

"You know, I might call Wes and his wife. I'd like to introduce him to Mel and talk about the magazine. Hey! What about your sister? Let's invite them."

"Sure, if you want to. So that's nine plus Wes and his wife is eleven. And Angel and Luis and the little one... makes thirteen and a half."

They both laughed.

Katy squinted as though she was pondering something. "Maybe Andre will bring a date. Why don't you mention it to him? Then we'll have an even fourteen."

"All right. Not sure where we'll put them all. But we'd better start planning the menu and prepping pretty quick. What time did we say? Six or so? It'll be here before we know it."

Back at the house they each made calls to those they hadn't already spoken to about the dinner. Katy texted to confirm with some. Although she had never been one to entertain much, she liked the idea of getting everyone together. It made her feel part of a community, a family, again. The last few years had tried to tear all that apart. Maybe it was time to rebuild, starting with her and Matt. She watched him on his phone as he sat at the kitchen island, smiling, joking with the person on the other end. Not only was he handsome and kind but she felt safe with him like he'd never hurt her. Sounded like a trifecta to her.

He ended the call and looked up at her, narrowing his eyes. "What?"

"Oh, nothing. Just admiring."

"Really? Now listen, woman, there's no time for me to be your eye candy."

She let out a whoosh of air. "Woman?"

"Well, that's what you are, right? And you're my eye candy. But we've got to be serious about the work ahead of us. No playing around."

"All right, all right. What are we going to serve everyone?"

"I say keep it simple. Steak, potato, salad. That's it."

"What about our vegans? Or vegetarians. Or whatever they are. Maybe they're pescatarians. Do you know what that is?"

"Ka—ty, you're getting off track. How about I'll take

care of the steak and maybe chicken, too, and potatoes. You make the salad and any other veggie-type thing you can think of. Maybe pasta. And everyone eats dessert, right?"

"Some people are off sugar." She grinned like a troublemaker.

He shook his head, then squeezed his eyes with his fingers, and held his head.

She massaged his shoulders. "Matt, no stress. We can do this. Let me check the fridge. Do I need to go to the store? What about wine?"

"I think we've got everything. No need for a store run."

AS THE DAY progressed Katy scurried around dusting and straightening the house, mopping the floor, and sanitizing the kitchen from top to bottom, including cleaning the refrigerator. The bathrooms were already sparkling, and the house was looking good. What with all the craziness in her life lately, some of the chores had been sorely neglected. Plus, with Rocky being on premises lately his dog hair was starting to take on a life of its own, like an additional puppy, or at least tumbleweeds floating around. But she loved him and wouldn't have it any other way.

She wasn't sure where Matt was or what he was doing. He had defrosted the steaks and chicken and set out enough baking potatoes to feed a small army. Earlier he made a quick run to town and purchased some potted flowers for the porches, front and back. She liked how he was sprucing things up and could tell he was looking forward to their soirée. They both had laughed at that word and kept repeating it to tease one another during their preparations.

~

FIRST TO ARRIVE WERE Melanie and Food Truck Jeff.

"Hey, guys! C'mon in." Katy answered the door and welcomed them. She hugged Melanie for a long time. "So good to see you." Then gave Jeff a hug. "How are you, dude?"

"Groovy, as always, ma'am...er, I mean, no ma'am." They all laughed.

Rocky ran around the guests and even leaped on Jeff in his excitement.

"Down, Rocky." Matt intervened and held his hand out to shake with Jeff. "How're ya doin', man?"

"Awesome, lawdog, being an upright citizen. Still groovy." Jeff gave an ear-to-ear smile.

Matt gave Jeff a stern look which caused Jeff to fluster.

"Oh, man," he said. "Is that a derogatory term? Hope not. That's not how I meant it, really!"

He was in an obvious tizzy, but Matt bailed him out. He grabbed hold of his hand to shake again.

"No worries. I'm not sure if it is or isn't. But Rocky might be offended at the use of the word 'dog' so maybe let's go with 'lawman' or PI or something like that."

They laughed, but Jeff still seemed unsure about his possible faux pas with Matt.

Katy escorted Melanie to the kitchen. "I've got a no-cheese, no-gluten, cauliflower crust, all-veggie pizza for you guys later. And a humongous salad. How does that sound?"

"It sounds amazing, Katy. But you didn't have to go to any special trouble for us."

"I wanted to, Mel. You are a dear friend. In fact, later I'd like to talk to you about something—journalism. But first, how is your dad doing?"

The girl lowered her eyes. "Let's save that for later, too, okay?"

"Sure, of course."

A knock and then the front door opened.

"Anybody home? You ready for the Martinez family?"

All smiles, Matt's sister stepped over the threshold carrying their six-month-old baby, Jon-Luis. Her husband, Luis, followed juggling two tote bags containing infant supplies as well as one other bag filled with food items.

"We brought two pies and a spinach dip," Angel said as she headed to the kitchen. Then gave instructions to her husband. "Put the food down here on the counter."

Katy moved in for a hug. "You didn't have to bring anything, just yourselves. Ooh, look at this little guy. He's growing so fast."

Luis said, "Yep, like a weed as they say." He shook Matt's hand, then introduced himself to Jeff and Melanie.

Stan and Lily appeared carrying a tote of food and flowers. "Hey, neighbors! We came through the back; hope you don't mind. Heard there was a party." Stan was larger than life, in size and voice, and towered over his petite wife.

Matt laughed. "We'll let anyone in off the street."

Katy hugged them. "Hope you rascals didn't bring any food. You were only supposed to bring yourselves."

Stan hugged Lily at his side. "By now you must know

my sweet wife is incapable of going anywhere empty-handed."

The front door had been left partially open and next to appear were Wes and his wife. Although the house was open concept, Katy didn't notice them until they quietly made their way to the kitchen. She hadn't seen Marjorie in a very long time and was overcome with emotion. Memories flooded her mind of when the Stevenses had been friends with her parents. She grasped a hold of the older woman.

"Oh, Miss Marjorie, it's so good to see you. Thank you both for coming."

"It's our pleasure, dear. Thank you for inviting us. I don't get out that much. Now don't go getting teary. This is a party."

Katy wiped her eyes and hugged Wes, muttering in his ear, "I'd like to talk to you later about the magazine."

He gave her a nod. "Sure thing."

"Everyone, make yourselves at home. There's a cooler with water, sodas, and we also have some wine and beer. We've got plenty of food, so you won't go hungry. Now, who's missing? Oh yeah, my brother." She rolled her eyes good-naturedly.

As if on a preplanned cue, Shawn came barreling through the front door, Tara following.

"Hey! You didn't all start without us, did ya?"

His auburn hair standing like spikes was different today. He must've been generous with the extreme-hold gel. With his black T-shirt, bulging biceps, and baggy khaki pants, Katy thought of the G.I. Joe doll he liked so much as a kid. She tried not to chuckle.

To her surprise, on their heels was Andre, also looking military casual in camo pants and a green T-shirt. Katy had prepared herself to see him make an entrance with some striking female, but instead…was that Pastor John?

"No party is a party without you, Shawn." Matt clapped him on the back, and both did a bro-hug. Handshakes and hugs went around to Andre and the pastor until everyone was properly greeted and introduced.

Katy hugged Tara. "Not sure how you put up with this lug. I hope you know what you're signing up for." They both smiled.

"Yeah, I know. But he seems to be worth it."

Shawn poked Katy's side. "You're not bad-mouthing me, are you, Sis?"

"Now, would I do that to you, big brother?"

Andre gave her a strong hug and she said she was happy he came.

"Pastor John, this is a pleasant surprise. It's been quite a while since we saw you last. Would you mind saying a blessing? I think we're about to start soon."

He took Katy's hand then gave her a sweet hug. "Hope you don't mind my tagging along, Katy. Andre couldn't find a date." He braced himself for Andre's shove. "I'd be honored to pray. How 'bout I'll end if Matt will start us off?"

Katy knew what he was doing, honoring Matt as though he were the head of household. Maybe he would be one day.

Matt nodded. "Let's pray."

Gathered around the kitchen island in a semicircle, some holding hands, everyone bowed their heads.

"Lord, thank you for bringing our friends and family to this home. Please bless them with health and happiness and love…" He raised his head toward Katy, then continued. "…all the days of their lives. Help them to know You and listen for Your will."

Pastor John took over for the close. "Heavenly Father, we thank You for all who are gathered here today. And we ask a special blessing upon Katy and Matt, for their safety and for wisdom and direction in the days ahead, as well as for those whose jobs take them into harm's way. Please bless this food and the hands that prepared it. And all of God's people said...Amen."

She knew he meant Shawn and Andre when he mentioned about going into harm's way.

The room was filled with "amens" which pleased Katy as she looked at all the faces. Her ranch was finally beginning to feel like a real home again.

# CHAPTER 37
## Friends and Family

SOME GUESTS HAD TAKEN THEIR PLATES TO CHAIRS ON THE back deck where Matt was manning the grill. Others were at the kitchen island bar, while a few more were sitting at the dining room table. Laughter filled the air and Katy enjoyed watching the diversity. She played the good hostess refilling plates and glasses. For a few seconds here and there, she thought of her parents and couldn't help wishing they were here too.

"Are you thinking of them?" Miss Marjorie brought her plate to the sink.

"Who? Oh, yes, I guess I am."

"You can't fool me, Katy. I'm thinking of your folks also. I remember when they built this house. Your mom and I shared many recipes in this kitchen, although it does look different since your dad had it remodeled for her. But the feelings and memories are still of her."

"They are. I'm glad I'm not the only one who thinks of her."

"Of course, you're not. Life is like that. You start out young, you build a family and memories. Sometimes bad things come along and interrupt your dream. We just have to adapt, roll with the punches, so to speak. Your folks wouldn't want you to stay depressed or grieving. They'd want you to go on, build a life for yourself here."

"I'm trying, Miss Marjorie. Lately so many strange things have been happening to me."

"I know. Wes told me. How's that young man of yours? He seems to be the real deal—honest and true. I see him looking at you with lots of love in his eyes. I hope you'll hold on to him. Love like that doesn't come along very often."

Katy wasn't exactly sure how to answer so she just smiled. Luckily, Wes came over and saved her.

"Good food, Katy. Hey, you wanted to talk about the magazine?"

"Let me get Mel over here also. I wanted her in on our discussion."

Soon Melanie and Jeff joined the little group. Again, Katy was tickled at the diversity—long-haired Jeff talking with older, conservative Wes Stevens and his wife.

"I think you all have met. Mel, you once said you wanted to take journalism classes at the community college. Is that right?" Katy nodded to encourage the girl who probably wasn't the most comfortable sharing her dreams with new people.

Melanie regarded the older couple, then nodded. "Yes to both."

"And your dad is recuperating?" Katy was trying to get the girl to engage with everyone.

"They said he'll make a full recovery. But there are legal matters for him to face." Melanie studied her manicured nails and Jeff placed an arm around her shoulders.

"Well..." Katy started. "I have an idea, a proposal, and

I wanted to run it by all of you."

They politely listened as Katy directed her attention to Melanie mostly.

"Mel, I'm glad your dad is doing better. And what I'm about to say, I'm hoping you can convey to him. If you need me to go with you, I will...although I'm not sure I'm his favorite person. Anyway, I'm thinking he may get tied up for a while with those legal matters you mentioned. So, I wondered about the magazine."

Wes spoke up. "It might have to fold."

"Maybe not. And that's where you come in. Mel, I'm not sure if you know this or not but your dad owes Wes a lot of money. He was supposed to purchase the magazine, but he never made any payments. I'm thinking Wes could take the magazine back and the three of us could run it. Mel, you'd learn a lot about journalism. Real-world experience. And Wes, if you and Miss Marjorie want to be semiretired and do a little traveling or whatever, Mel and I could take care of the business. It could be a great thing for all of us. What do you think?"

Wes glanced at Marjorie, and Melanie was quiet for a while until she focused on Wes.

"I'm sorry he never made any payments to you, Mr. Stevens."

Wes touched her hand gently. "It's not your fault, dear." Then to Katy, he said, "We'd have to have a lawyer set it up all legal, like maybe you and Melanie could own a percentage."

To his wife he said, "What do you think, sweetheart?"

Marjorie gazed intently into her husband's eyes. "I just don't want you doing too much, but this is something you love. And we trust Katy completely. If she thinks this is a good idea, I'm behind it one hundred percent."

"Thank you, Miss Marjorie." Katy touched the lady's hand.

Soon all eyes were on Melanie as if awaiting her thoughts.

When Jeff broke the ice with, "What do ya think, Punkin? Do you want to be Lois Lane and I'll be your Superman?"

Everyone chuckled and Melanie's face broke into a girlish giggle. Katy liked the gangly hippie guy and thought he seemed to be ever the protector since she had introduced him to Melanie.

Finally, the girl spoke. "It sounds like an interesting idea. I'd like to write for the magazine and learn more about the business. Like Mr. Stevens said, we'll have to find out the legal ins and outs...and also talk to my dad. I, too, have a feeling that he might be tied up with other things and not be able to pay attention to the magazine. So...I'm in."

Katy told the publishing group that they could reconvene after they knew more about the situation and excused herself. She was very encouraged.

Matt's laugh rang out across the living room and she saw him with his sister, Angel, her husband, and baby. Katy joined them and gave Angel a hug.

"I'm so glad you came. Did you all get enough to eat?"

"Yes, Katy, I'm stuffed." Angel patted her stomach. "That salad was really good and of course Matt did a great job on the grill."

Luis held the baby and Katy came close and put her finger in the boy's tiny fist.

"You are strong, little fella. Just like your uncle. And look at that dark hair." She fluttered her eyes at Matt.

Angel pulled her aside slightly. "Katy, are you guys

okay after all that crazy shooting stuff? When I heard about it, I was so worried for you."

"Thanks. It was pretty scary, but I think things are settling down now. The bad guys are in jail."

"Good. Maybe you and Matt can come visit more often now. We're not that far."

Katy wasn't sure how they'd juggle everything, but family was important and she really liked Matt's family.

"How's your mother doing?"

Angel was quiet at first. "We were just talking about that earlier. She's getting older and I sometimes worry about her. She misses seeing Matt."

He spoke up. "I'll try to visit her. You know we've had our hands full lately."

"I know," Angel said. "And Mom understands. Of course, we don't tell her everything or else she'd be scared to death for you. She knows you have a dangerous job."

Katy couldn't help but feel a little guilty. Over the past months she had taken up a lot of Matt's time.

Neighbors Stan and Lily had been chatting with Shawn and Tara, and although sometimes Shawn's extroverted personality seemed "out there," in this social setting Stan's loud laughter had him beat. She also knew, from what Andre had told her, that in his line of work he oftentimes had to be stealthy and calculating as well. He had practiced reining in some of his outgoing qualities for his leadership role in conducting a military-type team.

Katy joined them and Stan's howling quieted into serious talk.

"I was just telling Shawn that Lily and I are planning a trip to Ireland, and we wanted to ask if you could watch our horses and house. Our daughter said she'd help also with the house and check on it every so often. We might be gone a month. Hope that's not too big of an imposition."

Katy smiled. "I'll be glad to. No worries."

Lily touched Stan's arm. "Tell her the rest, hon."

"Okay. Well, Katy, when we return, we'd like to build a large arena between the two properties, maybe build a bigger barn. We can both use it for our horses, and maybe we'll get a few more boarders. What do you think?"

She was a little flummoxed. She loved her little barn. Her father had built it. And it had just recently been repaired after a fire had nearly consumed the whole thing. But she wanted to be supportive of Stan and Lily.

"Uh, well, we can always talk about it. I'd like to hear your ideas."

"I'll send you the report I've been working on," Stan said as though he were making a business presentation.

Lily smiled and nodded her head up and down about four times. "He has spreadsheets."

"Really?"

Katy moved toward Matt and put her hand in the crook of his elbow and held on to his strong bicep. They moved together toward Andre and Pastor John.

Matt and Andre jostled each other like guys do some-times, pushing and punching.

"So, you couldn't get a date to bring tonight?" Matt teased.

"Oh, I had one, but I brought the pastor instead since I figured you might want to confess your sins."

"But you know I don't have any. I'm a pure soul."

They all laughed, and Pastor John grabbed both of them. Katy thought she recalled he was ex-military too. He fit the bill.

"Now you guys settle down or I'll have to douse you with some holy water or something. Besides, we have a lady present." He winked at Katy.

"Pastor John, don't worry about me. I grew up with this one." She pointed with her thumb like a hitchhiker toward Shawn who was coming closer along with Tara.

"Just John is okay, Katy."

"All right. Just John. J.J." She chuckled then said to Andre, "I didn't realize you knew John."

Sometimes Andre was the strong, silent type. And things were still a little awkward between him and Katy even though they had only briefly dated two years ago after her parents' death.

"We all met at the support group he ran for vets when Shawn and I got out. John is an ex-vet too."

She knew he meant out of the military, and she knew it might also have to do with PTSD although none of them ever talked about it. Maybe they should, she thought.

"I'm glad you could join us tonight, er...John...J.J." She smiled at the pastor.

He touched her shoulder. "Well, I think Andre needed some moral support to ask his question tonight."

"What question?" She felt like everyone was staring at her.

Andre cleared his throat. "Katy, I don't want to upset you or ruin the dinner party...but, uh..."

"Oh, just spit it out, man." Shawn jumped in even though Tara tried holding him back. "We're going on a mission, and we want Matt to come along."

"What? Come where?" Her head swiveled from her brother to her boyfriend. "What is he talking about, Matt?"

"I didn't get a chance to tell you yet, Katy. I'm sorry."
He put his arm around her, but she stiffened.

Shawn continued. "You know we can't talk about it,
Sis. It could be out of the country. The three of us have
worked so well together the last few months, Matt just
fits the bill of what we need to get the job done. We'll
have him back before you know it. It might only be a few
months."

Clapping Andre on the back, he said it with a big
smile as though it was no big deal like he "and the boys"
were just having a night out or playing in a softball
league. Katy knew it could be life or death. It always was
with Shawn even though he didn't tell her about the
things he'd seen and done the way Andre had when they
were together for that short time. She wanted to smack
her brother but now noticed all her dinner guests were
gathered around and in on the conversation.

Matt's sister asked, "Is this spy stuff you're talking
about?"

Her husband interjected. "Honey, they're not spies."

"Well, mercenaries, hired guns, whatever you call
them. It's dangerous, right? Are you going to do it,
Matt?"

He watched as Katy moved away from him. "I haven't
decided yet and I haven't discussed it with Katy."

"I need to clean the kitchen."

Melanie stepped up. "I can help you, Katy."

"That's okay, Mel. I know you and Jeff need to get
going. He said he's got to get an early start tomorrow.
Thanks so much for coming. I'll talk to you soon."

She said a similar good night to all of them, almost
shooing them out the door.

She hugged Wes and his wife and told him she'd be in
touch about the magazine. Matt's sister said they had

made a reservation at a motel in town, kind of a getaway for her and Luis, now that the baby was sleeping better. It was a little awkward when Angel hugged Matt, and Katy wasn't sure what the sister whispered in his ear.

Neighbors Stan and Lily made their thanks and good night quick and said they'd text information about when they were scheduled to leave on their trip to Ireland and any last-minute instructions for care of their horses.

Pastor John hugged Katy and said he'd be praying for all of them, and Andre apologized. "I'm sorry. This wasn't the time or place to discuss our job. I hope you'll forgive me."

Shawn and Tara were the last to go. Tara said in Katy's ear, "This too shall pass. Call me anytime. I'm your friend. Remember that."

Shawn shook Matt's hand but when he came to hug Katy, her arms were folded across her chest.

"C'mon, Sis. I didn't think this would end your party. It's just that we need an answer from Matt. We're leaving in a few days."

She wasn't sure what to say to him and tried stuffing her hurt and anger, to no avail.

Her true feelings burst forth. "Are you always going to be leaving, Shawn? Sometimes you need to stay in one place to get close to people."

"It's my job, Katy. It's what I do." He appeared genuinely clueless.

"I just don't want you to wake up one day, old and regretful, with no family and no one to love. It would be like you're missing in action all over again. I don't know if I could handle that."

"That's a little dramatic, don't you think?"

"Good night, Shawn." She turned back to the kitchen.

## CHAPTER 38
# *Life Partners*

THE PARTY WAS OVER. A LITTLE SOONER THAN KATY HAD planned. And now, with just her and Matt, and Rocky of course, the quiet threatened to engulf them.

"I'm sorry, Katy."

She busied herself with dishes and cleaning up. Still upset, the sounds of her work were a bit noisier than normal—kitchen cabinets were shut more strenuously with a bang, silverware clanged in its drawer holder as she tried to set things in place. And her inhaled breath and subsequent sighs filled the room.

Finally, she spoke. "When were you going to tell me about this mission?"

"So much has been going on lately. And I hadn't made up my mind yet. I was planning to talk to you before the party but..."

"Well, have you made a decision? Will you be going with them?" Her lips were firmly pressed in a tight line across her face.

Matt picked up clutter from the living room and came toward her in the kitchen.

"Katy, I would never do anything without us both being in agreement. Honestly, I have been mulling it over. The mission didn't sound like anything where I would be in danger. It's not like I'd be a soldier or anything. They want me to pose as a businessman, meet someone for lunch, and try to get information out of that person. Then I'd come home."

She spoke quickly and glared. "Shawn said it could be a few months, not a one-hour lunch. Which is it?"

"You know how your brother gets. He's overenthusiastic and gets carried away. I think he was hoping to use me for other aspects of the mission, but I spoke to Andre and told him if I was going to be involved it would have to be short and sweet. In and out, and back home. He agreed."

"Humph," was all that came out of her mouth.

He faced her and took hold of her arms.

"Katy, you have a lot of things going on. You want to make a go of the magazine with Wes and Melanie, there will be court cases with Granger and Barker, your neighbors are going away and have big plans for an arena. I want to be with you for all of that. Right by your side. Helping. That is, if you'll have me."

He gave her that endearing tilt of his head he sometimes did. Darn, how could she resist him? She let him pull her closer and he kissed her forehead, then her cheek.

She looked up at him and he kissed her lips.

They stared into each other's eyes and smiled.

"Do you forgive me?"

"Hmm...let me think...maybe?"

He held her waist which produced squeals. This was one of their normal routines and she enjoyed making up.

"Promise me one thing, Matt."

"What's that, my love?"

She tried to remember, was that the first time he'd called her that? His love.

"Let's both promise to discuss things like this before either of us feels surprised or in the dark. Let's keep each other in the loop so that we're really a team, partners. Okay?"

"Roger that, ma'am. Partners, huh? I like the sound of that."

They sealed it with a kiss.

"So, what's next on your agenda, partner?" He stroked her hair away from her face.

"I need to talk to Shawn." She looked determined.

"Now? It's getting kind of late."

"Yes, now."

Matt continued cleaning up after the party and saw Katy pick up her phone.

"Hey, Shawn. I know, I know. You don't have to apologize anymore. Listen, I want to talk to you. Out at Mom and Dad's. Yes, the cemetery. First thing in the morning...say, about nine. No, it can't wait. I'll see you there tomorrow morning at nine. And you'd better be there."

She pressed end call.

# CHAPTER 39
## Brother and Sister

THE NEXT MORNING KATY TIPTOED PAST THE GUEST ROOM where Matt usually spent the night when he wasn't in the barn loft bedroom. She made her way to the kitchen and started the coffee machine hoping the sounds would not carry upstairs and wake him.

However, when she passed the couch, she jumped a little as Matt roused and struggled to his elbows, then almost to a sitting position.

"Uh, morning." He tried to clear his throat of the sleepy cobwebs.

"Oh my gosh, you scared me. Did you sleep there last night?"

"Well...kinda, sorta. I didn't really get much sleep."

"Sorry. Are you okay?"

"Just had a lot on my mind after last night."

As she watched him from the kitchen, she also pulled out the coffee mugs and creamer for her and started the machine.

"Did you get things figured out?"

"I'm working on it. I'd like to talk with you more about it…"

A knock interrupted his words.

Katy said, "Shawn's early," as she went to the door.

"Morning, guys. How is everyone?" He closed his eyes, raised his nose, and took in the aroma. "Yes, I'd love some coffee, thank you."

"C'mon in. It's almost ready." She shut the door after her brother.

Shawn watched Matt folding a blanket from the couch and teased, "Trouble in paradise, man?"

Matt's normally tidy appearance had taken a back seat this morning with his hair sticking up like a cockatoo and a five-o'clock shadow that was turning into a ten-o'clock shadow if that was even a thing. He had a very short beard which usually looked neat but now was rather scruffy.

"I think I'll take my coffee to the bathroom and grab a shower." He rubbed the palm of his hand over his whiskers.

Katy handed him his mug. "Shawn and I might be gone when you come out. We're going to ride to the cemetery."

Matt nodded. "All right. Be careful." He took his coffee and headed to the bathroom.

But Shawn was a little taken aback. "Ride? As in horses? Can't we take a vehicle over to that side road?"

"You're kidding me, right?" Katy's brows met in the middle as she stared at him. "When was the last time you were on a horse?"

"Uh, well, it's been a while. I do have a job you know."

"So do I. But I still find time for my horse." She slid a mug of coffee toward him. "We're doing this so drink up."

"What about breakfast?"

"When did you become such a baby? I thought you were a soldier."

"I am. Sorta." He grumbled and drank his coffee.

～

AT THE BARN she tacked up Cash and helped Shawn get one of her neighbor's horses ready.

"That one's pretty quiet. You should have no trouble. Let's warm them up with a slow jog first."

After just a minute, they were out of the barn and on their way. It seemed Shawn couldn't do anything slow. "Enough of this. I'll race you to the cemetery."

And before she could say anything, he and his horse were nearly across the pasture. That old competition fire just like when they were kids sparked within her. She couldn't let him outdo her so she prodded Cash into a lope, then gallop, after her brother.

She yelled after him. "Shawn, go easy with that horse."

He just grinned back at her from ear to ear. Sometimes she felt she acted more like the older, more responsible sibling than he did.

As they neared the cemetery she slowed and walked Cash in a circle.

"You let me win. That's not a real race," he complained.

She got off Cash and switched him to a halter and lead rope she had brought so he could graze while they visited with their parents. She didn't like horses eating grass with bits in their mouths and she thought it dangerous to tie reins to a fence. Anything could happen. They could spook and a bit could hurt their mouth if they tried to pull away. Some people thought her methods were unnecessary, silly even, but it was just the way her father had taught her.

"Walk him around a little, Shawn. You were running him pretty hard. Let him catch his breath. I've got a halter for him too."

He stayed on and walked the horse a while.

"I would've won fair and square."

"You had a head start, doofus." She rolled her eyes.

After a few minutes he dismounted, switched his horse to a halter to let him graze, and came over to the family cemetery.

"So, why'd you summon me here today, Katy?"

"Summon? That's kind of harsh."

"You know what I mean. You were kinda bossy last night."

"When was the last time you were here?" She took a blanket from Cash's saddlebag and spread it in front of her parents' grave markers so she and her brother could sit. Shawn stayed standing.

He got quiet. "I don't know. I was…uh…gone…when they died."

"That's two…actually, it's almost three years now. And you haven't been to visit? Why not?"

He didn't look at her. "You know why, Katy. It's been difficult the last few years. I've been busy with work. Besides, they're not here, right?"

"That's true. They're not here. But sometimes humans set aside one place where they can visit and reflect on what has been lost…or taken…from their lives. This is our place."

"You and I are different, Katy. Maybe it's a male/female thing, I don't know. You're all touchy-feely, or whatever they call it. I just want to put the bad stuff behind me and keep moving forward."

She took in the blue sky overhead and thought it was incredible. With a few white puffy clouds it was certainly postcard worthy. Although her brain told her people hardly ever sent those anymore.

"I get it. No one wants to dwell on the hurtful things in life. But I also think we should take the time and get off that wild roller coaster. Take stock of what's important—family, love, remembering. Not running all the time. You'll never outrun the pain, Shawn."

He said nothing.

"I want to say a few things. That's why I asked you here. I want to be clear on some things I'm feeling, and I want you to know what they are."

"Okay."

"When Mom and Dad passed away, you were around for a little while. I went to be with you in Florida and met Andre. He comforted me...more than you did, I might say. Then you both took off, leaving me alone. That year you up and disappeared. I know now that you were mixed up in dangerous things and with dangerous people. But then, in my compounded grief, I was told you were missing, presumably dead, and encouraged to have a memorial service for you. Do you know what a tailspin that put me in, Shawn?"

"I'm sorry, Katy."

"Then you turn up, with that Pastor John, and come back into my life. What am I supposed to do with that? Of course, I was overjoyed to have you back, but do you know how that messed with me?"

"Katy..."

She held her hands up. "No, wait. Let me finish. And even though you were 'back' so to speak, you continued going off on missions with Andre and now you want to involve Matt in your spy web."

Very quietly he mumbled, "It's not a spy web…"

But she cut him off and held up her hand for him to stop and she continued.

"Finally, I'm trying to rebuild my life and I've opened myself up to welcome love and you want him to take off with you for…what? months? And maybe get caught up in your dangerous life? Plus, you don't even talk to me about it. And he doesn't either. You *guys* just decide on your own, in your clandestine ring of secret missions, to go off to the other side of the world and…leave me here. Just like you always have. What happened to my brother?"

He was silent for a few seconds and toed the ground with his boot. She watched him and remembered when he was ten years old and had done something wrong or hurtful. He wore the same expression now.

"Katy, I'm still your brother and always will be. But when we work on these teams and put our lives in the hands of our mates, it becomes a brotherhood. It's a bond and we'd do anything for each other."

She fought against it, but a tear escaped from her eye and ran down her cheek as she lowered her head.

There was silence between them. Only the munching of the horses could be heard.

Shawn touched her shoulder.

"Katy, I don't know what to say. I'm really sorry. I never wanted to hurt you. I'm not sure how to make you understand. After the military, working with Andre in the private sector just seemed like a logical transition. It's the only job I know. What else would I do?"

She was quiet and wiped her face.

"And about involving Matt…I'm sorry. I didn't realize

how it might impact you. The three of us have worked on some cases together and we all get along great. We're good at what we do. It just seemed...again, logical...that he would be a perfect fit for a job we have coming up."

"What about Tara? How is she taking it?"

"To be honest, not very well. In fact, we've kind of broken up."

"Broken up? Why?"

"She didn't want to wait four months, or however long, while I went 'gallivanting' as she called it, around the world."

"I'm sorry, Shawn. Do you think you can talk to her more about it?"

"You know my track record with women, Sis. Maybe I won't settle down until I'm old and gray." He chuckled as he squatted, took a stick, and drew in the dirt.

She worried about him and pictured him as an old man. Her heart ached at the thought of him being alone.

"It doesn't have to be that way. You can change your future if you want. What about kids? A family? Do you think Tara wants that?"

"She definitely wants that. She's mentioned it a time or two."

"What do you think?"

"I think she's moving too fast. We haven't even dated that long and already she's planning a family?"

She turned closer to him.

"Shawn, sometimes people come along in our lives, and it's just meant to be. I know Tara is a special woman. It would be a shame to let her go. And you may never meet another who is more suitable for you."

"Like you and Matt? How did you know that he's the one for you?"

"At first, I kind of shied away from him. But he just

stuck with me. He was patient and loyal and kind. Finally, I wanted happiness, so I let go of my old habits where I always hid in my grief. And...to be honest...it helped to come here, to talk to Mom and Dad...and to God. It had been a long time, and I was angry with God. I blamed him for all the heartache in my life but eventually realized he doesn't want to hurt us. He doesn't cause the pain. He's the one who comforts us and carries us through the pain."

Shawn kept drawing with the stick in the sand but observed her. "I knew there was something different about you, Katy. I thought it was just that you had grown up."

"I guess that's part of it. But I decided I wanted to choose good things—happiness, love, family. And like an epiphany, it hit me—God is in all those things. Maybe it was Matt's influence. Or Mom and Dad's. I just remembered when we were kids and went to church as a family. I thought of some of the things Mom and Dad taught us. They were such good people. To each other, to their kids, to people in the community. I'm sure they had God in their hearts. I want that for my family, for my kids."

His eyes got big, and his eyebrows lifted.

She laughed. "Well, future kids that is. Don't start imagining things that aren't there."

He wasn't laughing and his low voice took on a serious tone. "So, what are you saying? That I need to settle down, get married, have a bunch of kids?"

She shook her head.

"No, Shawn. I'm not trying to tell you what to do or how to live your life. You've got to figure that out for yourself. I am saying that I love you and miss you and I only want the best for you. And while I'm at it and being honest, I don't like the idea of you and Andre recruiting Matt for your missions. There, I said it."

He stood and threw the stick away. "Sis, I don't think we pressured Matt. We have a business. He's helped us before. We presented this new case to him. And that's that. If he doesn't want to do it, fine. About all that other stuff—Tara…family…God. I'll try to be a better person, but it may not be for me, the whole package. I am who I am."

"That's just it. You don't have to be a better person. We can't earn our way to God by doing good things. I just want you to have peace and not hide from your past in these missions. Maybe you could talk to Pastor John. He works with vets."

"I talked to him once and he leaves messages for me. I'll contact him. But first we have this mission."

"Shawn, there's always going to be another mission. Just remember to take care of your health, physical and mental. Don't get stuck on a wheel doing the job and not caring for your own life. Will you do that for me? Please."

As he stared into space across the pasture, she could see their conversation had touched a nerve with him. And that's all she could ask…for him just to think about things and not bury his feelings. Or wear a false mask as though everything was okay in his life.

She wanted the best for him and didn't want to lose him like before. They were the only close family each of them had left.

He said one more thing before getting on his horse. "You know, Katy, most of the time on our missions we rescue people. We're their only hope in a world of evil. It's not like we're out there playing shoot 'em up for fun. We're doing real good."

"I know you are, Shawn. I just wonder…who's going to rescue you?"

He walked over to the horse, then looked back at her.

"Katy? I've got to do this, you know. Andre and I have been working on the logistics for months. We've hired other members of the team. Everything's nearly in place. And even if Matt doesn't go with us…lives are at stake. People might die if we don't go."

She loved her brother. And she learned a long time ago, you can't live someone else's life. You can encourage them, advise them, even chastise them…but you can't make them do what you think is best. They need to arrive at their own decision, and it could very well be the complete opposite of what you might choose for your life.

She had to let him go.

"Shawn, I love you. I understand and I'll be praying for you. Please come home soon, safe and sound. I'll be waiting for you." Then she added, "I'm sure Tara will be waiting, too, no matter what she said."

# CHAPTER 40
## *Gift from the Heart*

SHAWN CLIMBED ON THE HORSE AND HEADED HOME. HIS sister watched him, and he gave her a slight nod.

Matt rode toward him and the two slowed their horses to meet. "Hey, man, how's everything?"

"Pretty good. She's waiting for you. I'll talk to you later."

SHE WAS SURPRISED to see Matt riding the neighbors' other horse. They hadn't talked about him joining them.

"What are you doing? Didn't think you were going to ride."

"I just thought it would be nice. Hope it's okay I took this horse. He was kind of lonely in the barn anyway."

"I'm sure Stan and Lily would be glad to have their horses exercised. Anytime."

"Hope I didn't interrupt anything with you and Shawn."

"No. We were done. For now."

"Did you have a good talk?"

"I guess so. Shawn has some stuff to work through. But then, don't we all?"

"Katy, can we talk?"

"Of course."

"I've got a little gift for you."

"What? Why?"

He grinned. "Why not? Because I care for you."

He got off the horse, looped reins around the saddle horn, then retrieved a rectangular shaped item wrapped in brown paper like a grocery bag which she liked better than the more commonly used plastic. It reminded her of when she and her brother used the same paper to cover their school textbooks. Not many kids did. It was old-school, something their dad had taught them.

The small package was tied with what appeared to be the red string off a hay bale. He sat on the blanket next to her and handed her the gift.

She smiled and started to untie the string and unwrap the paper.

"Nice wrapping job." She grinned.

When she realized it was a book, her eyes glassed over with the beginning of tears, but she held them back.

"Dorothy M. Johnson. 'The Man Who Shot Liberty Valance.'"

She studied his face and tried to take it all in. Who was he and how did he "get her" so precisely?

"Matt, I love this. Female author...not that I don't also like the male authors. A Western. She's one of my favorites. I read it when I was a teenager. But this is such a nice copy." She held it to her chest. "Thank you so much. I will cherish it."

He reached for her hand. "I'm so glad you like it,

Katy. I want to give you things that mean a lot to you and make you happy."

She smiled and leaned toward him for a kiss.

"There's something else," he said. "The other night when we talked, I told you I didn't want to go away. On that mission. I wanted to stay right here with you."

"Do you still feel that way?"

He took her hand. "Yes. For sure. But I also wanted to say that someday if the circumstances are different and if I'd only be gone a few days to a week rather than four months...and if the mission really needed me...I hope you'd understand if I had to go."

"Matt, I'd understand."

"And, Katy?"

"Yes?"

"Katy, your parents are here...well, in heaven, I mean. And your brother is busy with his life, sometimes here, most of the time gone...although I'm hoping he'll stick around for you more often. My family loves you. I love you. Maybe you could be part of a new family. I don't mean any disrespect to your folks or brother. I just don't want you to feel like you're all alone in the world. We're here for you. I'm here for you. And I'm not going anywhere."

Her big eyes followed him, and she tried to prevent a thimble-sized droplet from leaving her lid.

"And that magazine, *Pegasus*. Instead of it falling to the earth and crashing because of everything that has happened, I know you'll be able to resurrect it, breathe new life into it. It'll be *Pegasus Rising* instead of falling. What do you think? I'll help you however I can."

"Or...*Pegasus Flying*...instead of 'rising' like flour. Everyone knows I'm not an expert cook." She chuckled.

Matt burst out laughing. "You do just fine, Katy." He

patted his middle section which was still in great shape. "It doesn't look like I'm starving or anything, does it?"

"That's because you're the main chef."

"We're a team. We cook together. Ride together. Let's do life together. I love you, Katy."

He leaned in to kiss her again and she gratefully accepted. She could get lost in him and forget life's heartaches.

"I love you, too, Matt. Okay. *Pegasus Flying* it is."

# Acknowledgements

My appreciation to Caroline Elizabeth Lawrence for helping with my travel tablet so I could keep up with my writing schedule. It pays to have a young person around to teach us about these "newfangled" electronic devices. *(wink)*

Thanks to Mary Lawrence for inviting me to borrow an evening dress and sparkly shoes to wear to the 2023 Western Writers of America convention in Rapid City, South Dakota…and to Sue Croft for her kind advice and fashion sense. You can't show up to a fancy event wearing your daily writing outfit.

Thanks to Janis Parkhill for her continued support. Unbeknownst to her, I used her last name in this story for Parkhill Stables.

Good friend Aaron Friesen from Bluffton, South Carolina, and now Boise, Idaho, grew up in Redding, California. He gave me valuable tidbits about that area of Northern California.

Many thanks to Grace, Connie, Joy, Chris, Beverly, Barbara, Lois, Carol, Teresa, Linda, and Jamie from my Bible study group "Sew & Serve" (I don't sew!), as well as Rui, Teresa, Steve, Andrea, Gary, Janet, Gerald, Cheryl, Henry, Gerri, Sue, Mary, Janis, Charles, Josette, and Kierston from my 12Stone Church group (Joshua 4:2-9), "Living Stones"—all who have been praying for my writing journey.

And to you, Dear Reader. Thanks for spending time in my fictional world. Writers try so hard to connect, entertain, and tell a good story. We spend hours, days, years at this. Hopefully, you have received a positive experience and blessing.

Mark Twain said, "To get the right word in the right place is a rare achievement...anybody can have ideas—the difficulty is to express them..."

Thank you all!

# A Look at Book Three

## HERO BROTHERS

*The true journey of a hero lies in discovering one's faith and family...*

Katy McKim and Detective Matt Hartman are enjoying life. With Katy's brother, Shawn, alive and well, everything seems to be heading in the right direction. But happiness is short-lived—and nothing stays perfect forever.

As Shawn departs on yet another mission, obstacles threaten to shatter the peace Katy has worked so hard to maintain. With each new challenge, she and Matt find themselves grappling with the fragility of their contentment.

Traversing a rocky relationship, relentless stalkers, and professional setbacks, the arrival of a cryptic package threatens the last straw. Katy's desire to be the peacemaker and help everyone is at an all-time high. And when a loved one lands in the hospital, she realizes that, more than ever before, being a hero isn't all it's cracked up to be.

*"... an irresistible mystery that leaves you eagerly awaiting further adventures in the continuing series featuring a charming equestrian turned detective."* **—Chris Enss, New York Times bestselling author, on Stalker or Saint**

*AVAILABLE MAY 2024*

# About Denise F. McAllister

Lovers of the West can be born in the most unlikely of places. For Denise F. McAllister, her start was in Miami, Florida, surrounded by beaches and the Everglades.

But the marvels of television transported her to stories of the West—such as *Bonanza*, *Gunsmoke*, *The Virginian*, and many others—which she fondly recalls watching with her brother every Saturday morning.

After being in the working world for some years, Denise applied her life experience to study for degrees in communications and professional writing. She loved going back to college later in life and hardly ever skipped a class, as opposed to in her younger years. She credits her love of horseback riding and fifteen years of showing in Atlanta, Georgia, to her heartfelt connection of all things Western.

Denise's faith is important to her, and she loves to write about characters's journeys as they navigate real-world challenges. She prays that readers will enjoy her books and—more importantly—experience a blessed connection with our Heavenly Father.

# Helpline Resources

If you need any help or know someone who does, please
contact one of these organizations:

Anorexia Nervosa & Associated Disorders
1-888-375-7767
https://anad.org/get-help/eating-disorders-helpline/

The National Alliance for Eating Disorders Awareness Helpline
1-866-662-1235
https://www.allianceforeatingdisorders.com

National Sexual Assault Hotline
800-656-HOPE (800-656-4673)
https://www.rainn.org/about-national-sexual-assault-online-hotline

PTSD - Wounded Warrior Project® (WWP) Resource Center
888-997-2586
resourcecenter@woundedwarriorproject.org
https://www.woundedwarriorproject.org

www.ingramcontent.com/pod-product-compliance
Lightning Source LLC
Chambersburg PA
CBHW011431240626
47153CB00011B/2944